Diverted Traffic

AVRIL DUNCAN

Lullaby
Press

Diverted Traffic by Avril Duncan
Copyright © 2020. All rights reserved.
The right of Avril Duncan to be identified as the author of
the Work has been asserted by her.
This first edition published and copyright 2020 by Lullaby Press
(an imprint of Tippermuir Books Ltd, Perth, Scotland).
mail@tippermuirbooks.co.uk
www.tippermuirbooks.co.uk

ISBN 978-1-9164778-9-6 (Paperback Book)
A CIP catalogue record for this book is available from the British Library.

Project coordination by Dr Paul S Philippou.
Cover design by Matthew Mackie.
Editorial support: Alan Laing, Mary Alexander and Steve Zajda.
Design, layout and artwork by Bernard Chandler.
Text set in Sabon 10.5/13pt.
Printed and bound by Ashford Colour Press, Gosport.

There can be no keener revelation of a society's soul than the way in which it treats its children.

NELSON MANDELA

Modern Slavery, be it bonded labour, involuntary servitude, or sexual slavery, is a crime and cannot be tolerated in any culture, community or country. It is an affront to our values and our commitment to human rights.

HILLARY CLINTON

This novel is packed with emotion, excitement and detailed knowledge of poverty in rural India and counterfeit Scotch whisky – strange and uncomfortable bedfellows – until the book's triumphal end.

Avril is a natural storyteller who draws the reader into this fast-paced and gripping tale of modern slavery spanning two continents. Her knowledge of her subject is obvious in every word and she offers an eye-opening glimpse into this horrific trade that continues to blight our modern world. A must-read thriller with a distinctive Scottish voice.

Prepare to be appalled and captivated in equal measure as the contrasting lives of a Scotch whisky counterfeit expert and a victim of the obscenity that is human slavery become intertwined in Amsterdam's seedy underbelly. This is a fast-paced thriller oozing authenticity.

Set between the contrasting worlds of Edinburgh, Amsterdam and Mumbai, *Diverted Traffic* brings together two equally captivating heroines: the astute and ambitious Ellie, an anti-counterfeit officer working in the whisky industry; and Suman, the feisty eight-year-old victim of sex-traffickers. When their worlds collide, prepare yourself for a roller-coaster journey that reveals the best and worst of humanity.

ACKNOWLEDGEMENTS

My sincerest thanks to the following people:

My publishers, Paul Philippou and all his colleagues,
Matthew Mackie and Rob Hands, at Tippermuir Books
and to everyone who helped prepare my book for
publication including Mary Alexander,
Bernard Chandler, Laura Jones, Alan Laing,
and Steve Zajda.

Jean Chapman, my mentor and driving force.

David Longmuir, my godson –
the real anti-counterfeit officer!

Bill, my rock, and all my fantastic family, near and far.

Maggie for her help, my fellow 'Scribblers', my brave
friends who come to India with me and see things
no one should ever see.

To Sangam Guide World Centre in India, my grateful
thanks for the opportunity to help us get little ones out
of the hands of traffickers, and to 'The Free to Live
Trust' for the work being done.

And to my two gorgeous granddaughters, Elinor and
Josephine, may you grow up in a world that will
eradicate human trafficking completely.

To everyone, our Girlguiding prayer:

Go well and safely
Sleep well and safely
Stay well and safely
The Lord be ever with you

India

The Festival of Holi, heralding the beginning of spring and the end of the winter season, was an eagerly awaited time of celebration in the village. Kanya, along with the other mothers of the village, had been collecting the vibrant orange heads of the tesu and palash flowers which grew in abundance near the river and, once gathered, she would crush the petals to make the coloured powders for Holi which Suman and her brothers and sisters would throw over each other amid screams of laughter.

On the day of the festival, once the bonfires had cooled, the ashes would be collected by the children to be smeared on the limbs of each family member, a traditional ritual believed to bring good luck into the family.

Kanya, so called because she had been born during the monsoon season, was heavily pregnant with her ninth child. At twenty-eight years old, having been given in marriage at the age of fourteen, she had known no other life than that of constant childbirth and caring for her ever-growing family. Her skin had been darkened and lined prematurely by the searing heat of the sun, and her body wearied by the many pregnancies and the hard toil of her daily life.

Suman, Kanya's eldest daughter, was nine years old. Typical of a village girl, Suman was small for her age and undernourished, but with a delicacy and gracefulness that characterises the girls and women of her region.

Kanya looked up and frowned as her daughter approached with a heavy jug of water balanced on her head. The two-mile walk to the river was one of Suman's daily chores and she enjoyed the fun of going with her friends, laughing and giggling as they splashed water at each other, luxuriating in a dip in the cool of the water under the blazing sun. Feeling clean and refreshed, they had stayed a little longer than normal, enjoying their girlish chatter by the edge of the Mula River.

'Where have you been, Suman?' Kanya asked sharply. 'You take longer and longer each day. Come, give me the water.'

She helped lift the water pitcher off the roughly made *indhi* on Suman's head and laid it by the side of the hut.

'Here,' she said, handing a stick to her daughter. 'Keep turning the bread on the fire and make sure it doesn't burn. When it's all done, go find your brothers and sisters and call them home for their meal.'

Leaving Suman to her task, Kanya made her way over to a rope where the daily washing was hanging out to dry and began to fold the garments that she had washed that morning. She sighed heavily, her unborn baby moving in her belly, reminding her that soon there would be yet another mouth to feed, another child to look after, and another strain on their limited resources.

In the dusk, the family gathered around the fire in the corner of the hut. Being their only meal of the day, Kanya loved this family time with her eight children squatted around, her husband, Mukesh on a stool with his back against the wall. She stood by the fire, placing the freshly made puri bread onto rough plates made from thick, strong banana leaves moulded together into a flat disc shape. As well as bread, Kanya put a small spoonful of white boiled rice laced with peppers onto the plate and drizzled over a sauce made from chilli, turmeric, cumin seed and coriander. As custom dictates, the children broke up the flatbread and scooped up the rice using only their right hands, their small grubby fingers moving speedily at their task.

Kanya looked around at them all. Today was a good day. Today she had been able to provide food to fill the hungry tummies of her family. Suman and Vada, the two eldest girls, helped their mother by passing out the plates. Their father was served first, with Suman's three brothers, Hira the oldest, then Manu and Cabir receiving their food next. The boys sat close together, the younger two watching Hira closely and copying his every action. Hira was twelve, growing taller daily it seemed, and developing a handsome physique from his hard toil every day out in the fields at the back of the house. To his two younger brothers, he was a figure to be hero-worshipped and to his parents, their pride and joy.

Once Mukesh and the boys were served, the girls came next; Rohini, six years of age, Gulabasha, three, and the baby of the family, two-year-old Rupal. The children, except for Hira, were barefoot, shoes being a luxury the family could not afford. All sat crossed legged with their plates on their laps.

The younger girls wore thin dresses, well-worn hand-me-downs from other homes in the village, but pretty, nonetheless. Suman, approaching the age of ten, had begun to wear a traditional Punjabi suit, a tunic and trousers outfit considered suitable for girls of her age. The suit was also second-hand, with patches holding together the torn or frayed parts and ill-fitting her slender frame.

Not that Suman ever noticed or cared what she wore; if everyone had something to wear each day, she was happy. She seemed to have a natural maternal instinct and enjoyed her role as her siblings' second mother, looking after their needs and loving them as Kanya did. Speaking only Marathi, the local language of Maharashtra, the children called their mother Aayi, meaning beloved mother. Suman also loved the nickname they gave her, Taayee, elder sister.

The family ate in silence, one of their father's many rules. The children had learned early in life that Mukesh's will was not to be crossed. Even Rupal, cuddled on Suman's knee to eat her rice from Suman's fingers, knew that chatter was not permitted until the meal was over and she could go outside to play on the dusty track until the sun began to disappear from the sky.

Darkness came down early on the village that night and slowly the noise and activity in each household died down. The cow had been tethered outside the hut, and the poultry settled for the night. Mukesh climbed onto the only bed in the house, quickly falling into a deep sleep. With the coming of Holi, Mukesh spent most of his days with the other men in the village drinking bhang, an intoxicating concoction specially prepared for the festival. It was made from the leaves of the marijuana plant mixed with some milk, masala powder and a little root ginger. The strong drink took effect after just one or two glasses, leaving Mukesh incapable of carrying out his daily work in the fields and adding to his wife's already heavy burden.

Kanya eyed him angrily then nudged him fiercely, trying to curb the sound of his rumbling snores which filled the house. He grunted and rolled over, oblivious of her presence, but the noise subsided significantly. She settled the children on the floor of the hut, onto rough, tattered bamboo matting. She herself lay down beside her daughters, curling her body into a ball and listening to the crickets outside making their nightly din. Eventually peace descended on the family as they slumbered.

Suman woke early, rising silently and rolling her mat up carefully before stowing it under her father's bed. As the eldest daughter, the bulk of the responsibility for helping her mother with domestic chores was hers, as was the care of her younger siblings with their basic needs. Gently she began to wake them, helping them dress and dishing out breakfast in the form of pan biscuits from a tin on the shelf. Her final task was to sweep the floors with the broom made from grasses and reeds, making as little sound as possible, careful not to disturb her father's sleep, knowing this would earn her a fist across her back.

Running quickly, she joined her mother in the field beside the house to tend the crops peeping through the dusty soil. And by late morning, she was once again wending her way along the track in the direction of the river, an empty water pot under her arm.

The noon sun was relentless, and the villagers retreated to their huts and houses to escape the searing heat of midday. Inside the Sudra household, Kanya was settling her little ones down for an afternoon nap, the older boys still working in the field, tending the crops. Mukesh was missing and she suspected he would be found somewhere around the village sleeping off the effects of the bhang. Feeling guilty, she prayed silently to be spared his company until she could herself rest for a short time in order to regain her energy after a very busy morning. Chores completed, she crossed the room to stand in front of a small shrine, arranged on a cloth in an alcove on the wall. She lit a candle and bowed her head. A picture of Lord Krishna stood in the centre of the shrine and Kanya offered her *Puja* in silence. With head bent, she sprinkled some grain around the candle and laid down a flower she had plucked earlier from the bushes outside. Her hands together in prayer, she thanked God for the gifts of her children and for the new baby growing in her belly. At last, satisfied that everyone was safe and well, Kanya lay down beside her children and closed her eyes.

A couple of hours later, as the sleepy villagers began to return to life, a large battered truck arrived at the entrance to the village, a loud tooting of the horn heralding its arrival. Two men dressed in

4

jeans and open-necked shirts climbed down from the front and stretched their limbs, as if they had been in the truck for a considerable time. Unknown visitors were a rare occurrence and several villagers stopped their tasks to watch. The strangers looked very out of place, their western clothes contrasting strongly with the white kurtas of the village men.

Approaching a couple of youths, the strangers asked to speak to the Sarpanch, the head man of the community. On being introduced to Deepak Mandani, respected head of the village council, the men explained they had come from a government organisation based in Mumbai. The organisation was one with money to give away to villages such as this. Money to pay for the education of the children – particularly girls around the ages of eight to twelve - who would not otherwise receive schooling. They had been given the task of distributing this funding and taking the chosen children to a centre in Mumbai for a short period, until they could read and write.

Delighted with this news and knowing that there were several girls in the village who would never learn these skills otherwise, Deepak, an uneducated man himself, led the two around the poverty-stricken community. Starting with the poorest families living in houses made of corrugated metal sheets or tarpaulin tents, they met with parents, impressing them with their stories of the centre where their girls would be given an education, food and shelter, and also earn money to send back to their families to supplement their meagre incomes.

Deepak himself, spurred on by the promise of rupees for his own family, and funding for a village hall in return for the encouragement he gave to parents, was loud in his praise for the wonderful opportunity that had come their way. Before long, two households had taken up the opportunity, and excitement began to spread through the village.

Reaching Kanya's house, she and Mukesh listened carefully, but Kanya dismissed the offer and backed away, the thought of losing any of her children striking fear into her heart. She pulled at Mukesh's arm, urging him away from the strangers. Ignoring his wife's plea, Mukesh, seeing this as an opportunity to relieve himself of some of his more pressing debts, negotiated a small sum of money up front in exchange for their eldest daughter. Kanya watched the transaction in silence, but as she saw him count out the rupees he had been given, her terror grew, and she cried out against his actions.

'No, Mukesh. No, no,' she pleaded, her tears beginning to fall. 'Give the money back, I beg of you. We must not let Suman go in this way. We do not know these men.'

Once indoors, Mukesh silenced his weeping wife with a slap, informing her that their daughter would now have a future; she would learn to read and write and make him a proud father. Kanya pleaded with him some more, to no avail. With fear in her eyes, knowing that Suman had returned from the river earlier in the afternoon, she watched as he left the house to search for her, silently praying that her treasured daughter would not be found.

Despite Kanya's prayers, Mukesh soon returned with Suman at his heels. Alerted by the villagers, he had found her with some of her friends amongst the colourful flowers of the forest, making garlands and hair ornaments with nimble fingers to wear at the forthcoming Holi celebrations in the village.

Kanya's heart broke as she tried unsuccessfully to convince herself that they were giving Suman a chance that no-one else in the family had ever had. Her devastation was eased only slightly by knowing that Suman would not be going alone, that there would be at least two other girls from the village with her. As she quickly packed the few belongings that Suman possessed and added some food to the bag for her daughter's journey, Suman watched her, a puzzled look in her eyes.

At last Kanya stopped, to kneel in front of her daughter and hold her tight.

'Suman, I need you to be strong for me,' she whispered softly. 'There's something I have to tell you.'

CHAPTER 1

Amsterdam

Emerging from a deep sleep, Suman lay still for a moment, her eyes coming slowly into focus on a ray of light dancing on the floor nearby. She turned her head a little in the hazy expectation of seeing her brothers and sisters lying beside her. But she was alone. Half-remembered events flitted through her mind as her eyes remained fixed on the beam. Was she so far away from home, so many hundreds of miles from her family and from the only life she had ever known? Had she really endured that long, uncomfortable ride in the back of a truck, and the unspeakable horrors that had greeted her when the truck had reached its destination? Nausea rose in her throat as reality seeped slowly into her thoughts, the reality of being sold at the end of the journey, like a piece of fruit at the market.

She had watched and listened to the bartering, not realising at first that *she* was the commodity on sale. Not until the transaction had taken place and she was handed over forcefully by the two men in the truck to some others. She had watched as the money changed hands. She had watched as the truck drivers scurried away, counting their rupees.

Then she had realised and knew she had been betrayed. Under the hands of the other men, she had been stripped, used and abused. She was hurt badly, lashing out and screaming with pain and fear, but her captors had ignored her. Then she was silent.

She turned over, her face pointed towards a stark white wall, her eyes closed tightly as she tried unsuccessfully to thrust these unwanted memories away. Her thoughts moved painfully through the dark days after her 'sale': men coming and going from the room she was kept in, the violence inflicted on her body, and the heart-wrenching, desperate longing for her mother.

Lying on the floor, still not fully awake, Suman desperately willed it to be just a dream, a horrible nightmare. Then she could awaken and be back in India, living with her family, her mother gently rousing her from sleep. Memories of the aeroplane that had brought her to this place suddenly entered her thoughts. She thought of the cold, cold air that had attacked her body as she was brought out of the airport and into a car which had carried her to yet another locked room, another prison, and she shivered.

Risking a peep through her fingers, wet with tears, she saw the blurred outline of the room's walls, and blinked hard. No, it was no dream. Everything had been real, the painful goodbye to her mother, being forced into the dirty lorry with two other girls from the village. For a moment, she wondered where her friends Karima and Neha were. They were the two girls who had travelled with her, full of trepidation at where they were going. They had been taken away by one of the truck drivers as soon as they arrived at their destination and she had listened in fear to their terrified screams and sobs. When the cries subsided, she had heard nothing more than the loud bang of a slammed door, then silence. Long ago, it seemed.

Suman turned and stretched out on her back, looking up at the light hanging from the ceiling. If she concentrated hard, she could pretend she was in her own home. She could picture the hut so clearly if she kept her eyes on the bulb. There she was, inside the cool dimness of her house, lit only with one tungsten bulb dangling from the ceiling, awaiting its infrequent supply of power. In her mind, she turned to look at her mother's dented *handis* arranged so neatly on a shelf on the wall. Part of her mother's dowry, the aluminium pots were Kanya's pride and joy, used daily to cook for her family on the open fire in a corner of the small room.

Suman sniffed, trying to capture the scent of the rice bubbling in the pot and the aroma of wood smoke filling the house. She tried also to conjure up the distinctive smell of the house itself, the cow-dung blocks on the walls and the clay and mud which formed the floor. Outside, in the morning light, she pictured Manoratha, the family's aged skeletal cow grazing lazily amongst the rubbish strewn about, a couple of hens scratching at her side. For a moment she felt safe as her thoughts of home intensified.

Still in her imagination, she could see the garden, a small area of crops which gave the family their living. Beyond that, she pictured the cement structure of the communal village toilet, a facility of which the villagers were immensely proud. No longer did the women and girls of the village have to visit the fields early in the morning, out of sight of the men, to carry out their daily ablutions. The advent of the communal toilet had seemed a godsend to the females, including Kanya and all her daughters, at the mercy of snakes, bladder infections, mosquito bites and sexual predators.

Suman's daydreams stopped abruptly. The noise of people passing by the door quickly dispersed her memories of home. She sat up, gently rubbing a swollen cheek which had begun to throb painfully, at the same time becoming aware of several other injuries on her body. Her arm had begun to ache, and bruising was showing around her elbow. She touched it gingerly, staring at the multi-coloured patches on her skin. Other parts of her body were sore too, not least the deep, desperate ache inside, an ache to go home, to the sunshine, to her mother.

Suman had never known such sadness, being so alone with no-one to help her and no way to escape. The nightmarish events she'd experienced since being taken away from the home she loved crowded her mind. She closed her eyes tightly against these terrible thoughts and dropped her head into her hands. The tears came rapidly, and sobs shook her small body as she cried out in despair, her mother's name on her lips. No-one came; no-one heard her cries nor her pleas for help.

In time her sobs subsided, and the tears stopped cascading down her cheeks. She wiped her face with the back of her hands, leaving streaks of dust across her face. Knuckling her eyes hard until they were red and sore, she lifted her head and looked cautiously around the room to which she had been brought last night.

It was a sparsely furnished room with a solid wooden table to one side and a few broken chairs dotted about. A thick, dusty blanket lay nearby and she vaguely remembered someone throwing her on top of it before leaving and locking the door from the outside.

She rose and tried the handle, but it was still locked. Her eyes swept upwards to a high window through which she could see the brightness of daylight outside. As carefully and quietly as possible, she pushed the small table along the floor until it sat directly below the window. Climbing up, her head reached the window but not high enough for her to see out.

Placing one of the broken chairs on top of the table, she tried again. Now her chin reached well above the windowsill and wiping the grimy glass with the side of her hand, she stared out at the scene below.

On the opposite side of the road, Suman could see a long terrace of houses stretching far into the distance. On the near side a row of shops and office buildings caught her eye, with brightly coloured canopies and the street busy with people milling about. She spotted a small grassy area nearby overlooked by a very large building with coloured windows and a tall steeple. She stood for a long time, watching in wonder all these things that were new to her. A pram was not something she had seen before and she gasped as she spotted a baby sitting inside. She watched a man walking a dog on a lead and wondered why he felt the need to tie his dog up in this way.

As she took in the details of the street below, her mind again began to conjure up another, more familiar scene. A scene where dogs ran around as free as air and babies were wrapped against their mothers' bodies inside a shawl; a scene where the neighbour's cow ambled its way along the track, a bell jangling from its neck.

Suman turned abruptly away from the window, unwilling to cry again. She climbed down from the chair, making as little noise as possible, and jumped onto the floor, then lifted the chair back to where it had been. With her teeth clenched tightly and a determined look in her eyes, the thought uppermost in her mind was that she had to get away from here, had to try to escape from these people who were keeping her captive.

She didn't know anything or anyone out there, she realised desolately, so where could she go? And where was here? What was this place? She shivered again and rubbed her arms briskly. Ever since being brought off the aeroplane, it had been so cold.

Alternating between sleep and long periods of boredom, the day progressed with no sign of life other than the passers-by outside the window. Hunger pangs began to gnaw at her empty stomach, and she longed for a drink of water to relieve the dryness in her mouth. Ideas of escape were fading and although she had slept on and off all afternoon, Suman's body was growing weaker and every injury was making itself known.

Her swollen cheek still throbbed painfully where she had been hit, a result of Suman biting down hard on one of her abuser's fingers which were closed tightly around her mouth. The man had lashed out, but Suman had no regrets and resolved to do it again if necessary. Some of her other injuries had been sustained during the rapes she had had to endure, and her aching arm brought back the memory of being thrown into a corner of the room and crashing against the wall.

Her contemplation of her injuries continued until interrupted suddenly by the sound of footsteps outside the door and the rattle of a key in the lock. However, instead of relief, the terror returned, and she scrambled over the floor as fast as she could to cower under the small table, the only protection in the room. She hid her face in her hands and pushed herself into the wall.

'Now what's all this?' she heard a woman's voice say. 'We can't have this, can we? You must be terrified, you poor thing. Come out of there and let me see you.'

Suman's eyes flew open at the sound of the voice, taken aback by the fact that it was a woman who had entered the room. Unsure and afraid, she didn't move.

'Come on, child, you've nothing to be afraid of. Sit up and let me see you.'

Suman stared at the tall, smartly dressed woman who was addressing her. She was wearing a green, heavily embroidered sari and was decked from head to toe in gold jewellery. Her hair had been cut into a short stylish bob with highlights of gold added throughout, something Suman had never seen before. She was familiar only with the jet black, uncut hair of the women of her village, worn flowing down their backs or pleated into a large pigtail. The woman's red bindi on her forehead proclaimed her a married woman, and Suman's eyes widened in astonishment as she took in the heavily made-up face, thick with foundation cream, garish lipstick, and her colourful eyeshadow. The woman laid a canvas bag on the floor and knelt to pull Suman out from under the table.

'That's better,' she said, cupping Suman's chin with a gentle movement. 'Now I can see your face. And what a pretty face it is. Relax, child, you're safe with me.'

'My name is Geeta and I'm here to look after you and get you all cleaned up. And what about something nice to eat, eh? I'm sure you must be very hungry.'

Suspicion and distrust were written on Suman's face as she watched Geeta lift her bag and pull out some bread and cheese.

'Come, child, eat. You must be hungry after your long journey. While you are enjoying your food, I'll explain where we are going and what you need to know. Then we'll get you all cleaned up and into some new clothes. You'd like that, wouldn't you?'

Suman remained still, watching Geeta from the corner of her eye, not nearly ready to trust but hoping with all her heart that this was indeed someone who had come to rescue and look after her. The woman spoke with an unfamiliar accent, in a dialect slightly different to the one that Suman was familiar with, but she understood most of what was being said.

Geeta asked Suman her name and her age. With a guarded look, Suman did not answer at first, but eventually asked a question of her own.

'Are you taking me home? Or to school? Will I learn to read and write?'

Amusement lit up Geeta's eyes as she answered.

'Oh, yes. You'll be learning a lot of new things. You may not get to read and write but there is one thing you will learn ...'

She paused, leaning forward as she spoke, her voice and face changing to a threatening demeanour. 'And that is to do everything you are told to do, exactly when you are told to do it.' Her tone hardened. 'If I am disobeyed at all, in any way, the punishment will be severe. Is that clear?'

Suman's eyes narrowed with suspicion as she realised that she had been right in thinking that this woman had not come to rescue her.

'Is that clear?' The repeated question was even more menacing and Suman, remaining silent, nodded her head.

Satisfied, Geeta resumed a more relaxed stance.

'Good, now we've got that sorted out, eat your food and then clear up all the crumbs from the floor. There will be no more food for quite some time.'

She paused.

'And then I will take you to your... school.'

A shiver ran through Suman's body as Geeta's laugh accompanied her exit from the room.

It was some minutes after Geeta's departure before Suman began to eat her bread and drink the water the woman had left. Starving, she quickly devoured everything she had been given.

Her mind was in turmoil. Realising that this was not going to be a rescue from her captors Suman could only hope that there would be someone soon that she would meet, someone who might help her get back home.

It was two hours before she again heard footsteps and the turning of the key in the lock. Geeta had changed her clothes before returning to Suman's room, and Suman took in the sumptuousness of the woman's beautiful, heavily embroidered jacket and golden-threaded dress. Over her arm, she carried an armful of clothes which she laid down on the floor beside Suman.

Turning, Geeta called out through the open door and another young woman entered, not looking at Suman but keeping her eyes on Geeta as she received curt instructions.

Just as Geeta had said, Suman was taken to a bathroom within the building to be washed in a warm overhead shower, a new experience for her as she had only ever washed in the river before. Her hair was scrubbed clean and brushed by the girl, who explained during the procedure that her name was Angena and that she was also from India, from the state of Rajasthan. She also spoke a slightly different dialect from Suman but was able to make herself understood, adding gestures to explain what she wanted Suman to do. Once dry, Angena applied cream to Suman's injuries, and perfume to her skin, before asking her to get dressed in one of the jewelled outfits that Geeta had supplied.

Ignoring Suman's appeals to help her go home, Angena took a firm grip of Suman's arm.

'We must all obey Geeta's instructions,' she said sternly. 'We have no choice. Come.'

Keeping a strong grip on Suman, Angena forced her back to the room where Geeta waited. Commanding Suman to sit on the floor, Geeta began to talk. Suman, struggling at first to take in what she was saying, listened with a slowly breaking heart as understanding dawned on what her life was to be like. More abuse like the abuse she had already suffered, more pain, and worse still, punishment not only to Suman, but to her parents and siblings back in India if she failed to obey the instructions of the people who now owned her.

Hideous pictures crowded into Suman's mind as she gazed at Geeta. Her small hands unconsciously closed around her body to protect herself. How well she remembered the blows rained down on her back and arms, the beatings she had endured when she had tried to defy her captors. Striking out in defence had proved futile and her screams had been silenced with more violence. Was Geeta right? Could these evil people do something terrible to her mother and father and to her siblings back home in their village?

She closed her eyes, overwhelming fear mingling with sadness as Geeta's voice invaded her thoughts. With her hands held tightly over her mouth, she whispered for her mother.

Furious, Geeta grabbed hold of Suman's thin arms and hauled her to her feet.

'Your mother cannot help you. You will do what I tell you to do. Do you understand?' Geeta's words were terrifying, but Suman stared back defiantly.

'I want to go home,' she shouted.

Leaning down, Geeta tightened her grip, digging her long, lacquered nails into Suman's tender skin. She shook the child hard, before delivering a resounding slap to Suman's face.

'There is no going home. Do you understand?' she repeated through clenched teeth.

Suman did not respond. Frustrated by her silence Geeta gave another slap. Not a sound came from Suman's mouth, and her eyes were filled with loathing and defiance as she looked at the tall woman in front of her. Blood began to trickle from her nose.

Geeta swore, the obscenity bursting loudly from her mouth. Turning, she addressed Angena, still hovering by the door.

'Clean her up quickly then take her to the Studio. They are waiting for her.'

Suman remained impassive as Geeta strode from the room. She stayed silent as Angena cleaned the blood from her nose. When she had finished, the Indian girl leaned forward and, gently taking Suman's face in her hands, whispered, 'Do what she says, it's the only way you'll survive.'

Suman looked into Angena's dark, heavily-kohled eyes. The two stared at each other, Suman recognising for the first time since her nightmare had begun, a spark of compassion and concern.

Then Angena repeated softly, 'Do what they say. These are bad people and they do a lot of very cruel things.

They own you now. Remember that. If you give them any trouble, they will hurt your family back home, even kill them if they must. There have been many children who have come here. The ones who stay alive are the ones like me, who obey the rules. This building is a nightclub; you'll soon find out what that is. It's also a brothel where men pay money to come and be with you.'

Her voice was low and compelling. 'I was brought here just like you, about your age, and I had to learn too. The ones who fight against them are killed. These are powerful men so there's no guardian angel going to come along and rescue you. Your life and the lives of your family depend on what you do now.'

Suman's body began to shake as tears fell from her huge eyes. She stared in horror at Angena who groaned, leaning forward to enfold Suman in her arms.

'Now do you understand?' she asked gently. Suman nodded. 'I'll be here for you when things get too bad. Remember.'

Then, moving soundlessly, she took Suman by the hand and led her out of the door, her heart aching at the thought of the ordeal that was about to be inflicted on the innocent child.

CHAPTER 2

Edinburgh

Collecting her suitcase from the carousel at Edinburgh Airport, Ellie sighed and stifled a yawn. She was on her way home from a work assignment in Mumbai, tired, sticky, and longing for her bed. She had been airborne for almost ten and a half hours, during which time she had caught up with a lot of her paperwork.

Looking at her watch, she was surprised to find it was only nine thirty in the morning. Knowing she should check in at the office, to let them know she had arrived home safely, she debated about doing it by phone instead of a visit. As always, her conscience won over her physical wellbeing and she soon found herself negotiating the thirty-minute drive from the airport into the city. Traffic was lighter than normal, the sun was shining, and she promised herself that this would be a quick visit to let them know she was home and to check that all was well with her colleagues who had returned from Mumbai some days earlier.

She was the last member of the team to return from this assignment, having remained behind to carry out some much-needed training courses to local customs and excise staff in Mumbai and to wrap up the investigation they had been working on.

Ellie's job was a complicated one, sometimes extremely challenging, sometimes dangerous, often exciting, but never boring. Her employer was United Brewers Inc., and for the last four years she had held the title of anti-counterfeit officer with a very dedicated team of six working under her lead. Her job took her to many of the largest cities in the world, India being the third country she had visited this year, and it was still only February.

The company's office was on Dundas Street, and as she entered the front door, she was greeted warmly by Jim Cumming, long-time doorman of UBI.

'Good to have you back, Miss Douglas. How was the trip?'

'Very interesting, Jim,' she replied as she signed herself in. 'I caught all the baddies and even got a tan while I was doing it,' she added with a twinkle.

The friendly doorman grinned. 'Aye, Miss Marple of UBI, that's who you are, Miss Douglas.'

'Welcome back, Ellie.' A less familiar voice made her turn to see who had spoken. 'The office has been quiet without you. How was India?'

Geoff Mendez, one of the company's IT specialists was approaching the desk. Normally a very quiet, serious man, she was surprised to find him so genial.

'Too much sun, too much heat and too many people, as usual. It's been a tough trip this time; a bit more stressful and dangerous than normal.'

Geoff's eyebrows lifted in surprise. 'In what way?'

'Have you ever been to India?' she asked as they began to walk along the corridor together.

He shook his head.

'Well, there are the rickshaws for a start. Getting around is quite an adventure if you use the motorised rickshaws. You take your life in your hands when you climb aboard and this trip, we had three near misses with other cars before we decided taxis were slower but much safer. It was as if someone was out to get us. It was scary. They seemed to be trying to knock us off the road.

The work was dangerous too,' she continued. 'We tested random bottles from about three hundred and fifty outlets and found nearly fifty per cent counterfeit.'

'That's a lot of whisky. Who buys it all for you?'

'We use students if there are universities or colleges nearby. Or, more often we just use enforcement agencies, you know, private detectives who do the leg work for us before we arrive.'

'And is fifty a high percentage? What do you normally find?'

'Fifty is very high. Most areas of Europe will show only about eight per cent counterfeit, but the Middle and Far East are usually a bit higher.'

'That points to a lot of lost revenue for us, doesn't it? Not to mention the risk to UBI's reputation.'

She nodded. 'When these figures are so high it's common for

them to be linked to other types of criminal activity in the area. And once word gets out that we're there testing, the counterfeiters start to get nervous. That brings the danger in to the job. In Mumbai, we think we've uncovered a big operation out at a place called Nariman Point. That's where the statistics show up the most concentrated number of outlets. We've handed it all over to the Mumbai police who were brilliant after our three misses in the rickshaws. They provided some guards for us while we were working and followed our taxis every time we were on the move.'

'God, Ellie. What I wouldn't give to come on these assignments as part of your team.' His enthusiasm surprised Ellie, knowing him only as a private, reticent man not given to expressing his feelings like this.

'I'm sure your job is just as exciting in its own way.'

'Well, I wouldn't say exciting, exactly.' He gave a wry smile. 'Maybe more 'interesting' than exciting. The tension's been building here too, in the office, and the old man's been desperate for you to return and take control. The Amsterdam job's been giving problems,' he explained as he saw her puzzled look. 'You could be heading off to the Netherlands this week.'

'I haven't even been home yet,' she replied, surprised by his words. 'I hope you're wrong.'

'Well, I can't see them sending anyone else. Good luck with it all. If I can help in any way, just shout.'

'Thanks Geoff, I will.'

With a nod, Ellie turned away from Geoff to make her way to her office. The news that she was heading straight back into more problems was worrying, and Ellie hoped that Geoff was mistaken in his prediction. She would like some time to catch her breath after her India trip and to make some inroads on her huge backlog of paperwork.

A backward glance showed that Geoff had disappeared in another direction, and she wondered for a moment about why he had been so chatty. He was a man who usually kept himself to himself, known more for his silence than for any casual banter with other staff members. Highly intelligent and reputed to be a mastermind in the field of computer science, his nickname around the office was 'The Professor', a title Ellie suspected was indeed a factual one, gained during his time at University College London prior to joining UBI. She was also aware, despite his very attractive appearance, that Geoff was unmarried, unattached, and pretty much unavailable according to the few brave female employees who had tried to get to know him.

Shame, thought Ellie, who in keeping with these other women had been known to feel a pull towards this likeable man. However, total dedication to her job and a keen ambition meant she was not looking for any romantic attachments at this stage in her career. Once into her office and the door closed, Geoff was dismissed from her thoughts.

The old man that Geoff had referred to was in fact John Anderson, chief executive of UBI and Ellie's immediate boss. Ellie's work ethic and commitment to the company had helped her rise through the ranks from humble beginnings as a secretary up to the position of personal assistant to the manager of the Overseas Affairs Division. This was where she had first come to the attention of John, then new to the role of chief executive. Within a short space of time, Ellie had been offered the post of anti-counterfeit officer, a position that had been created in response to the rising problem of counterfeit whisky throughout the world.

It was around the late 1990s when the whisky corporations had first identified the extent of counterfeiting, reputed even then to cost the industry somewhere in the region of a hundred million pounds each year. Within UBI, a fraud research department had been set up, employing scientists and technical experts like Geoff to find ways to expose and limit the problem.

Ellie had been excited to be offered the opportunity to join the department and was now heading up her own team of diligent, committed employees of whom she was extremely proud.

Reaching the secretary's office, she knocked and opened the door.

'Is John free, Gina? Can I have a word?'

'I'm sorry, Ellie, he's in a meeting at the moment. Would you like to speak to someone else?'

'I'll wait for John. Can you tell him I'm home from Mumbai and would like to see him later if he has time? I'll be here 'til about lunchtime, then I may have to go home and put my head down for a while.' She grimaced. 'Jet lag. No sleep on the plane home.'

'No problem. I'll tell him as soon as I can. Glad you're home. We've all missed you.'

For the next hour or so, Ellie's head was down over her desk, checking through the backlog of correspondence that had gathered while she'd been away. She found time for some quick calls with a few of the company's overseas directors, including Archie Wallis, director of the Amsterdam office. From Archie, she learned that the information given by Geoff earlier was correct, and that the Dutch office was in fact expecting a visit from her in the very near future.

'Looking forward to your team's visit,' he confirmed. 'I'll email details of the accommodation where you and the team will be staying and get the sample bottles bought before you come. I'm sure it'll turn out to be nothing much, just a storm in a teacup. You didn't find much wrong the last time you were here.'

Ellie answered sharply, 'I wouldn't be sent back so soon if it was *nothing much*, Archie.' She emphasised the last words of her sentence. 'My time's too precious. Tell me what the problems are exactly?'

Realising he had erred in trivialising the troubles he was experiencing, Archie began to explain that they had recently had an outbreak of food poisoning in the city which was being investigated by health services and police. Halfway through a question to him, Ellie stopped, suddenly aware that Archie was no longer on the other end of the line. The phone had gone dead. Annoyed, she immediately phoned him back, only to hear the engaged signal. She tried a second time, again unsuccessfully. Had Archie deliberately ended their call she asked herself. He had certainly seemed a bit reticent in wanting to discuss his problems, but why on earth would he not want to bring her up to speed before her impending visit? Checking the Netherlands file, she located Archie's personal mobile number and tried a third time to get back to him. This time she was rewarded with an answer from him.

'I'm so sorry, Ellie, all our phone lines went down as we were speaking. There are roadworks outside the office and I think they must have cut the lines. I tried but couldn't get back to you.'

Ellie accepted Archie's apology and reason for the termination of the call, but a little of her earlier suspicion remained implanted in her mind. This suspicion was not allayed with their subsequent conversation as Archie gave her scant information on the food poisoning outbreak before steering the chat on to a very different topic.

UBI research scientists had very recently come up with new technology which involved using brand packaging security marks to help the company identify whisky bottles that had been tampered with. Just like bank notes contain water marks, UBI now had labels with covert marks to help identification along with new security caps for their bottles. Some of these were external marks, but some were disguised, identifiable only with the new tools being perfected by the researchers and being trialled by Ellie's team. Archie's interest in how these trials were going formed the rest of their conversation and although Ellie tried again to discuss the food poisoning outbreak, rather than do this, he apologised and said that one of his staff had entered his office and he would have to go.

It was with annoyance that Ellie put the phone down, frustration showing on her face. Archie's attitude concerned her a great deal, and the suspicion that he had ended the first call remained in her mind.

Keen to discuss this with her boss, Ellie was pleased when very soon afterwards Gina called to say that John was ready to see her. She hastily gathered up the documents scattered on her desk and slid them into her briefcase before grabbing her jacket and heading along the corridor to her boss's office.

'Good morning,' John greeted her as she entered. 'Good to have you back. Get yourself a coffee before you sit down. You look like you need one.'

'Thanks, but I'll skip the coffee, John,' she responded. 'It's a holiday I need!'

'Ah, well, I might be able to help with that one, in a manner of speaking. I'm sending you off to the Netherlands, to Amsterdam to be precise. Not a holiday, but we could look at a few days off at the end of your assignment.'

Ellie was pleased. 'Okay, I'll settle for that. Tell me about Amsterdam and then I'll tell you what's made me feel the need for a holiday.'

John sat back in his chair and took a drink from his coffee cup. He was a handsome man, in his late fifties, with a charisma and personality that encouraged his employees to regard him with both respect and admiration.

'You know the background to this assignment; you were in the Netherlands only three months ago. Your research showed that we did have some problems there, but not major ones. However, while you were out in India, we received a request from the Amsterdam Trading Standards office asking us to go back and have another look. They've had a worrying outbreak of illness related to food poisoning in a heavily populated area of the city. It's a bad one, Ellie, with a number of people being hospitalised and one death reported.'

Ellie's face registered some of the shock she felt when she heard this last piece of news.

'I did hear some of this when I spoke to Archie Wallis about twenty minutes ago, but he didn't mention the severity of it; no mention that there were people in hospital or that someone had died. In fact, he seemed to make light of the whole thing, using the words 'a storm in a teacup'. That's what upset me so much earlier. Is he aware of everything that's going on?'

'Of course, he reported it in the first place. I'll have a word with him once we've finished here to find out what's going on. That's certainly not the attitude he should be taking. Leave that one with me.'

Ellie nodded. 'Tell me more about the outbreak. I take it they suspect it's because of tampered whisky?'

'No doubt about it.'

'What did they use?'

'The usual diluting substances, methanol for flavour and caramel to colour. Only they've used too high a percentage of methanol. And what's bad for us is that the source has been traced back to a number of clubs and supermarkets selling what Trading Standards are calling 'bad quality' Glen Lomond Whisky – our newest brand.'

'That's very similar to what we've just found in Mumbai,' Ellie interposed. 'We're coming up with a lot of Glen Lomond with dangerous percentages of methanol there too.'

'In that case it's critical I get your reports before you go.'

Ellie was deeply concerned: poisonous whisky was devastating news for the company. Her heart went out to the people who had suffered as a result of drinking counterfeit whisky and the family who had lost a loved one.

She could also understand John's unease that the publicity surrounding the outbreak might have a devastating effect on their export figures to the Netherlands. And now there was a possibility it could be linked to Mumbai as well.

'Presumably the police and local authorities are involved. How far forward are they in finding the source?'

John sighed before replying.

'They're struggling, although they've recovered well over a hundred cases of the illicit whisky so far. It's looking like this is just the tip of the iceberg. There have also been suggestions that the people involved in distributing the whisky may have links to some of the other countries we've been working in. Like Taiwan and of course, India. Customs and excise in all these countries are heavily involved in the investigations as well as police and, if what I hear is correct, Interpol have been advised although they have not been officially brought in yet.

I'd like you and your team to go back to Amsterdam to do a lot more investigating. They need your expertise. The counterfeiters seem to be making everything from caps to labels, and even the outer cases of the contraband have our stamp on them. Authentic looking, but obviously forged.'

Ellie was listening carefully to John's words, biting her top lip, an unconscious habit she'd had from childhood.

'Are you worrying about the timescale?' he asked as he watched her. 'As I said before, it's essential I have all your reports before you go. If there's a link between the Netherlands and Mumbai, your findings could be critical. I can only give you a few days and then I'd like you and the team to get to Amsterdam. What do you think?'

'I'm just slightly concerned about the timing. There should be enough time to do my reports and give you the figures from Mumbai, but I'll need to do a good bit of reading to bring me right up to date with the Dutch situation. That'll take a bit of time as I can't afford to skim over it. Could you spare someone to give me a hand with my stats?'

John leaned back in his chair, a relieved look crossing his craggy brow.

'Sure, no problem. I'll speak to Geoff and see what his diary is like this week. I know it's way under-utilising his skills, but Geoff's keen to help us with this investigation. As you know, he created the initial programmes to link all your stats and give reports on the similarities in counterfeiting and he's developing better programmes which can pick up on all the small nuances that your reports throw up. How would you feel if we asked him to help you?'

Ellie nodded. 'Sounds good to me, although I think analysing my stats and typing up my reports will be a huge demotion for the Professor. Very mundane, but if he's willing, it would be a great help. Sounds as if he's taking all the data we have to a whole new level.'

'He is. I'll see if he's got time this week to help you. If not, I'll get someone else. Now I'll let you go home to get some rest.' John stood as he spoke, and Ellie lifted her briefcase and jacket and headed for the door.

'Take care out there, Ellie and don't take any chances. Stay in touch daily. And regarding Archie, I'll speak to him, but you'll be working with him while you're out there so give me a ring if you have any more concerns.'

He paused before continuing thoughtfully, 'I'm going to give you one of the protection officers with you this time. If you find any similarities at all to the Mumbai assignment or even the Taiwan one, we could be looking at something much bigger than we imagined. Back out quickly if there's any threat or any sign of danger to you and the team.'

Leaving the office, Ellie thought about John's last words. She was keen to get started on what looked like being one of the most challenging jobs she had ever worked on. However, his remarks made her remember that some of the most demanding assignments she had been on had also been the most dangerous. The Venezuela job three years ago had been her introduction to the high risks she and her team sometimes had to face. The counterfeiters had openly threatened the team with guns after gaining access to their testing headquarters in Caracas and destroying all their equipment and samples. Only the bravery of the armed guards in getting them quickly away from the situation had averted a major disaster for Ellie and her courageous team members.

She remembered the armoured vehicles they were obliged to travel in and the constant presence of bodyguards. With Caracas having the highest homicide rate of any city she had ever visited, and major crime rampant in Venezuela, it was with relief they had boarded their plane home at the end of a difficult assignment.

Yangon in Myanmar hadn't been much better. The risks of investigating counterfeit whisky in one of the most corrupt countries in the world had again been brought home to the UBI employees working in Ellie's team at that time. For a second time, Ellie had experienced the fear of being threatened and having a gun pointed in her face. Remaining calm, she had negotiated with her masked assailants and thankfully gained the team's freedom in exchange for the fifty cases of whisky they were about to test and all the money the team possessed.

About a year later, when word came to the company that the guerrilla group responsible - organised and run by a group of corrupt officials in the Burmese Army – had been tracked down, the counterfeiting had turned out to be just one of their operations. The group's activities included money laundering and trafficking of women and girls into China and Ellie remembered the pride she had felt for her team who had helped to bring them to justice.

Yes, she thought, nothing like a good challenge to keep me on my toes.

CHAPTER 3

Edinburgh

The traffic around the city centre was heavy and the pavements congested with local shoppers and tourists as Ellie drove along Princes Street and then out of the city towards Queensferry Road, taking her eventually to the quieter streets of Barnton, the attractive suburb she called home. She steered her car into a space in the underground parking lot of an apartment block, unloaded the luggage from the boot and made her way up to her flat on the second floor.

Exhaustion was really setting in by the time she unlocked the door, but she knew that if she sat down at this moment, she would fall asleep immediately. With an effort, she unpacked her bags, filled the washing machine and switched it on. She travelled light on her trips abroad yet somehow still managed to bring home a huge amount of dirty washing in her suitcase.

Waiting for the kettle to boil for a much-needed cup of tea, Ellie curled her legs under her on the sofa and lifted the phone. Now that she had reported in at the office to say that she was safely home there were two other phone calls she had to make before she hit the pillow.

The first one was to her mother. Evelyn Hamilton, divorced from Ellie's father and now married to Matt Hamilton, lived in Anstruther in Fife. Evelyn and Matt were the proud owners of an elegant house overlooking the harbour and marina, with stunning views out over the North Sea. Her divorce and subsequent single parent status had resulted in a struggle to provide the education and lifestyle she wanted for her daughter. Undeterred, on completion of a course at Stirling University, she gained a BSc (Hons) and a job teaching history at one of the local secondary schools which made life easier for them both. Her mother's intrepid strength of character was one of the things that Ellie had inherited along with the ability to face life's challenges head on. Accepting wholeheartedly her daughter's chosen employment and the dangers that came with it, Evelyn would nevertheless be waiting for the call that told her all was well in her daughter's world. They chatted for only a short time but caught up with a lot of news during the call.

The second phone call Ellie had to make was a much longer one. Her best friend, Sara, had also been waiting for the news that Ellie was home. The two were as close as sisters, and although both had demanding jobs and busy lives, constant phone calls and regular lunch meetings in Edinburgh were permanently on their agendas. At first, conversation was centred round Ellie's India trip, but soon moved on to Sara's recent break up with a long-time partner. Sara was struggling to come to terms with this and was looking forward to a catch up. She was disappointed when Ellie explained that she was being sent off again to Amsterdam at the end of the week but was appeased when Ellie promised to organise some time off after this assignment so that they could have a holiday together.

This second phone call lasted at least three times the length of her first one, and by the time she hung up, Ellie knew she couldn't stay awake any longer and the cup of tea would have to wait. Ten minutes later she was tucked up in bed, fast asleep, the problems of counterfeit whisky and her best friend's love life cast aside for the moment.

Ellie awoke early. An exhilarating hot shower, and fresh, clean clothes soon banished all remnants of exhaustion and jet lag. Breakfast was an easy one of cereal, fruit, and toast. Enjoying the simplicity of her meal, Ellie thought back to the breakfasts she had eaten recently in India: hot puri bread, paper masala dosas and the light, little idlis of which she had become extremely fond. Her mouth watered at the thought.

By eight o'clock, Ellie was back in the office, her briefcase contents spread out on the desk, her computer revving up and a piping hot coffee in her hand. At eleven, she was on her third cup of coffee and oblivious to everything around her except the mountain of files and paperwork she was methodically working her way through.

The firing of the 'One O'clock Gun' on the north side of Edinburgh Castle reminded her it was lunchtime and she decided to take a short break if for no other reason than to have a walk in the fresh air and grab a sandwich to keep her going through the rest of the day. Ellie found the sound of the gun firing every day a comfort, a feeling of security, and as all Edinburghers do, she checked her watch to make sure it was at the right time.

She signed out at reception and headed for the exit which took her out onto Dundas Street.

'Going somewhere nice for lunch?' The question came from behind and Ellie turned to see Geoff coming along the corridor towards her. She waited for him to catch up.

'Just getting a sandwich to eat at my desk. What about you? You don't normally go out, do you?'

'Only when the sun is shining. You must have brought it back from India with you.'

Geoff paused then continued. 'I thought I'd take a walk down to the Gardens and share my sandwich with the squirrels. They're always pleased to see me.'

She chuckled. 'I'm sure they are if you share your sandwiches with them.'

They walked in companionable silence for a short way before Geoff spoke again.

'John tells me you'd like some help with your paperwork. I've had some meetings this morning, but I could come and look at it this afternoon if that would help?'

'I'd be really grateful. John has been telling me about the new programme you've developed which can go further into the analysis of the department's stats and reports. It sounds as if they could minimise the amount of manual work I've to do, but there's an awful lot of data to input from my notes. Might be tedious for you.'

'I'm pleased to help. It will give me the chance to trial my new software properly and an opportunity to work with you and your team.'

Noting that he had put some emphasis on the word 'you', Ellie looked away quickly, annoyed to feel a very faint flush coming to her cheeks.

'Well, that's kind of you. I'd appreciate it.' She kept her tone light, trying to ignore the embarrassing flush and very grateful that the sandwich shop was in view. At the shop, she left him quickly with the words, 'See you later,' and went in to buy her snack without a backward glance.

True to his word, Geoff appeared after lunch at her desk and Ellie handed over the workbooks and memory sticks she had brought back from Mumbai. He worked swiftly and skilfully, using his own programmes for collection and analysis to produce a range of charts, maps and diagrams which he hoped would prove of help to the counterfeit department. With what he had done so far, he could see at a glance that the problems of counterfeiting were on a surprisingly large scale in certain areas of Maharashtra, all within a hundred-mile radius of Mumbai. As he sat working, Geoff found himself more and more fascinated by the picture that was building up on the screen from Ellie's detailed research, making him understand a bit more the importance of her role and that of her team.

By late afternoon, he had introduced another of his new analysis programmes, capable of interpreting both descriptive statistics and inferential statistics. Each of these two systems gave him a different insight into the nature of the data Ellie had gathered, with the inferential statistics capable of drawing random samples from Ellie's figures and making an inference about the whole. The descriptive stats helped him produce histograms and ogive graphs and together they provided a powerful tool for both description of the problems and a prediction of how they could escalate enormously.

What he now had in front of him was a comprehensive picture of a criminal trade operating in and around Mumbai, including a map highlighting the exact spots where the counterfeit whisky was being traded. Key risk markets, he thought, full of nightclubs, clubs, pubs, shopping malls and supermarkets. UBI as a company investigating counterfeit crime also had access to information on other crimes in certain parts of the world, and using this alongside Ellie's research, Geoff realised that the whisky counterfeiting appeared to be linked to a high incidence of other criminal activity around the same areas, in particular drug dealing and human trafficking. Ellie's research was very thorough, with many photographs to back up her findings, and Geoff's respect for her deepened the more he read.

'Time you had a break, Geoff,' she instructed, appearing suddenly at his side with two cups of coffee. 'You've been at that screen for hours.'

He pushed his chair back slightly and stretched, rubbing the back of his neck before accepting the cup she held out to him. Then, without looking at her, he immediately became engrossed again in the screen in front of him, seemingly unaware she was still standing beside him.

Ellie smiled to herself. This is more like the Professor I'm used to, she thought. No chit-chat, just work, work, work.

CHAPTER 4

Amsterdam

The flight from Edinburgh took off on time and Ellie settled into her seat with her laptop in front of her. The others in the team were scattered around her, two men a few rows in front and one directly behind, and she welcomed the chance of an hour of solitude to do a bit of preparation for the task ahead of them.

Dr Ken Mailer was the scientist assigned to the team, whose remit was to identify the chemicals and additives found in any of the whisky bottles and other spirits provided by the Dutch staff. With this information he would then be able to advise on the effects that these additives could have on the innocent drinkers of the counterfeit alcohol.

A tall, thin man, always noticeable by his height in a crowd, Ellie could see his head jutting above the seat, his grey, wiry hair in its usual untidy state. Ken was the quiet gentleman of the group, the team's very own 'boffin', studious if somewhat nervous amongst people that he didn't know. That nervousness and untidiness, Ellie knew well, hid an immense intellect and she was pleased to have Ken along on this assignment. His knowledge of the job was second to none and she knew that knowledge would be needed very soon.

In the seat adjacent to Ken was Alan Polson, the technician whose expertise was needed to ascertain how the brand identity copying was being carried out. In polar opposition in looks to his colleague, Alan was a short, stout man with a liking for bow ties and smart checked suits. A very dependable man, sometimes cheeky but never offensive, Ellie had developed a fondness for her technician and the family of whom he was very proud. She had met Alan's wife and two boys on numerous occasions and knew how much they missed him during his work overseas with UBI. Both men had travelled many times as part of Ellie's team, and she knew their skills would be critical to the success of this trip.

The third man from UBI, Sandy Weir, was sitting directly behind Ellie and, strictly speaking, was not a member of Ellie's team, but was the protection officer promised by John Anderson. Protection officers did not normally accompany the counterfeit teams on their travels, especially in Europe. It was more usual to employ a bodyguard in the cities where they were working, particularly in the Middle East and Latin America, where economies were generally less developed and political systems more volatile, places where violence is more prevalent. The team's wellbeing was always the number one priority for UBI, and safety training courses were intense for Ellie and her colleagues prior to being sent out to any areas considered to be risky. Sandy's presence added to their awareness of the possible risks on this assignment.

A hired car collected them at Schiphol Airport and took them to their city centre hotel, one at which Ellie had stayed previously in Amsterdam. She had been allocated a twin room and was happy to have the extra space in the room for all her work kit. She had just unpacked and was relaxing in the armchair in the room, a glass of juice in her hand when a knock at the bedroom door announced the arrival of Ken and Alan, visiting to check that all was well.

'Orange juice?' queried Alan, glancing at the glass in her hand as they entered. 'Thought you only drank whisky.'

She laughed. 'No, I don't. Just because we work for a whisky firm doesn't mean we have to drink it all the time, does it? And anyway, we're on duty, so I'm sticking to the soft stuff. Would you two like a drink?'

'Not if it's orange juice that's on offer,' replied Alan with a twinkle. 'I'll take a beer if there's one in your mini-fridge. If I remember right, there's a nice cocktail bar downstairs, and, I think, a dedicated whisky bar, so we can have something later.'

'Is anyone hungry?' asked Ken, as they got their drinks and sat down on Ellie's spare bed. 'These aeroplane meals wouldn't feed a mouse.'

'I'm ravenous,' Ellie replied. 'It's been hours since we ate.'

The two men grinned at her reply.

'I can't think how you stay so slim, Ellie, the amount you eat!' teased Alan. 'I only have to look at food to put on weight.' He patted his protruding stomach.

'Ah, that's beer and take-aways that have done that to you, Alan, so I'll be fine,' she countered back with a grin. 'I read in the brochure they have a high-tech gym in the hotel. We'd better make sure you get a chance to use it while we're here!'

'Well, being here for so long we'll have to do something to keep busy in the evenings. Hope you've brought your trainers!'

'Certainly have. I put them in just in case we need any quick getaways!'

'Wouldn't be the first time we've had one of those, would it?' Alan's comment drew rueful smiles from the other two.

'Speaking of which,' Ken exclaimed, 'where's our protection officer? Has anyone seen Sandy?'

'His room's next door,' Ellie replied, pointing behind her. 'He'll come through once he's checked the whole place out. Should we have a quick planning meeting while we're waiting?'

'You're a slave-driver, boss.'

'Got to earn my big salary,' she joked, reaching for her briefcase. 'We'll go for something to eat as soon as Sandy comes.'

The planning meeting lasted for around thirty minutes, and as if on cue, Sandy's knock came right on time.

A delicious meal in the roof-top restaurant was followed by a good night's sleep and a hearty breakfast the next morning. By eight thirty, the four UBI employees were in the foyer waiting to be collected by an appointed driver and taken to their destination. Thoughts of security were high on Ellie's agenda, but an assurance from Sandy that he was in control of safety arrangements, and that he was discreetly armed, put her mind at rest for the moment.

The unmarked six-seater car made its way along Prins Hendrikkade, turning left onto Spuistraat, at one point passing Ellie's favourite eating place, the Grand Café Ovidius. She pointed the café out to her three colleagues, causing another barrage of teasing comments about her love of food. Winding their way through the vast network of canals and wide streets, the journey was slow with the rush hour at its peak and the roads congested with the morning traffic. Ellie gazed out of the window, feeling a slight apprehension at the thought of what lay ahead.

Their first task of the day was to set up an investigation into the whisky and vodka sales of a local businessman and nightclub owner,

Arne van Breda. Amongst his enterprises were three huge nightclubs in the central area of the city, eight large supermarkets and various small clubs and pubs spread throughout the district.

Van Breda was also known to have fingers in lots of other pies, some of which had been brought to the attention of the police on various occasions. One of these was his most notorious and popular nightclub, The Furnace, in the Centrium district of the city. On this occasion it was in one of his supermarkets that the discovery of counterfeit spirits had been reported, and local customs and excise personnel had been called in to follow this up.

UBI's first round of testing was to be done using random bottles of both whisky and vodka which had been bought from each one of Van Breda's enterprises. Alongside the testing Ellie had been asked to do a course of training programmes with local customs staff on how to use the equipment to identify the counterfeit spirits.

Van Breda was a high-profile figure in the town, well-known not only to the local police and the Dutch authorities, but as a socialite amongst the citizens of Amsterdam as well. In recent years he had twice been under investigation by Interpol for serious cases of drug dealing, but with a lack of evidence against him he had never been convicted of any crimes. In this latest round of testing, Ellie's team was under orders to report back to the police on all they discovered, the authorities being keen to try to find proof of a link between the counterfeiting and the Van Breda Corporation, and to identify any other companies associated with him.

Arriving in New West, the car stopped in front of a large, modern office block, directly opposite Sloterpark, an attractive parkland with its world-famous Botanical Gardens. The building belonged to the local customs and excise department, and Archie Wallis, UBI director in the Netherlands had reserved a few rooms in the office block for Ellie and her team to carry out their testing. Alighting from the car, the team unloaded their equipment and entered the building where Ellie gave her name to a young receptionist behind the desk in the foyer.

As was normal practice, in the days prior to the anti-counterfeit team's visit their Dutch director had employed a local detective agency to visit several Amsterdam venues in order to surreptitiously buy a large quantity of whisky and vodka bottles. Every one of Van

Breda's outlets and premises within Amsterdam had been visited and the bottles bought at these establishments had been brought into the customs office, alongside bottles bought at other random outlets in the city.

The team were shown the allocated rooms by a member of staff. For Ellie, Ken, and Alan this would be a long, laborious job, recording where each bottle had been bought, testing the alcohol in each, and cataloguing their findings. Stacked high against the walls in one of the three rooms were around three hundred bottles, most in crates and some in presentation boxes lying alongside. All the bottles were numbered and labelled showing the date and name of the establishment where they had been bought.

'We might not make the gym tonight, guys,' Alan warned. 'There are a lot of bottles here. Better get started.'

Ellie nodded. 'Okay. I'll leave you two to get the equipment set up. I've to attend a meeting somewhere in the building.'

She checked her watch as she spoke. 'As soon as I'm clear, I'll come and give you both a hand. Sandy, are you coming with me or will you stay here?'

'I'll stay around here for the moment,' Sandy answered. 'Once they're all set up, I'll disappear for a while. I'm glad to see there are keys in the locks, so once you're in your rooms, guys, keep the doors locked at all times.'

He turned back to face Ellie. 'I believe we're getting a visit from Archie Wallis this morning. Do you know what time he's coming?'

'No,' she replied, looking perplexed. 'I've no idea when he's coming in. Have you been speaking to him? I haven't managed to get him on the phone since we arrived, and he really should have been in touch with me. I left a number of messages for him to ring me.'

'Don't worry. I spoke to him last night and he said he'd be here at some point.'

He turned as if to leave but Ellie continued.

'That's not good enough, Sandy. He's in charge here in the Netherlands and he's supposed to liaise with me and the team while we're working in this area and give us any help we need. He's been very evasive, and I need to know why. I've got an uneasy feeling about his lack of communication. I wish you'd told me you'd spoken to him last night.'

The burly security officer drew himself up to his full height before answering.

'I'd no idea you were having any difficulties, did I? Archie certainly didn't mention anything. Don't worry, we'll get them sorted out when he arrives.'

With this, he closed the door behind him, giving Ellie no chance to comment further.

Ellie was not happy at this abrupt departure but decided she would corner him later to discuss it. Yes, there was something disturbing her about the Amsterdam manager's elusiveness and she really needed to get to the bottom of it, but for the time being, Ken and Alan were trying unobtrusively to get their instruments set up and she urgently needed to be somewhere else.

'Right, guys. I'll let you two get organised. It's time I was at my meeting. I've also to set up the training course but it shouldn't take too long. I'll see you later.'

In the testing area, Alan had been given the room next door to Ken to carry out his examination of the alcohol which involved testing the labelling and capping on every bottle. Counterfeiters' techniques of replicating caps and labels were becoming more and more sophisticated and major whisky companies constantly had to develop new ways to protect their brands.

Innovative security measures had been introduced by UBI some time ago and, to test for authenticity, Alan used a mini UV light on both the labels and the screw caps to check the company's covert identification marks were there. The testing of such a vast number of bottles was arduous, but he was adept at using the equipment and worked his way through the task quickly. Recording the results was also very repetitive and, once completed, he took batches of the bottles through to Ken for the second part of the process.

The scientific part of the testing was done with the use of UBI's own whisky authenticators. These were mini gas chromatographs and Ken had set up the machines on a table in his room alongside his test tubes and chemicals, ready to go.

Gas chromatographs had first been used by UBI in the 1990s and were invaluable to the whisky industry. During Ellie's training for her anti-counterfeit work, she had been taught how to use the apparatus, and how their mechanics worked. She knew from her research that these machines had been used in the 1980s by medical technicians for testing blood samples, and it quickly became apparent to the whisky industry that the same technique could be used to test for authenticity of their spirits.

As a novice, Ellie had been fascinated when Ken Mailer had first taken her through the process to train her in the job. He had explained in detail how the machine could separate different liquids while being passed through various phases at different speeds. This meant the operator could see straight away if there were any liquids present other than neat whisky, showing they had a counterfeit bottle on their hands. The machine then went on to check for the relative proportions of these other liquids in the mixture.

Ken had been the company's leading instigator in the use of chromatograph machines. A hard-working, courteous man, Ellie found him a pleasure to work with, even enjoying his endearing habit of humming while he worked, his way of keeping calm and concentrating.

Donning his white overall, Ken began the mammoth task of testing the many hundreds of bottles, his soft humming already started. With the first two bottles, Ken discovered that one whisky was genuine, and one was not. He moved the bottle containing the additives to a separate table, to begin his search to identify which chemicals or liquids had been used to top up the real whisky in the bottle. The machine had already given him a reading on the proportions and he now needed to find out what substances he was dealing with.

He was totally absorbed in his work when Ellie returned from her meeting and she smiled as she heard the familiar humming from some distance away. She knocked on his door and heard him ask who was there.

'It's Ellie, Ken.'

He turned the key and opened the door for her to enter.

'How are you getting on?'

'Busy, busy,' he replied, bustling back to his table.

Ellie looked round the cluttered room. 'As I can see. Anything dramatic about the results so far?'

'Early days, but certainly higher than normal positives.'

She nodded. 'As suspected.'

Ellie looked at the engrossed scientist for a moment. 'Have you had a break, Ken?'

When there was no reply she added, 'I'll go and get you a coffee, or would you rather have water?'

He looked up. 'I've got water, thanks, but I'd love a coffee.'

She left him to his work and headed to Alan's room next door.

Alan was having a break from the humdrum routine of testing the whisky bottle caps and labels and had moved on to testing the vodka bottles. For vodka testing, the team used a different technique and Alan was in the middle of lowering a dipstick, about the size of a cigarette, with glucose coating at one end, into the clear liquid in the bottle. The dipsticks changed colour to green or red to determine whether the alcohol was pure or not. A nice easy process and a non-stressed Alan greeted Ellie as she entered the room.

'Hi, boss. This is some job you've given us this time. Almost seventy per cent counterfeit so far and I've only just started. These are the highest figures I've ever seen. Could be we've got a major crime on our hands here.'

'Yes, I think everyone suspected that when they called us in. It'll be interesting to see the end results. Anyway, can I get you a coffee? I need one and I'm getting one for Ken.'

'Coffee sounds great. If I get any thirstier, I'll be testing these bottles in a different way!' He grinned at Ellie. 'I'll go and get them if you tell me where. I need to stretch my legs anyway, if you know what I mean,' he added with a wink.

As Alan headed off to the staff area, Ellie used her mobile to have yet another attempt at phoning Archie at the Amsterdam UBI office and was rewarded at long last by hearing his voice give a cheery good morning.

'Archie,' she began, 'it's Ellie. What a job I've had contacting you. Did you get any of the messages I left for you?'

'Hello. My apologies, my dear, I had a meeting with some of our retailers this morning and I've only just come into the office. Helen, my secretary told me that you had been phoning. How are things going?'

'Going fine so far,' Ellie replied shortly, returning to the question he had not answered. 'I left a number of messages for you on your mobile, Archie. Did you get them?'

'I did and I didn't. I saw them coming through but haven't had time to read them yet. Was there something urgent?'

'Well, yes. I hoped you would be here when we arrived so I could go over a few things with you. Are you managing to come along this morning?'

'I'll be there as quickly as I can.'

'Okay, then I'll see you shortly.' Ellie felt a bit happier now that she had spoken to Archie, and added, 'You did a good job with the quantity of drink you bought. Ken and Alan are a bit stunned at the number of bottles there are. Did you manage to get them all from the venues on the list we gave you?'

'We did. My helpers were mostly from a local detective agency and students from the university. They did a grand job. Would you like any help with the testing? I could spare a couple of people from the office if that would help?'

'Definitely. We'd appreciate that.'

Immediately identifying two of his staff, his office administrator, Jane Gibson and his finance officer, a local man named Lucas Decker, he promised to bring them over in his car as soon as he could.

Jane proved a godsend to the team, working quickly and efficiently with Alan. However, Decker, as he asked to be called, turned out to be a brusque, surly man, with a bit of a chip on his shoulder at having been asked to help in this way. Halfway through the afternoon, Archie replaced him with another member of his staff, explaining to Ellie that Decker had requested to be taken out and wouldn't be coming back.

'I'm not surprised at this, Archie,' she informed him. 'He was a very difficult man. I don't think I met him the last time I was here. Has he been with you for long?'

'No, couple of months. Came with good credentials and good references but he's certainly not the easiest person to get along with. Keeps himself to himself and doesn't mix with the other staff except when he has to.'

'What did he do before he came to UBI?' Ellie asked curiously.

'I believe he was a financial adviser, self-employed. Must have made a lot of money out of it, judging by his lifestyle; he owns several flashy cars and the staff tell me he owns a few bits of property too. I was surprised when he applied to come and work with us.

Not that I can complain about his work, he does it well.'

'Well I shouldn't complain about him either, Archie, but I'm a bit relieved he's gone. He gave us all the distinct impression he didn't want to be here. Not like Jane; she's doing well, helping with recording the test results. Hopefully your new chap will prove good too.'

Even with this extra help, the team came to terms with the fact that the testing exercise was going to take a few days to complete. First results had confirmed what they suspected, that most bottles contained counterfeit spirits, but by the end of the week, the results had still to be collated and analysed to show the complete picture. Ellie had anticipated a busy assignment and was not surprised by this. What did surprise her was an unexpected invitation from some of the customs and excise staff asking the team to join them for a night out on the town on Saturday.

They were delighted to accept, feeling in need of a break away from the intense testing during the week. The work itself was not difficult, but the quantities they were dealing with made the job repetitive and long. Everyone agreed that a night out was just what they needed and looked forward to it with anticipation.

What no-one had anticipated, however, was that on being collected on Saturday night they discovered that the venue for the evening's entertainment was none other than Van Breda's biggest nightclub, The Furnace.

CHAPTER 5

Amsterdam

In the minibus, hired for the evening, there was an air of excitement and anticipation amongst the six customs staff, soon shared by the four UBI colleagues. Exchanging a glance with Sandy at the first mention of The Furnace, Ellie's misgivings about visiting a venue under investigation disappeared with his reassuring nod. If she was truthful, as soon as they were on their way, she found herself pleased to be given a chance to see it for herself. The Furnace's reputation as an exciting venue had spread far and wide although Ellie's interest in it was more because of the suspected illegal activities happening within the building. She looked forward to an interesting evening. The minibus driver dropped the group near the entrance, and they joined the long queue waiting to get in.

About fifty yards away, outside a more discreet entrance at the back of the club, another group of ten were waiting for admittance to the nightclub. The attire of these ten businessmen was in marked contrast to the people in the queue at the front, their smart suits, white shirts and ties looking out of place for a night on the town. On entering, the men were taken along a corridor by a beautiful young Thai woman in an evening gown who opened the door to a large sitting room and ushered them in.

The room was furnished with dark brown, leather sofas and long, ornately carved coffee tables in front of each. Around the walls were bookshelves, housing a great many books in a variety of different languages. In one corner, there was a well-appointed bar, where another attractive young girl was pouring drinks. The room gave off an aura of wealth and affluence, with the appearance of an exclusive London gentleman's club.

Once the ten were seated and being served their drinks, soft music began to play, and jackets and ties were quickly removed. The drinks were topped up continuously and cigarettes were offered from silver boxes. It wasn't long before the smell of cannabis filled the air and the men's voices became louder with bawdy laughter resounding around the room.

After a short time, the two girls began to circulate, handing out a book of photographs to each of the men. The noise dulled as they began to study the pictures inside.

Once they had made their choice from the many girls and young women featured in the books, the two hostesses began to escort them, one by one, along to a suite of rooms on a different floor of the building.

Only one comment was heard during the exodus, made by the executive of the company who had organised the outing to The Furnace.

'One of the perks of the job, eh, fellows?' There was a cacophony of ribald replies.

Meanwhile, at the front of the building, Ellie and her friends had gained entrance to the Disco Hall in the huge nightclub and were making their way to a balcony overlooking the dance floor to find a table. Looking stunning in a striking mini-dress with her blonde hair left to fall in glossy, loose curls over her shoulders, Ellie was attracting a good number of glances from club-goers as she fought her way through the huge crowd. Her team, all married men, closed protectively around her, much to her amusement. She was appreciative of their ring of defence but hoped it wouldn't last for long. No chance of meeting up with a good-looking Dutch lad with all these 'dads' round about her, she thought wryly.

Once up to the balcony, they managed to find an empty table which had no chairs, but with a bit of searching they managed to acquire seats; the women sat, while the men stood around them. A waiter approached to take their order for drinks and while they waited, Ellie's eyes travelled all round the club, becoming mesmerized by the walls with their moving images of flames and fire that seemed to leap up all around the dancers. The red strobe lighting gave the place a vibrant, exciting feel and the heat was intense. Ellie was thankful her dress was made of a thin material and that she hadn't worn trousers which had been her first choice of outfit that night. The club was thronging with people of all ages and the boom of the music made conversation difficult.

Over the next couple of hours Ellie, who loved to dance, was frequently invited onto the dance floor and accepted willingly under the watchful eyes of her colleagues. She found she was enjoying herself greatly and wished Sara could have been with her.

Around eleven o'clock, she decided to visit the washroom, and made her way through the crowds to one of the many rest rooms up on the third floor of the club. She was surprised to find it empty apart from one person, a young, attractive Asian girl standing looking up at the ceiling at the far end of the room. Slightly startled at someone coming in, the girl moved quickly over to a row of wash-hand basins and turned on the tap, watching Ellie out of the corner of her eye. Thinking that this was a bit strange, Ellie smiled to the girl, and said hello, at which the young girl turned with a jump, inadvertently splashing water over herself.

'Are you okay? You look a bit worried.'

Ellie could see now that the girl was slightly older than she had at first thought and reckoned her to be in her late teens.

'I am okay, thank you,' the young girl answered politely, drying her dress with one of the paper towels from the machine.

Although she had answered the question, Ellie still felt that the girl looked terrified and instinct told her that there was something amiss. An inherent curiosity made her move a little closer to the girl and continue the conversation.

'Are you feeling unwell? It's very hot out there and there's a lack of air in the place, isn't there?'

This time the girl did not answer.

Ellie tried another question. 'Are you enjoying the night club?'

Again, there was no reply, but Ellie received what she could only interpret as a very frightened look. She gave it one last go.

'You look gorgeous by the way. I love your dress. Did you buy it here in Amsterdam?'

This time the girl did answer. 'I was given the dress, so I do not know where it was bought,' she said, speaking in English but with a very noticeable accent.

'Well, it's fabulous,' replied Ellie wanting to keep the conversation going. 'Are you from India?'

The girl nodded, but voices outside the rest room brought back her terrified look.

'I have to go,' she said as she moved away from Ellie. 'I am working and will be missed.'

'You work here at the club?'

Still backing away, the girl made no reply but nodded before slipping out through the door. Ellie remained by the basin for a moment, looking at herself in the mirror, but not really seeing her reflection. Her thoughts were on the very unusual behaviour of the girl, and she wondered what had caused this.

Inquisitively, she walked across to the far side of the rest room and glanced up at the same spot on the ceiling she thought the girl had been looking at. As there was nothing to see apart from a grid with wide metal vents which she assumed was the air conditioning unit, she continued into the cubicle.

Presently drying her hands at the dryer, Ellie glanced up once more at the vents, and something seemed to draw her over to them again. Staring up into the metal slats, she was astonished to see what looked like a little girl's face staring down at her. She took a small step back to see better and two dark eyes followed her movement.

'Hello.'

There was a slight movement from above and Ellie repeated softly, 'Hello. Who are you? What are you doing in there?'

The door of the rest room suddenly opened, and Ellie was surprised to see the young Asian girl return, this time moving with more confidence, almost anger, straight over to where Ellie stood. Looking up at the vent, she spoke sharply in what Ellie thought might be a dialect of Hindi; her trips out to India had taught her one or two words that she recognised. A scuttling noise came from above and the small face disappeared. Ellie turned questioningly to the girl standing beside her.

'I'm sorry,' the girl began, 'that was just a little friend of mine who would be in trouble for being up there.'

At that moment, the main door burst open once again and about half a dozen young women plunged into the room, making a lot of noise with their laughter and chatter. Ellie looked at the girl beside her and met a beseeching, almost pleading look. She nodded towards to the row of wash hand basins and they walked over to the mirrors where they made a pretence of fixing their hair and washing their hands. After what seemed an interminably long time, the young women left, as noisily as they had entered. Ellie looked at the girl and gave a grin.

'Busy place,' she remarked. 'Not a place to be exchanging confidences, is it?'

'No, and I would be in trouble for talking to you, but I want to thank you for not saying anything,' the girl spoke hurriedly. 'It's really important to my friend that you do not speak of seeing her there. Please, I feel I can trust you. It would be very bad for us both if you told anyone that you saw her there or that you have been speaking to me. Will you do this for me?' she asked with an imploring look in her eyes.

'Of course, don't worry,' replied Ellie at once. 'Can you tell me who you are and if you are in danger? Can I help with anything?'

'No, no,' the girl said hurriedly. 'My name is Angena and I work here in The Furnace. You cannot help except to say nothing about meeting me or my friend. I beg of you,' she whispered, really frightened now. 'Our lives depend on this.'

Ellie gasped, taken aback by this comment. 'You have my word,' she promised. 'I won't say anything, but tell me quickly, before anyone else comes in, you say you work here, what do you do?'

'I work in the casino. I must go now. They will be looking for me. My gratitude and my thousand thanks.'

With these words she fled through the door. Ellie remained where she was for a moment, and then made her way thoughtfully back to where her friends were sitting.

'Are you okay?' asked Sandy as she sat down beside him. 'We were worried about you. I was about to send someone into the Ladies to look for you.'

Ellie thought for a moment, wondering what to do. Normally she would have had no hesitation in telling him about what had just happened, but with the promise she had made to the girl, this was impossible.

'I'm fine, Sandy. Nothing to worry about.'

'Would you like me to take you back to the hotel? These guys will be here for a while. In fact, I think they're going to visit the casino, but I could take you home if you've had enough here.'

'No, I'm perfectly fine,' she replied firmly. 'I'd actually like to see the casino too, check it out while we're here.'

Ellie's comments reached Alan's ears and she heard him chortle.

'Well, well, boss,' he teased as he leaned forward. 'You want to waste some of that hard-earned cash of yours on the roulette table, do you?'

'Well no, but I'll come and watch you waste yours,' she countered. 'Seriously though, I'd like to see what else is going on here apart from the dancing. I'm interested to see if there's anything illicit happening.'

'I've checked a bit of it out already,' Sandy remarked. 'No way of knowing what's illicit and what's not, Ellie. Anything illegal is not going to be on view to the public. There's a separate club behind the gaming tables which has lap dancers and strippers, but nothing that's illegal that I could see. It isn't private. It's open to anyone willing to pay the entrance fee.'

'Well, I'd like to check it out myself. The place has got a bit of an evil feel about it, a sort of sinister air. Can you not feel that too?'

Both her colleagues agreed.

'Come on then,' said Sandy, as he drained his glass and laid it on the table. 'Let's go and see what we can see. Have you ever been to a strip club before?'

'Nope, not my scene.' Ellie rose from her chair. 'But I'm really curious to see more of this place.'

And, she thought to herself, if I'm honest, I'm curious to see where Angena is working, and what is frightening her so much.

The terror she had seen in Angena's face had aroused many suspicions in Ellie's mind, suspicions of exploitation of women and possibly girls as well, if the little face in the vent belonged to someone who also lived and, God forbid, worked here too.

Her sense of wanting to help someone who may be in trouble was roused and it was with a determined step that she followed the others through the nightclub to a large doorway at the far end of the crowded dancefloor. Beyond this doorway Ellie could see another huge hall full of one-arm bandits and gambling tables, all busy with customers, and a few circular bars serving drinks dotted here and there. Paying the entrance fee at a reception desk, they were led to seats beside one of the ornately decorated bars. The low-level lighting gave the place a very smoky, even sinister atmosphere.

She gazed around the crowded hall with a rising sense of unease, taking in the many raised podiums dotted around the cavernous hall, with pole dancers and strippers moving to the sensuous music that was playing. Standing close by were several security guards, burly men dressed in black with their arms crossed ominously.

'Are they protecting the dancers, or are they making sure the dancers stay there?' Ellie whispered to Sandy. 'Bodyguards or gaolers?'

He looked over to where she pointed. 'Both probably.'

Ellie felt a shiver of apprehension run down her spine.

A waitress dressed in very little appeared at their table and asked what they would like to drink.

'Champagne for everyone, please,' Alan ordered.

'Champagne? Is that not a bit extravagant?' Ellie asked him once the waitress had moved away. 'I'm in need of a glass of water.'

Alan and Ken exchanged amused glances.

'Ellie,' Alan said quietly into her ear, 'we don't want to look out of place.'

'Okay,' Ellie agreed with a laugh. 'Point taken.'

While waiting for their champagne to arrive, Ellie found herself checking out the faces of the croupiers working on the tables. Some were too crowded for her to see, and some were too far away and hazy, but she was certain that Angena was not working on any of the tables close to where they were sitting. Perhaps she works in one of the bars, Ellie thought. Maybe she's not a croupier.

Waiting for their drinks to come, she sat in silence, her thoughts on Angena's terror that Ellie might tell someone of their encounter, and the idea went through her head that perhaps it would be better to just mind her own business. However, as quickly as this entered her head, it disappeared. Ellie's job with UBI came with its own dangers and challenges; its main element was investigation, and investigating was what Ellie loved best about it.

The Miss Marple inside her wouldn't walk away without finding out more and solving the case!

CHAPTER 6

Amsterdam

The champagne was on ice and Ellie settled down to enjoy her bubbly as the four colleagues toasted each other with a clink of glasses.

'Here's to a successful assignment,' declared Ken.

'And a safe one,' added Sandy, sipping his one and only alcoholic drink of the evening.

Some of their group began to wander over to the gaming tables and slot machines, and Ellie decided to go with one of the young women for a walk round to see what games were on offer, and to buy some casino chips to be able to play. Eva, one of the customs staff who had been many times to The Furnace was pleased to be able to show Ellie the ropes. She explained very simply the rules of blackjack, baccarat, and craps, but Ellie wasn't interested in these and steered Eva in the direction of some roulette tables a little further away, ostensibly to gamble on the 'little wheel' but really to search for Angena.

After several tries without winning, Ellie left Eva happily gambling and, with her chips tucked into her bag under her arm, she began to wander round the other tables. She passed some podiums with pole dancers and came to a small stage where a strip show was in progress. As she walked by, her attention was drawn to a group of young lads watching the show. A very disorderly crowd, what Ellie's mother would call a drunken rabble, they were obviously enjoying the strip show very much. She was not surprised to see three burly security men in dark suits standing nearby to keep a watch on them.

Out of keeping with the whole ambience of the place, she could appreciate that a drunken boys' night out, with raucous laughter and innuendos was not likely to go down well with the management. As she watched, the shouts from the lads grew louder and more strident, but the security men seemed to handle the situation well and moved in to quieten the group down very quickly. She walked slowly on but within moments noticed that the boys were being shepherded by the security men and were coming in her direction. She slipped out of the way to allow them to pass, hearing snippets of their conversation as they walked by. From what she heard, she realised that they were not in fact being thrown out of the club as she had first thought but were being taken somewhere where they would be able to buy 'extras' as one of the lads phrased it.

Ellie knew she had been right in thinking there was more investigating needed in this venue and began to wonder how the frightened young woman she had met in the toilet was involved in it all, and if the child whose eyes she had seen through the vent was here legally or otherwise. She started to look harder for Angena, checking out each gaming table she passed, and the face of each pole dancer and stripper that she could see.

As she stopped at a table where poker was being played, a touch on her shoulder made her jump. Her heart missed a beat as she turned, and it was with relief she saw Sandy standing beside her.

'Just keeping an eye on you, boss,' he said quietly into her ear. 'Not too sure about this place.'

'No, it's definitely got sinister depths. Thanks for looking out for me.'

'My job,' he answered as they began to walk slowly back towards the area where they had been sitting. 'Did you win any money?'

'No, I had no luck at all. What about you?'

'I'm no gambler. It's just throwing your money away.'

Grasping his arm, she chuckled. 'Och, come on, old skinflint. Let's have one last flutter before we go home.'

She pulled him firmly over to one of the roulette tables she had spotted half hidden in an alcove, not giving him the chance to complain. Unknown to Sandy, it had suddenly become imperative that she had another gamble, and essential that it was at this roulette table. Ellie had recognised the croupier and was desperate to have one more chance to speak to her before heading back to the hotel.

With no clear idea how she was going to achieve this, Ellie took a vacant seat at the table, and set about getting her casino chips out of her handbag, as Sandy sat down in the seat next to hers. She didn't have many chips left after her earlier bets but thought that might work in her favour. Sure enough, when she had played and lost all her remaining chips, she took some cash from her handbag and turned to Sandy.

'Would you mind going to buy me some more chips, Sandy? I'm pretty sure I'm about to have a lovely big win. I can feel it in my bones.' She handed him some twenty-Euro notes, keeping her fingers crossed that he would take the bait.

With a look of resignation, Sandy accepted the notes and went over to one of the casino's cash booths. As soon as he was away, Ellie dug in the handbag on her knee again, and discreetly removed one of her small business cards, keeping it tightly clenched in her hand.

Ellie had realised when first approaching the table that Angena was aware of her presence. The occasional glances they exchanged as Ellie had placed her chips on the roulette numbers were enough to show her that Angena was agitated, and she longed to let the young girl know that she was in no danger from anything Ellie might do or say.

She slipped off her seat and slowly moved round the table, trying to be as inconspicuous as possible, knowing that there were probably security cameras watching all tables, as well as security officers milling about the vast casino.

At the end of the semi-circular table, she sidled round as far as she dared until she was quite close to Angena. The table was not a huge one but was shaped in such a way that Ellie could go no further without being obviously where she shouldn't be. How could she get her card to Angena, she wondered?

As if by accident, Ellie allowed her handbag to slip out of her hand and looking embarrassed, she bent down to retrieve it. Out of sight under the table, she flicked the card in Angena's direction along the floor. In the wink of an eye, Angena's foot covered the card, making no obvious sign to the customers that anything had happened.

'*Rien ne va plus*,' she called out, 'no more bets.'

The girl's swift fingers spun the first ball into the wheel and the second ball into the groove, as all eyes were on the roulette to see if they had been lucky or not.

From the corner of her eye, with no movement of her head, Angena saw Ellie walk away from the table to go and join a middle-aged man coming towards her, with a container of chips clasped in his hand.

Ellie took hold of Sandy's arm and carefully steered him away from Angena's roulette table and across to another table some distance away.

'I've decided that's not a lucky table after all, Sandy,' she explained. 'I'm moving to another one, and I'm going to let you play all my chips for me. I want you to put them all on black thirteen, my lucky number.'

'All of them?' Sandy asked in surprise. 'All on the same number? Now that's not a good idea, Ellie. The odds are against it.'

'All of them,' stressed Ellie, with a huge grin. 'The odds are with me. I can feel it in my bones.'

Sandy groaned, wondering what on earth had possessed Ellie to make such a decision. He sighed, blaming the champagne.

———————————

CHAPTER 7

Amsterdam

Ellie turned over in bed, reaching out to switch off the alarm clock ringing loudly in her ear and gave a soft groan into her pillow. Memories of the previous night flooded back, and she knew it had been a mistake to drink as much as she had. It was about four in the morning when they had finally left the noise and clamour of the nightclub behind and climbed into a taxi to take them to the hotel. Her head pounded, and it was with difficulty that she drew back the covers and slowly swung her legs over the side of the bed.

'Just as well it's Sunday and we've got a day off,' she thought.

Looking at the clock, she saw it was after nine and moving rather lethargically, she showered and washed her hair. Once dressed, her headache had dulled to a distant throb and she felt prepared to face a coffee and croissant for breakfast. Lifting the phone, she dialled Ken and Alan's room.

The two men were not quite ready and arranged to meet her down in the restaurant as soon as they could. They didn't know Sandy's whereabouts but assumed he would meet them in the restaurant as well.

Taking the lift down to the ground floor dining room, she gave her name and room number and asked for a table for four, not seeing Sandy in the room. Ellie was nestling a cup of coffee in her hands when Ken and Alan arrived, looking every bit as hung over as she was. They slipped into their seats and ordered coffees and full English breakfasts from the waitress nearby.

'How on earth can you manage a cooked breakfast this morning?' she asked with a pained expression. 'I don't think I can face anything.'

'You don't deserve breakfast after all you drank last night, boss,' teased Alan as he looked at her white face. 'Get some eggs and bacon to set you up for the day and make you feel better. Take it from an old hand at the drinking game.'

Ellie groaned. 'I just couldn't. And don't let me have any more nights out or any drink for that matter, while we're here, please. My system won't stand it. And neither will my purse! How much did I lose last night?'

'A lot,' Ken exclaimed. 'When I came through you were at least three hundred down and still throwing your money away, although you did round it off nicely with a sizeable win.'

Ellie gave a grimace. 'Do you think it was bad champagne?'

The men laughed. 'I don't think you can blame counterfeit champagne for last night's losses,' said Ken as he shook his head.

Their breakfast arrived and at the same time, Sandy joined them at the table. His only comment of 'Glad you all got home safely last night,' drew nothing but sardonic grins from the others and the rest of the meal was consumed in relative silence. A decision was made at the end of the meal to get a bit of fresh air by having a walk along the canals outside, and to see a bit of Amsterdam during their day off.

The day was cold as they left the hotel, crossing over Europa Boulevard and entering Amstelpark. They walked along the side of the canal, which according to Alan was the North Holland Canal. He had taken on the role of tour guide for the group, clutching his map and pointing out various landmarks along the way.

'I fancy a sail in one of the canal boats,' he stated, with various grunts and nods of agreement coming from the others.

Strolling for some time at a leisurely pace was certainly helping Ellie to feel a lot better and as they approached a small pier where a couple of boats were moored, she felt she would enjoy a sail along the canals.

Spotting a set of steps and a pathway down to the ticket booth, Alan offered to be the one to go and purchase the tickets for the next sailing available. Sandy decided to go with him. The men had only been gone a few minutes when Ellie realised they had turned around and were running back.

'Check your phone,' cried Alan as they came within earshot. Ellie pulled out her mobile and seeing lots of messages, began to open them as quickly as she could.

'There's been an explosion at the customs office,' she heard Sandy tell the others. 'John's been in touch to alert us. He was contacted by the Amsterdam police as they think Archie's been hurt. We need to stay together and get to the police station as quickly as possible. Might be nothing to do with us, but best to find that out before we do anything else. What did John say to you, Ellie?'

'The same. That we should head for the national police regional office and stay safe until he can get more information to us.'

'I think he's sent the same text to us all,' Ken added as he too checked his phone.

They hastily made their way back up to the main road and headed for the hotel. No taxis passed, so they entered the hotel lobby and Sandy asked the receptionist to call one. Within five minutes the cab appeared, and the four colleagues climbed in, sitting in silence as they were driven to the central police office. It was hard to accept that something like this had happened without knowing any of the details and Ellie sat on the edge of the seat, biting her lip as the taxi drove them through the Amsterdam streets.

As they neared their destination, the cab driver turned a corner and came to an abrupt halt, giving everyone a slight jolt. A traffic jam had caused the sudden stop and further ahead, Ellie could see a police cordon across the wide street. The driver left the cab for a moment to go and see what the hold-up was and, on his return, explained that there had been some sort of incident in the city centre, and he was going to take a detour as some of the roads were closed to traffic. He didn't seem to know any other details, except that he thought it had happened within the last hour. The four exchanged worried glances but said nothing.

At the police station, they introduced themselves to the constable at the desk, and explained what had brought them here. After asking advice, he ushered them through to a room at the back where he told them to wait for someone in authority who would come and talk to them. He offered the four of them coffee, but they declined, just wanting to find out what was happening.

The group were seated at a table, although both Ken and Sandy had taken to pacing the floor before an official eventually joined them, introducing himself as Unit Chief Janssen, Head of Landelijke Eenheid, or LE as it was referred to. Chief Janssen quickly explained that LE was the National Unit of the police force in the Netherlands, dealing with special investigative services and counterterrorism amongst other things. A second, non-uniformed officer entered, and he too shook hands with the group, giving his name as Senior Officer Daan Meijer, from Dienst IPOL, the International arm of LE.

Before giving out any information, Janssen asked if they had brought their passports with them. Just to prove their identity, he explained. Both Sandy and Ellie had theirs, but unfortunately Alan and Ken had left their passports behind in the hotel bedroom safe. Alan offered to go back for them, but was told that he could do this later, once some paperwork had been completed and questions answered.

It was some time later that the four began to learn the facts of what had happened. Janssen confirmed that an explosion had occurred at the customs and excise offices, thought to be a bomb or maybe more than one, and that a small number of people had been hurt, including their local UBI colleague, Archie Wallis. The Chief was not able to say how badly he had been injured only that he was in hospital and in a serious condition. Ellie's heart lurched as she heard this news and she hoped very much that it was not as bad as it sounded.

Unable to answer Ellie's question of why Archie had been in the building on a Sunday, all Janssen could say was that this was being investigated. It was too early for any suspects to be identified yet, he informed them, but did mention that there was one mystery they needed to clear up quickly. Apparently, the CCTV camera covering the front of the building had picked up Archie entering the main door alone, and a few moments later another man had entered behind him. The camera had failed to pick up a clear image of the second man's face as he had been wearing a hat pulled low over his face. The Chief indicated that this man might be able to help with their enquiries and showed the group some footage of the mystery man. Unfortunately, they too were unable to identify him.

John Anderson called while they were in discussion with the officers, and Ellie was given permission to bring him up to date with the situation. On being told about the seriousness of Archie's condition, John's reassurance that he was flying out to Amsterdam on an early flight next morning was welcomed by them all.

It was early afternoon when the group eventually returned to their hotel, courtesy of a police vehicle and accompanied by a young constable who was coming to take possession of Ken and Alan's passports. Sandy and Ellie's passports also remained with the police for the moment and a polite order had been given that they were not to leave Amsterdam until they had permission to do so.

Entering the hotel, Ken suggested they go to the restaurant for something to eat.

'I'm not very hungry!' Ellie exclaimed.

'You should try,' Ken urged. 'It's been a long morning and you look like death warmed up. Even if it's just a coffee and a bun, you'll feel the better of it.' He turned to Sandy. 'Do you think we should phone the hospital and see if we can get any more news on Archie?'

'Definitely. John asked me to try to get some more news of him, so I'll go and do it now. Keep a seat for me in the restaurant.'

Although not hungry, Ellie was cajoled into ordering some sandwiches and coffee, and was grateful when a large pot was laid on the table, along with a couple of bottles of mineral water. She poured herself a glass and sipped it slowly, chewing thoughtfully on her lower lip.

'You know,' she said eventually, leaning her elbows heavily on the table, 'I'm confused by all this. The police are convinced the bombing is linked to our assignment here and I can understand why. There's obviously something huge going on. My confusion is Archie. What was he doing there this morning? It's Sunday so he didn't go looking for us because he knew we were off for the day.'

Ken answered. 'I don't know. What I do know is that the testing we did this week points to something major in the criminal world, so I think we must be extra careful of our own safety while we're here. Although that might not be for very long. If all our equipment has been destroyed in the bombing, John will ship us all home as soon as we're given permission by the police. Are all your findings and reports from the investigation safe?'

'Yes. Everything's on my PC and in my briefcase, which are both locked up in the hotel room safe. I always take every scrap of paperwork away with me at nights.' She paused before asking the questions uppermost in her mind.

'Do you guys think Archie was targeted deliberately? Do you think he's involved in some way?'

She watched her colleagues' faces searchingly as she spoke but didn't need any verbal answers to tell her that their suspicions were the same as hers.

'Well, we won't know any more until the police have investigated,' Alan stated. 'Don't go doing any detective work on your own, Ellie. I know you. You don't have enough information about it all and it could be dangerous for you to try. Don't you go around asking too many questions while we're here. Leave it to the experts.'

She didn't answer and after a moment, he changed the subject. 'What time did John say he was coming tomorrow?'

'He didn't. He just said he'd be coming on the early flight so he should be here by breakfast time.' Ellie had answered his question, but her thoughts were still on Alan's last remarks.

'I know what you're saying, Alan, that I shouldn't try to investigate things myself, but I hope John doesn't send us home right away. I'd like to finish what we've started here, the testing if it's possible to do any more, and all the training courses with customs and excise that I had planned to do.'

Ellie put up a hand to stop both Ken and Alan interrupting, seeing that both were indignantly going to refute what she was saying.

'Don't worry,' she continued. 'I know, we all know, that John won't leave us here if he suspects it would be dangerous. And yes, there may be no equipment left to do the testing so it's maybe not a possibility.'

'Here's Sandy.' Ken raised his hand to attract Sandy's attention and discussion at the table halted abruptly when they noticed an extremely solemn look on Sandy's face as he approached.

The big protection officer sat down heavily in the fourth chair. 'It's terrible news,' he stated bluntly. 'I'm afraid Archie has died in hospital as a result of his injuries. The doctors tried their best to save him, but he was too seriously injured.'

'Oh God, that's awful.' Ellie's hands went to her face, shocked at this horrendous news. 'Poor Archie. And his family. Were they with him in the hospital, Sandy?'

'I'm not sure about that. It was Daan Meijer who told me the news. You know, the senior officer from IPOL that we met at the police station. The hospital wouldn't give me any information at all, so I called Daan to see if he knew anything. When I asked him about Archie, he told me the news. I've called John too, to let him know. He's going to try to get an earlier flight and come today.'

There was a depressed aura around the group as they left the restaurant after their lunch and headed to the hotel lounge bar. Sandy had suggested a stiff drink, and everyone agreed, wanting to stay together at this time as much for comfort and support as for their safety.

During the afternoon John sent a text to say that he had booked a flight from Edinburgh that evening, and would be arriving at Schiphol Airport around eight o'clock. He had organised transport to the hotel, booked a room and expected to be with them just before nine.

At around three in the afternoon, Ellie left the others to go up to her room. Her headache from the morning had returned and she needed some painkillers to stop the throbbing in her temple. She made one quick phone call to her mother to say that she was well; a bombing in Amsterdam may well be an item on the news in Scotland and she didn't want her mother to be worried about her. She sent another quick message, this time by text, to Sara, again to say that she was safe and well. Then before she knew what had happened, she was asleep on her bed, not waking until the sun was well down and the shadows lengthening in the dimness of the room. The sleep had done much to restore her to normality, and chase the headache away completely, although the sadness of Archie's death still pervaded her mind.

A quick wash and her make-up refreshed, Ellie was ready to go and find the others, and ready to face John when he arrived later that night. She found them in the bar of the hotel, sitting in silence, each nursing a tall glass of beer and eating nuts from a dish on the table.

'Hi guys,' she said quietly. 'Everyone okay?'

Sandy stood to greet her and drew in another chair to the table. 'We're fine. How are you? I knocked on your door but got no answer, so hoped you were maybe asleep.'

'I was. And feel the better of it, thanks. Any word from John?'

Ken answered her question with a nod.

'He asked us to book a table in the restaurant for nine o'clock. Plane's on time so all being well, he'll be here soon to eat with us.' He pushed the dish of nuts towards Ellie while he spoke, but she politely declined. 'He's bringing someone with him. Asked us to book the table for six people but didn't say who he was bringing.'

Ellie's eyebrows rose slightly as she pondered this. 'I wonder who it is. And I wonder why.'

'I think it may be another of my team,' offered Sandy. 'John knows I've got another security job booked in for Tuesday which I need to go back for. If I'm allowed to leave the country,' he added.

The four continued to chat quietly for some time, each quite subdued after the events of the day. They spoke of Archie, their unfortunate colleague, and of the sadness his family must be feeling at this time. They also touched on the fact that, had the bomb been planted just one day later, their own lives would have been endangered, a thought that was very difficult to contemplate.

Thoughts of Archie losing his life possibly in the course of his work brought Ellie's mind back to the girl she had met in the nightclub. She wondered about Angena and her little friend up in the ceiling. Were their lives really in danger, or had the girl exaggerated just to keep herself out of trouble? She thought about how she had thrown her business card to Angena under the roulette table and wondered if anything would come of this.

At eight thirty, the team made their way to the comfortable seats in the hotel lobby to await the arrival of their chief executive and his mysterious companion. Ellie realised she was very curious about who this was and found her heart skipping a beat when the revolving doors turned to reveal John Anderson accompanied by the Professor.

The group moved forward to greet the new arrivals, Ellie being warmly embraced by John, who offered both condolences and understanding of what the team had been through. Not keen on receiving the same warm greeting from Geoff, she quickly proffered her hand instead. Geoff took it in a tight clasp.

'What brings you here, Geoff?' she asked in a voice as normal as she could make it.

Before he could reply, John interrupted.

'I've co-opted him onto your anti-counterfeiting team, Ellie. I'll tell you all about it, but just let us get checked in first and put our cases in the rooms. Then we'll meet you in the dining room.'

Ellie watched them move across to reception and turned to follow Ken, Alan and Sandy into the hotel restaurant, mixed thoughts all vying with one another about the arrival of the Professor.

CHAPTER 8

Amsterdam

The meal was good but short, the restaurant being too small to allow any private discussions. They had decided to have a meeting in Sandy's room, his being the largest of the bedrooms. Sandy had checked the room thoroughly for any kind of listening device, a task which would not have been considered necessary some days ago. Things had changed, as John stated more than once during the evening, so no chances should be taken with their safety. He began the meeting by explaining the presence of Geoff.

'After you all left last week, Geoff and I had a meeting regarding Ellie's reports and stats from Mumbai. I gave Geoff permission to continue working on these for as long as necessary and to incorporate the reports from your Taiwan assignment. Piecing them all together, he came up with some results that linked the two assignments together. Very astute young man.' John turned to nod at Geoff as he spoke.

'What were the links?' Ellie asked impatiently.

'Well,' Geoff began, 'working with your figures from both countries, I found two links, the identical chemicals and percentages they are using to doctor the whisky, plus identical branding on the bottles. The labels and caps on the counterfeit bottles are all the same. Not in the same language, of course, but the same brand marks, same colours, same type of print. And now Holland as well. We've had a quick look at the initial reports you sent back and these tie in with the other two countries. Same chemicals again, same brand marks.'

John took over the story. 'Once we had all these facts and figures, I then brought in another couple of members of the anti-counterfeit department to work with Geoff and bring him up to speed with the type of investigations we carry out on a day to day basis, and how these progress. Like me, they were impressed by the way Geoff had analysed your findings, Ellie, and we realised that his expertise in setting up more advanced software for us could be used for investigations in the future. I've co-opted him onto the team for the present time.'

Everyone seemed pleased to have Geoff joining them and offered a word of welcome. Geoff nodded his thanks in a sombre fashion.

'Glad you're pleased,' said John. 'So were the other members of the department back home, and, like me, they are all backing Geoff's theory that you seem to have uncovered a major criminal operation stretching over the three countries. Might be even more, we don't know yet. Could be we're looking at an organisation involved in the big crimes, like human trafficking, drug running and arms smuggling. Serious, serious stuff.'

He leaned back in his chair, looking at the grave faces around him before continuing.

'What happens now? Well, you all know that investigating these activities is *not* something UBI get involved in, so we're going to withdraw from this one. To do this safely, we'll have to take guidance from the authorities. With Archie's death today, and the bombing of the customs building, it's become much more dangerous than any of us had imagined. Therefore, the time is right to hand it over to an organisation capable of dealing with it. Luckily, we can do this right here in Amsterdam.

I know you all met Daan Meijer today. Daan is a senior officer with IPOL, a department in the National Police Service. Their headquarters are in The Hague, although Daan is working here in Amsterdam for the time being. I have an appointment with him tomorrow and I'll take Ellie and Geoff with me.'

John turned to the others. 'Ken, Alan, Sandy, I've booked you on flights home tomorrow. I know you've done a massive amount of work since coming here, and it's probably not finished. But you won't be able to get into the customs offices any time soon; they are part of a crime scene and unsafe to enter. There's nothing to keep you here and I know you're needed back in Edinburgh. I'll organise the return of your passports in time for your flights.

The three of us can handle what's necessary here. Tomorrow's meeting will be a handover of everything we know, all notes, reports, stats, and anything else in your head, Ellie, from the three last assignments. I'm assuming you have your laptop and all paperwork safe? You didn't leave anything behind in the customs office?'

Ellie nodded. 'It's all in the safe in my room.'

'Good, I knew you would have it in a secure place. Geoff and I will come along to your room now, and we can go over the details for tomorrow.'

'What about Archie's wife and family, John?' asked Ellie.

'Yes, I should have said. I've arranged to go and visit her tomorrow morning, prior to the meeting. There's a lot to talk about and sort out, so I've scheduled the meeting with Daan Meijer and his staff for twelve noon. Want to come with me to see Nan Wallis?'

'Yes, I would. I've met her a few times, and I'd like the chance to see how she's doing. It must be a nightmare for her.'

A general sadness pervaded over the rest of the meeting as each of the team had known and worked with Archie at some point over the last few years. It wasn't long afterwards when they called it a day and headed back to their own rooms.

The visit next morning to Nan's house was a difficult one, but Archie's wife seemed to be coping as well as she could with lots of support from family members, some of whom were flying over from Scotland to be with her. John gave assurances of UBI's help and support, both financial and otherwise and promised to visit again before he left Holland on Wednesday. Ellie realised the poor woman was still in a state of shock over her husband's death, and not really taking in any information. However, Nan seemed comforted by John's assurance that the company would look after her and her family.

Nan was unable to tell Ellie and John why Archie had visited the customs offices the previous day, but she did explain the circumstances leading up to it. She told them that Archie had received a phone call while she'd been in the shower, and he had popped his head round the bathroom door to say that he was going out to meet someone from UBI and wouldn't be long. He had not said who the caller was, and she hadn't asked. As Nan began to cry again, John and Ellie did not push her for any more information.

More tears were shed, and hugs shared when the visit came to an end. As Ellie stood back to allow John a chance to say goodbye, she caught sight of a very elaborately framed photograph sitting on Nan's sideboard. The frame had caught her eye, but it was the picture that she stared at for a moment or two. Apart from Archie, the people in the photograph were unknown to Ellie, but what had caught her attention was the fact that the group were standing in front of the nightclub that Ellie and her team had visited on Saturday. The neon sign for The Furnace was blazing above their heads and the man standing next to Archie was looking at him with a wide smile on his face. Archie too was grinning widely, and the two men looked like they were sharing a joke between them.

Nan spotted Ellie staring at the photo.

'It's a good photo of him, isn't it?' she said sadly. 'It was taken about a year ago when they had a night out for one of the UBI staff who was leaving. He loved his job and his staff so much.' Nan's voice ended on a quiver and Ellie moved forward to give her another hug.

'He looks very happy in the photo, Nan,' Ellie said gently, her arm still round Nan's shoulders. 'We know he was much respected by all his staff here in Amsterdam and the ones in Scotland who knew him too. Who is that beside him, the one laughing with him? I don't recognise him.'

'That's not one of the staff. That's the owner of the nightclub they were visiting, Arne Van Breda. We've known him for a while now, at least Archie has.' Nan hesitated. 'Had,' she corrected herself softly.

Ellie's arm tightened round Nan and her heart went out to her. Thoughts of Nan stayed with her as they left the house and climbed into the private hired car waiting at the door.

Once inside the car, she raised her concerns with John.

'It seems Archie and Van Breda were possibly good friends. And Van Breda is one of the men under investigation by IPOL. What do you think this means, John? Could Archie have been involved in something sinister with Van Breda? Do you think he was killed deliberately?'

'I don't know the answers,' John replied after a moment. 'It may mean something or nothing, but I think it's crucial we pass the information on to Daan Meijer today and let the police deal with it as part of their investigation. For my part, having known Archie for many years, I always found him an honest, trustworthy employee. I'm hoping that maybe he was just in the wrong place at the wrong time. I don't like to think he was involved in anything crooked. However, we can't rule it out.'

CHAPTER 9

Amsterdam

Geoff was waiting at the hotel entrance for them and climbed into the car as his boss got out.

'I won't be minutes,' John told him, turning to ask the driver to wait, and then hurrying into the hotel.

Geoff looked enquiringly at Ellie.

'He's forgotten his phone. He doesn't like to be without it. How are you this morning?'

'I'm good,' he replied, settling into his seat, and fastening his seat belt.

'Has John given you any indication how long we'll be here in Amsterdam once this meeting is over?' Ellie asked.

'Not in so many words. I expect it will depend on what the police say we can and can't do. Are you anxious to get home?'

Ellie sighed. 'From my point of view, I'd love to stick around for a few days to give me the chance to tidy up the investigation and deliver some of the training I was supposed to be doing.'

'Workaholic,' accused Geoff with a chuckle. 'Well, if it's any help, I was told to pack for at least a week, so I'd be happy to stay on as well if necessary.'

'That would be good.' Ellie was pleased at his offer of help. 'There are so many loose ends to tie up here.'

For a moment her mind wandered back to one or two of the events that had occurred over the last few days but before she could say any more, John was taking his seat in the car.

The drive to the police station was a quick one, the traffic having calmed down considerably since the earlier rush hour. On arrival, the group found Daan Meijer was waiting to take them to his office where some of Daan's colleagues joined them and the meeting began.

Meijer opened the meeting by explaining his role in IPOL and his current job as head of one of the department's biggest investigations over the last few years. This investigation, in conjunction with Interpol, had stretched over countries throughout Europe and the Far East, and concerned what he called a massive criminal enterprise involved in multiple nefarious occupations.

UBI's own investigations, Daan told them, could be critical in helping IPOL piece together certain aspects of the criminal organisation and help to bring the leading figures to justice. Evidence, he went on to say, was crucial to achieve this end, and evidence was what he believed UBI might hold in their findings from Ellie's last three assignments.

Ellie glanced down at the laptop sitting on the table in front of her and reached out a hand to touch it lightly. Thank goodness for her habit of never leaving it anywhere, always taking it home with her at night and keeping it close at all times. Same with the paperwork in the sturdy briefcase she used. Until this moment she hadn't realised just how vitally important her investigations could be to anyone other than UBI and the whisky industry.

The meeting progressed slowly into the afternoon, with each of them being grilled thoroughly about their part in the investigations. Ellie's laptop and all files were taken away to be copied as necessary, with a promise that these would be returned as soon as possible. John and Geoff had also been thorough in finding and bringing along all files from her two previous assignments, anything they could find in her filing cabinet in the office in Edinburgh.

The IPOL officers seemed extremely pleased with the quantity of relevant information and Ellie hoped they would be just as pleased with the quality once they began the task of sifting through it.

At no time during the interrogation did Ellie mention the existence of Angena and her friend in the nightclub. A promise was a promise and Ellie found herself unable to break Angena's trust. However, she was given an opportunity when talking about Archie Wallis to mention seeing the photograph of him and Van Breda together and the fact that no-one seemed to know the reason for Archie's visit to the customs office on Sunday. Both these things, they were assured, would be investigated and hopefully, thought Ellie, there would turn out to be an innocent explanation for both.

Darkness had descended as the three rose to take their leave of the IPOL officers who thanked them profusely for the help they had given, and confidently assured them that the police investigation had taken a huge, satisfying leap forward today.

First thing next morning, John left to catch a flight to Edinburgh, work developments making it necessary for him to return home earlier than planned. Daan had been in contact with him late last night, requesting that Ellie and Geoff be allowed to remain for a couple of days, there being a need to bring them back to the IPOL office to clarify some of the data that had been downloaded. Following this decision, Ellie contacted customs staff and organised to deliver the UBI training course to the relevant employees that afternoon.

A busy day ensued for the two of them, with another meeting in the morning at the IPOL offices followed by a second visit to Nan Wallis to give John's apologies for not managing to return as he had promised. Ellie was pleased to see Archie's wife surrounded by friends and family and looking less fragile than she had the previous day.

As the afternoon training course ended, Helen Koster, Archie's secretary appeared to ask if the pair would like to visit the damaged offices to see whether there was anything belonging to UBI which was recoverable among the ruins. The area was still sealed off but under the guidance of fire officers, they were taken through the rubble and up some stairs which were still standing, to the offices where the testing had been carried out.

Ellie found the visit quite emotional, conscious of the fact that Archie had been fatally injured amongst all this mess and could tell by Helen's face that she was feeling the same way. A warm hug was exchanged before they began to explore.

She could see from a glance around that the bottles they had been testing were no more, with shattered glass everywhere. And although parts of the testing equipment and machinery could be seen in bits amongst broken furniture and bricks, one of the machines had been rescued by the firemen and laid on a makeshift table made of planks of wood. On inspection, Ellie deemed the machine too badly damaged, and shook her head at the destruction in front of her.

As she had suspected, there was nothing there for her to take away and she thanked Helen and the firemen for organising their tour of the site. She and Geoff returned to the hotel, subdued and downcast at what they had seen.

Back in her bedroom, Ellie threw her bag onto the bed and sat down heavily in one of the easy chairs. Her shoes were pinching since she had been on her feet most of the day, and she blissfully kicked them off, stretching out her ankles and wiggling her toes.

Knowing she had some time to spare before meeting Geoff for dinner, she decided on a quick shower and change of clothes as much to shake off the melancholy she felt as to freshen up for the evening. With her wet hair wrapped in a towel and clad in a cosy hotel bathrobe, she sat down on the bed with her mobile phone to see if there had been any recent messages.

She was cheered to see a text from Sara, a long, chatty text bringing her up to date with all the news of friends and family in Edinburgh. From the wording of the text, Ellie could tell that her friend seemed happy and was obviously recovering well from her broken relationship.

She put through a quick call to Evelyn as well, aware that her mother would most likely still be worrying about her. The call was short, Evelyn being on the point of going out, but Ellie knew she was relieved to get the call.

Checking her call log further, she noticed that she had missed an incoming call from a number she didn't recognise, and no message had been left. The suspicion that the code could be an Amsterdam one and that it may have come from Angena crossed her mind and after a few seconds indecision, she lifted the hotel phone and dialled the number displayed on her mobile.

The phone rang several times before someone answered.

'Hallo,' said a woman's voice. 'Wie is er?'

Ellie hesitated, unsure what this meant. 'Do you speak English?' she asked after a moment.

'Eenglish, geen. No, no Eenglish. Wie wilt u spreken?'

Ellie knew a pang of regret that she had not learned a few phrases in Dutch, taking it for granted that the people she met here would speak English. An arrogant view, she admitted to herself.

'Is there someone who can speak English?' she asked slowly and optimistically.

'Wachtaub,' the woman's voice commanded, and Ellie heard the phone being laid down onto a hard surface, still connected. She waited hopefully and was rewarded after a few minutes when a second

67

voice, a younger sounding woman, came on the line.

'May I help you? I speak a little English. Who is this please?'

Ellie thought it prudent not to give her name for the moment as she was still unsure who she was connected to. Instead, she asked the woman where she was speaking from.

'I speak from the nightclub. It is The Furnace Nightclub,' came the accented reply. Ellie hung up immediately, her suspicions confirmed.

Let's hope Angena gets in touch with me again very soon, she thought as she began to dry her long hair and get dressed for the evening.

The strident ring of the bedroom doorbell at eight o'clock precisely told her that Geoff had arrived to take her down to dinner. Crossing to the door, she hastily checked her appearance in the mirror on the wall before peeping through the spy hole. Assured that it was him, she opened the door.

'You... you look fabulous.'

'Thanks Geoff, that's a nice thing to say. And you look pretty good yourself,' she added, lifting her bag from the dresser before joining him outside the door.

Geoff breathed an inward sigh of relief. He hadn't meant to say anything controversial to her to spoil the good relationship he was slowly building up, and he was very thankful that she had taken his comment so lightly.

The pair enjoyed dinner in the rooftop restaurant of the hotel, in any other circumstances the perfect place for a romantic evening, but the conversation between them stayed friendly and casual.

He did manage to learn a good bit about Ellie herself, about her childhood in Edinburgh and her family and friends. He was amused as she admitted that her proper name was Elizabeth, a name she felt was too grand and formal, preferring the shorter name her mother had used when Ellie was very young. She spoke warmly of her mother and he learned that Evelyn had been divorced when Ellie was just a toddler and had been left with many debts to settle. He could see the pride in Ellie's eyes as she told him how inspiring a role model her mother had been, bringing Ellie up singlehandedly in the city, while holding down a demanding job. Her mother had been a history teacher during Ellie's childhood and her no-nonsense approach to life had rubbed off on her daughter, she informed him with pride.

Ellie told him that Evelyn had met and married a teacher

colleague, Matt Hamilton, Head of Science at the same school as Evelyn. Now retired, they were busy running a small guest house down in Anstruther on the Fife coast. He gathered Ellie was a frequent visitor there and could hear the happiness in her voice as she spoke of her family.

Ellie on the other hand still knew very little about the man opposite her, but as the bottle of wine they shared began to take effect, she found herself asking more and more questions. She discovered they had a lot in common, including a shared love of the cinema, and of reading travel books, and both were amazed to discover a mutual adulation for hard rock. He didn't talk much of his childhood or his family, but she learned a little more about his views on life and ended the evening with the feeling of having found a new friend, someone she could rely on and trust.

Just before midnight, Geoff said goodnight at Ellie's bedroom door and walked back to his own room happier than he had been for a long time. Ellie closed and locked her bedroom door, wondering how she had previously failed to spot what a kind person he was behind his quietness. As she undressed for bed, she knew in her heart that she was attracted to him and was very glad that he had joined the team. In her pyjamas and cleaning her teeth she was deep in thought when her mobile phone rang, the shrill, tinkling sound startling her for a moment.

Her heart began to race as she dried her mouth with the towel and hurried to pick up her phone.

'Is that Ellie?' a quiet voice asked in her ear. She recognised Angena's voice at once.

'Yes, it is. Did you call me earlier? I tried to phone you back but didn't leave my name.'

'I know,' replied Angena in her soft accent. 'I heard the dancers talk of the phone call in English and guessed it might be you. Is it safe to talk? Can anyone else hear me?'

'No, I'm on my own; it's fine to talk. How can I help you?'

'We are in a lot of trouble here and you were so kind to me. And I know you have been very secret about our speaking together.' Angena's words speeded up as she spoke, as if there was suddenly a lack of time, and her immaculate English slipped slightly.

'I am trusting you again and praying that you will be able to help with a very bad problem I am having. It is my friend, Suman, the girl you saw.' She paused for a moment.

'What's happened to her?' Ellie prompted.

'Her life is in danger, and I am afraid that they will kill her very soon. I need you to help me escaping her.'

'Angena, slow down, you're speaking too fast for me. You're saying Suman's life is in danger. Who from? Who is going to kill her and what does she need to escape from?'

'I am not sure what I can tell you. I am not sure about anything. And I cannot speak much on this phone. Please, I am begging of you, will you help me?'

'Of course I will. I want to help if I possibly can. Tell me the whole story.'

Ellie heard a sigh of relief from the other end of the phone.

'Can you come here again; can you come to The Furnace, tomorrow night? We could meet in the same place and I will tell you more then.'

'Well...' She hesitated for only a second. 'I'll be there, and you can tell me everything and then we can work out some solution. I'll meet you where we met before. What time?'

'Eleven o'clock is good.'

'And how can I contact you if there are any problems?'

'Oh please, do not fail me. We need you so badly. I will be there at eleven o'clock. Do not contact me. I will just pray that you will come. Thank you from my soul.'

The phone went dead as Angena said the last words, and Ellie closed her mobile. Still clutching the towel, she sat down for a moment.

What was she getting involved in? Why was the child's life in danger and how could she help the girl escape? Should she tell anyone what she was going to do? All these thoughts were running wild in her head. Maybe I could tell Geoff, she thought fleetingly, but quickly dismissed the idea. If there was to be any danger, then Ellie felt it would be unfair to drag him into such a daring escapade as she was imagining this to be. She had also given her word to Angena that she would not tell anyone, and she would not break that promise.

CHAPTER 10

Amsterdam

The following day dawned bright and sunny and began with a visit to the hotel from Daan, returning Ellie's laptop and her files. He stayed to eat breakfast with them and managed to consume a huge quantity of sausage, bacon and eggs whilst giving them some more information about how the investigations were going.

After his second croissant and fourth cup of coffee, just to wash everything down, he told them with a wink, the IPOL man made his departure leaving them chuckling at his voracious appetite. With nothing on the agenda for the day, Geoff suggested they do some of the sights of Amsterdam, this being his very first visit there. Ellie readily agreed and, with no guilt about taking a day off from work, she guided him around the city, taking in a visit to the Van Gogh Museum and to the Dam, a cobbled square right in the heart of town, and home to the striking Royal Palace.

'Do you like pancakes?' Ellie asked Geoff, looking at her watch. 'They've got some fabulous pannenkoeken in that café over there, and it *is* lunchtime,' she prompted with a grin.

It seemed so natural for him to steer her across the street to the café she had pointed out, and she made no remark as he slipped his arm around her shoulders to do so. By the afternoon, neither was interested in seeing any more tourist attractions in the beautiful, cultural city and sat down to enjoy a long, ice cold glass of locally made Heineken beer in one of the bars.

The daytime ended too soon for both, but dinner in the hotel had been reserved at eight o'clock and Ellie and Geoff made their way down in the lift to the restaurant. Ellie was relieved to have brought something else to wear for dinner, her small store of clothes sadly almost exhausted. Nonetheless she looked extremely beautiful in her black, fitted trousers and shimmering white silk blouse, the sheen giving her skin a glow, under a very light dusting of make-up.

Geoff, conscious of his mistake last night, commented only on how 'nice' she looked though his eyes were telling her more. Ellie however, whilst not oblivious of his admiring look, did not give it a second thought, her mind now beginning to veer towards the events planned for eleven that evening.

'I was thinking I'd have an earlier night, tonight,' she said apologetically as the lift descended. 'I've been a bit tired and not sleeping too well. And we were very late last night,' she added with a twinkle.

'We were,' he agreed, with a playful hug. 'Then we'd better get Cinderella home before midnight tonight.'

To his delight, she did not shrug off his arm, but nudged him softly as she continued, 'I was thinking more about ten o'clock. I need my beauty sleep, you know, Prince Charming!'

His arm tightened as their eyes met for a moment and Ellie's heart gave a huge lurch, the feeling taking her unawares. Leaving the lift, he removed his arm, but they walked closely together into the dining room.

Towards nine forty-five, Ellie became aware of a strong feeling of trepidation in the pit of her stomach as the time approached for her to leave Geoff and thoughts of the evening ahead made her slightly edgy and more distant from him. She rose from the table, thanking him for his company at dinner, a bit more formally than she would normally have done so. For a moment he looked surprised, almost upset, but his frown was only fleeting as he rose to accompany her upstairs.

'You don't have to come up with me. If you want to stay in the bar and have a drink, that's fine. I can manage.'

'I'll see you up to your room and maybe come back down later. I'll see how I feel.'

She said goodnight to him at her bedroom door, aware of a certain disappointment that their time together could not have been longer. She had too much on her mind to worry for long, and thoughts of him receded as she put on a coat to go out into the night.

As surreptitiously as she could, she made her way out of the hotel and flagged down a taxi to take her to the nightclub. They arrived soon at The Furnace, and she was pleased to see only a small queue at the door this time. A group of women in their early twenties was in front of her in the queue, and she deliberately began a conversation with them, hoping that no-one would notice she was on her own. Once inside, she checked her watch, and saw that she had ten minutes to spare before meeting Angena in the ladies' room. The music was loud, and the dance floor as crowded as before and she decided to watch from the side for a few moments. Suddenly she became aware of a young man clutching a beer in his hand and bearing down on her. She tensed.

'Wil je dansen? Of eendrankje?' he asked, coming up very close and lifting his beer mug.

She stepped back, realising that he was asking her to dance or have a drink, which she declined with a shake of her head. She spoke no words, feeling it was probably safer for no-one to know that she wasn't Dutch.

She turned quickly and made her way to the ladies' room. She was only a few minutes early and decided that she would be less noticeable away from the dance floor. There were only a handful of women in the room and Ellie saw Angena at once, putting on some make-up in the far corner. Their eyes met for a second as Ellie walked over to stand at a basin nearby.

Angena, again dressed in a stylish evening gown, put her lipstick back into her bag and indicated with her eyes for Ellie to follow her. She moved to a door at the back and held it open. Once through, she hurriedly led Ellie along a corridor, down a flight of stairs and into a small storage room. She pointed to a couple of crates for them to sit on.

'Thank you for this,' she whispered. 'I knew you would come, and I know you will help me.'

Ellie answered, 'Tell me quickly, what is the problem and what can I do to help?' She glanced around the room as she spoke. 'Are we quite safe to talk in here?'

'For a short time we are. So I will tell you and you must promise again to me that you will not speak a word of this to anyone. No-one,' she emphasised. 'It is too dangerous.'

Ellie looked into the young girl's eyes. 'I can't do that Angena, because I don't know what you're about to tell me. I will promise that I won't knowingly put you or Suman in any more danger than you seem to be in now. Please trust me.'

'I have to, I have no choice. I need help to get Suman out of here, and someone to keep her safe. I will explain.'

Ellie's eyes grew wide and her heart almost broke during Angena's tale, as she heard about how the child had been trafficked from her home in India, raped and abused and brought to Amsterdam to be put to work in the sex trade for the 'Organisation', as she called it.

'I too was trafficked, as were a lot of girls who work here. We have been through what Suman is going through. And we all realise that we have no choice, we cannot get away. Our families back home will suffer if we disobey. It is impossible to escape, and we have nowhere to go even if we could. These people do much killing and I know of some girls who have been killed here at the club as they caused too much trouble. That is what is going to happen to Suman. She is being used for terrible things, but she is not doing it willingly. She causes much bother and has been very badly hurt because of this. I know they will not allow this for many more days, we have heard them talk of what will happen soon. They will kill her, but I just cannot get her to understand this. She will not speak, not to me, not to anyone. She never makes a sound, just fights against them all the time.'

Angena stopped for a moment, shaking her head sadly, then reached out to Ellie, tears overflowing from her eyes.

'She is just a little girl and I do not want to see her put in the fire.'

Ellie drew back sharply, disbelief on her face.

'A fire?' she gasped. 'What fire? Surely not, no, no. They wouldn't do that, would they?'

'They will, as they have done to others. Underneath this building is a real furnace. Not just painted like the walls. You must help me get her away.'

'I find it hard to believe what you are saying, but if it's true, we must go at once to the authorities and report it. They will then move in and get you and the children out.'

Angena tumbled forward from the crate and knelt at Ellie's feet in a pleading gesture.

'No, no, no. That is the thing you must not do. *Never*! You do not understand. The man who runs this organisation is very friendly with the police and all the others.' She stopped. 'What did you call them? The authorities. He is very powerful man and the first thing he will do is kill us all, Ellie. No, no, no. I beg of you.'

Ellie realised that this must have been used as a threat to Angena and it would be hard to convince her otherwise, but she tried again to coax Angena to allow her to call in the authorities, seeing this as the only logical step.

'I have been working with a very important organisation called IPOL,' she explained, 'and they are more powerful than the criminals. You must trust me and allow me to contact them.'

Angena shook her head, tears pouring down her face.

'No, I should never have asked this of you. I see it is too dangerous, because I know Van Breda. I know he is friendly with this important organisation you talk about. I see them come here to this nightclub, to our casino, the politie and all the men in the suits. There is one man especially, who comes on his own. He comes to see Van Breda up in his offices and I know they are working together. And sometimes he comes to have sex with the girls in the brothels. He knows about us but does nothing. I think he is from this IPOL that you talk of, I am not sure. You do not understand how dangerous these men are. Please, please promise me,' she pleaded, staring hard into Ellie's eyes.

Angena's words made Ellie think hard, the realisation creeping over her that perhaps Angena was right. Perhaps she really didn't understand or know what went on in the criminals' world. Questioning Angena further, she could see that if she was to do what Angena was asking of her, to help get the child out, then it would have to be on Angena's terms, without the help of the team at IPOL or anyone else for that matter.

'Okay,' she said, swallowing hard, 'I'll do what you're asking. But how do we do it?'

Angena leaned in closer. 'You must come to the club as a customer and stay until the end. Just before we close, I will hide you in our dressing room and when it is quiet, you will leave with the other dancers, as if going home and take Suman with you. Can you bring a large bag, big enough for her to be inside?'

Ellie sat silently for a moment, the sheer audacity and danger of the exercise just beginning to hit her.

Never one to balk at something difficult that needed to be done, she nodded at Angena. 'I can bring a bag. Tell me more.'

CHAPTER 11

Amsterdam

For the next few minutes, Angena and Ellie discussed the plan to get Suman out and deliberated where Ellie should take the child once she was free. The hotel was to be a stop gap place of safety, until Ellie could contact one of the anti-trafficking organisations in the city and hand Suman over to them. It had to be tomorrow, urged Angena, explaining the urgency was due to Suman's life being in imminent danger. Ellie agreed as she knew she could be asked to return to the UK at any moment.

Whilst still rough around the edges and in need of a lot more thought and preparation, they agreed it was the best they could come up with in so short a time. A nervous glance at her watch told Angena that she would soon be missed, and the two girls rose quietly and made their way back out of the basement.

As they approached the ladies' room, Ellie turned to Angena and looked long and hard into the girl's eyes.

With a hug she whispered, 'Take care.'

Angena nodded. 'I thank you with all my heart. May your God take care of you and Suman.'

Ellie slipped warily back into the powder room alone, not looking round as Angena quietly closed the door behind her. No-one seemed to notice her entrance. She crossed the room and hurried out into the busy disco area, relieved to see no sign of the young man who had spoken to her earlier. The noise of the nightclub gradually receded as she walked to where the taxis were parked, waiting to pick up customers.

The cab took her back to the hotel where she was pleased to see only a few staff members and one or two guests milling around. She kept a sharp look-out in case Geoff was back downstairs in the cocktail bar or in the lounge but saw no-one she recognised. In her room undressing for bed, Ellie's brain was working overtime. The conversation with Angena and the plans they had made were swirling around in her head as she lay in bed and she knew with a certainty that it would be some time before she would get to sleep.

She woke with a start early in the morning, the memories of the meeting with Angena flooding back. She decided to get up and prepare for the difficult day ahead of her. Her apprehension had grown overnight into something approaching panic and she tried to quell the tension rising in her stomach.

Keep calm, she told herself, the dangers of her job paling into insignificance beside what she was attempting to do today.

In the bathroom brushing her hair, she heard the ring of her mobile phone and ran to pick it up, praying that it was Geoff but intuitively sensing something was wrong.

'Ellie, Ellie, is that you?' The angst in the words told her it was Angena.

Her nerve ends tingled; her mind fully alert as she replied.

'Yes, it's me. What's happened?'

'You must come now. Not later. It's got to be now, Ellie,' Angena whispered through tears. 'They're going to kill her. She is hurt and I have her here with me, but they will find her soon.'

Angena's next words were spoken in her own language and ended on a sob.

'Don't panic,' said Ellie gently. 'I'm coming right now. I'll get a taxi and be with you quickly. Tell me how to find you. Is The Furnace open as early as this?'

'No, it's not open until later. You must come to a back door. I'll be there waiting. Behind the casino look for a door which says 'Personeel' and I'll make sure it's unlocked. Don't let anyone see you. Please Ellie, be careful for yourself. And remember to bring the bag.'

'I will.'

'Please hurry.' Ellie heard the dialling tone on the line as Angena hung up.

Ellie sat for a few seconds after closing her phone, thinking swiftly but carefully about what she should do. Her absence was going to be noticed very quickly this morning, and she wanted to avoid a hue and cry about her disappearance. She lifted the hotel phone and dialled Geoff's room number.

'It's Ellie,' she began when he answered. 'I'm really sorry, but I'm afraid I'm going to have to stay in bed this morning. I've got one of my bad migraines, and I just know from experience that it won't go away. The only way I can cope is to take some painkillers and try to sleep it off. I'm so sorry, Geoff.'

He sounded worried as he answered. 'Don't apologise, you can't help if this happens. Is there anything at all I can do to help? Can I look in on you later, and maybe bring you something to eat?'

'No,' she said decisively, afraid of what might happen if he found her missing. 'I really need to stay quiet and sleep it off. I'll ring you later and speak to you then.'

Ellie hung up abruptly, leaving a very concerned Geoff on the other end of the phone. He laid the receiver down slowly, a deep frown on his brow.

For a moment he contemplated phoning John to let him know that Ellie was unwell and to discuss their return to Edinburgh once she was recovered. However, a look at the clock told him it was still very early in the morning and even earlier in Edinburgh. He doubted that John would welcome a phone call at this time in the morning.

A few doors along, there was frantic activity in Ellie's room. She was pulling her holdall out of the cupboard at the same time as grabbing her leather jacket and throwing herself into it. Her hair was still slightly damp from the shower and she had applied no make-up to her face. Unsurprisingly her looks were the last thing on her mind as she zipped her wallet and her mobile phone into the jacket pocket and rushed to the door.

She peeped out along the corridor towards Geoff's room, checking he was nowhere in sight. Coast clear, she closed the door quietly behind her and ran along the corridor, choosing to hurry down the hotel stairs instead of using the lift. Coming out at reception, she sped across to the concierge, standing at his desk. Her request for a taxi was quickly and efficiently dealt with, and she threw the elderly man a grateful thank you as she left the building.

In the back of the cab she tried in vain to collect her thoughts, but the danger that the child was in had taken complete control and she silently willed the taxi driver to speed up a bit. Once she had been dropped off and paid the fare, she began to walk quickly along the back of the casino, checking out all the doors she passed for the word 'Personeel' as she had been instructed. It was a scruffy door, but although the paint had faded and cracked, the sign itself was very visible.

Heart pounding, she pushed the door and slipped inside. The room she entered was vast. A warehouse of some kind, she thought. Filled with tall shelving units, and long, dusty aisles, the huge room appeared to be empty, with no sign of Angena.

It was stiflingly hot, the heat seeming to come from a network of silver metal pipes on the ceiling. Seeing this Ellie deduced that she was in the plant room of the nightclub, the pipes providing the heating to the huge venue above. Ellie wondered if she had come in the wrong door and was at a loss to know what to do when suddenly her ears picked up the creak of a door opening at the far end of the room. Swiftly she ducked behind one of the shelving units, hoping she was hidden from view. Her heart was pounding as she peeped through a tiny space in between the boxes on one of the shelves. A figure appeared in the distance.

'Angena,' she called out softly, standing up and moving out from her hiding place.

Angena, slightly startled, put a finger to her lips and motioned for Ellie not to make a sound. Beckoning Ellie to follow, she led her back along the aisles and out through a door. The cold air was a sharp contrast from the heat coming from the pipes as Ellie silently followed her through.

At the bottom of a set of stairs, they entered a large, dimly lit, dank cellar. Cautiously checking all around her, she led Ellie into another room leading off the cellar, shutting the door quietly behind them. Taking something from the pocket of her cardigan, she handed it to Ellie.

'This is Suman's passport, Ellie. It is a forged one, but you will need it in case you have to take her out of Holland.'

She continued, 'You must be very careful. I'll bring Suman here to you in a few moments. I don't know where you will take her, and this is probably best. I know you'll keep her safe, but you must remember, Ellie, she will not be able to go home to her village in India. She has been with many, many men who have done terrible things to her and she will never be accepted back.' Angena stressed these words carefully.

'This would bring shame on her whole family and her village and she would be thrown out and have no home. The traffickers may also go looking for her again in her village to kill her and her family.'

'Also,' she continued with barely a breath, 'you must be careful about the people you call IPOL. The man I spoke of, his name is Becker, or Decker, I'm not sure which.'

Ellie gasped. 'Lucas Decker?' she whispered. 'If it's him, he works for my company, UBI, not IPOL. Could it be Lucas Decker?'

'I'm not sure, but yes, I think that is the name. He is a very good friend of Van Breda and Madame Geeta who is in charge of us. I have seen him get money, lots of money. I thought he was working for this IPOL or Interpol as he comes here with one of them. And so you must not go to them, Ellie. You must take great care and go far, far away from here with Suman. Now I must go and bring her to you. She's been hurt very badly and doesn't look good, but I know you will take care of her.'

Angena's last words were said with a pleading look and Ellie moved forward to enfold the girl in her arms.

'I will,' she said earnestly. 'You're a wonderful person for trying to save the life of this little girl, Angena. Will you not come with me as well?'

'No, I cannot, I have others here I must take care of. But Suman is a very special and I must not let her be killed by them. I will pray very hard for you both.'

The minutes seemed to drag by as Ellie waited quietly in the dingy room, trying to process the information she had been given about Lucas Decker. She hadn't much liked the man when he had come to help her, but not for a moment did she suspect him of being a criminal.

Suddenly, she heard the clatter of a door closing and men's voices in the cellar. She looked for a place to hide but there was nothing in the room to conceal her and no lock on the door. She stood rooted to the spot as the voices drew nearer until they were outside the door of the room she was in. Her heart was thumping as they walked past talking loudly in Dutch.

Not until she heard the voices receding did she begin to breathe again, and her body relaxed as she heard a door shut in the distance, followed by silence.

Come on, Angena, she pleaded silently.

It was another five minutes of uneasy waiting before Ellie saw the handle turn and the door open to reveal Angena clutching Suman's hand tightly. Unable to stop herself, Ellie winced as she watched the little girl enter the room.

'What have they done to her?' she asked Angena, horror making her voice a bit shrill.

A mass of wounds and bruises covered Suman's face, and Ellie could see what looked like burn marks on her skinny little arms. There were also chunks of hair missing from her head. Her heart ached for the child.

Angena shook her head sadly at Ellie's shocked question, but had no time to answer it, knowing they must get Suman out as quickly as possible. She pointed to the hold-all at Ellie's feet. Quickly Ellie unzipped the bag, opening out a soft towel which she had stuffed into the bottom of the bag in haste.

Angena knelt and spoke softly to the child in Marathi, gave her a gentle hug and pointed to the bag.

'Go on,' she whispered as Suman hesitated. 'Ellie will look after you.'

Suman's lips moved as if trying to say something, but no sound came from her swollen mouth.

'I know,' Angena said tenderly, stroking her cheek then pushing her over to Ellie.

Reality hit quickly as it became obvious that the bag was going to be far too impractical, being too tight for the child to curl up in, and too heavy to carry. They rapidly realised that it would more likely impede the rescue than help. Angena lifted her out and threw the bag into a corner of the room.

'Here, put this on, Suman,' she ordered, pulling off her cardigan and helping put Suman's arms into it. Even with the cuffs turned back, it was ridiculously too big for Suman, but the child pulled it around her and Angena buttoned the lowest button behind the child's back.

Taking Suman's hand again, she opened the door and looked cautiously out. With Ellie at the back, the three of them walked through the cellar and climbed up the stairs as silently as possible. At the top, Angena turned left into a passageway, stopping beside a large, casement window which looked out onto the street a few feet below. She unlocked the catch of the window and swung it out as wide as it would go. With one last hug for Suman, Angena began to help both over the windowsill and onto the street below.

A sudden noise caught them unawares as a door opened into the corridor and a tall woman appeared. Angena looked round and uttered a strangled cry.

'Geeta!' she breathed, a look of terror on her face.

Frantically, she lowered the child down to Ellie, standing with her arms outstretched. 'Run. Run fast,' she shouted, panic in her voice.

Geeta had hesitated only for a second before running towards the window, realising that someone was trying to escape.

'Stop,' she yelled at the top of her voice, 'come back.'

Turning to face Geeta, Angena held out her arms to stop Geeta leaning out of the window, trying to give Ellie and Suman time to get as far away as they could. Geeta was furious. Spitting out obscenities, she flung out her fist and caught Angena a heavy blow to her face, causing her to fall back against the side of the window.

Suman, holding Ellie's hand tightly as they ran, heard Angena's cry and tried to pull Ellie to a stop. Knowing that they had to get away, Ellie resisted the pull and tightened her clasp of Suman's hand to force her to run faster. She could hear Geeta screeching through the window but didn't look back, knowing that the child's life and her own depended on them getting to somewhere safe.

In the corridor, the attack on Angena resumed. Geeta slapped and punched at her adversary and screamed out her name. As the woman's temper raged totally out of control, Angena's slender frame was no match for the ferocity of the blows raining down on her body. The young girl fell to the floor, curling up into a ball to try to protect herself. Geeta kicked out and Angena winced in pain, trying to crawl out of the way. It was too late as Geeta had lost control completely and threw herself on top of the injured girl, forcing her over to wildly reach for her neck. Winding both hands around the slim neck in a throttle hold, she began to squeeze tighter and tighter.

'No, Geeta, no,' Angena's voice was rasped and whispered.

Suddenly, the door at the end of the corridor was pushed open again with a clatter as two dark suited men entered, staring at the sight of Geeta and Angena on the floor under the open window.

'Get after that woman!' Geeta shrieked at the men. They hesitated, unsure of what she meant.

'You fools,' she hissed. 'A woman taking Suman away. Out of the window. Get after them.' Her voice rose hysterically.

The men ran to the window and climbed out, landing on the pavement below with a thud. Seeing this, Geeta's attention returned to Angena, now clawing desperately at the hands round her neck, her breathing becoming laboured.

'Who was that woman?' Geeta screamed loudly, her clammy face heavy with perspiration.

There was no reply from Angena. The fingers squeezed tighter.

'Who took Suman away?' Geeta strung the words out menacingly, her face inches from Angena's.

In the silence that followed, Geeta delivered a stinging slap to Angena's cheek. The girl's head snapped to one side, the blow drawing blood from the corner of her mouth. Geeta's hands returned to her neck to increase the pressure, the red painted nails on her hands cutting into Angena's skin. With hate in her eyes, she pressed harder and harder until at last, Angena's arms fell slowly to the floor. Her face had begun to swell, but as the last breath was squeezed from her body, her expression softened, and her bulging eyes gently closed.

Geeta rose clumsily as in a daze and brushed the dust from her skirt. She inhaled deeply and calmly began to smooth her ruffled hair, never once looking down at the dead girl at her feet. Moving to the window, her lips pursed as she saw no sign of the two men or Ellie and Suman.

Beginning to regain her composure, Geeta knew that it was imperative to bring Suman back. Van Breda would not tolerate Geeta's inefficiency if he discovered she had allowed someone to escape. A wave of fear ran through Geeta as she took a mobile phone from her pocket and began to make a call.

Within minutes of this call, one of the managers from the night club, Stefan Peters appeared in the corridor and ran quickly over to where she stood by the window. He looked down at the girl on the floor and back to Geeta, a question in his eyes.

'She is dead,' Geeta informed him unnecessarily. 'You will have to dispose of her.'

She gave him a curt explanation of what had happened, stating untruthfully that Angena had attacked her while helping the girl, Suman to escape.

'It was self-defence, I had no choice.'

Peters looked worried. 'I don't think Van Breda will be very happy about this, Geeta. This could cause problems.'

'You think I don't know this.' Her voice faltered. 'But it's not as important as getting that stupid girl back before he finds out she has gone. Get a search party organised and cars and find her quickly. Someone has helped her escape. We must find them both before they can get to the politie.'

Peters stroked his chin. 'Not your finest hour, Geeta, is it? A murder and a runaway, all on the same day. I wouldn't like to be in your shoes.'

He began to walk slowly away, a sardonic expression on his face. Turning back, he added nonchalantly, 'And Van Breda wants to see you in his office immediately. I nearly forgot to tell you.'

There was both anger and fear in Geeta's eyes as she swore long and hard.

'What about this?' she called after him, pointing to Angena's body on the floor. 'What are you going to do with this?'

'What do you want me to do with it?' he asked with no hesitation in his stride.

There was also no hesitation in her vicious reply. 'The furnace.'

CHAPTER 12

Amsterdam

Ellie and Suman ran until they were both out of breath. Feeling that she wasn't far enough away from the nightclub, Ellie began to search around desperately for some sort of hiding place, or any transport they could board to get away. As they reached a corner, she heard shouting from some way behind and glanced round, shocked to see a couple of men about two or three hundred metres away, running in hot pursuit. She pulled Suman around the corner quickly and set off at a fast run again, knowing that they would struggle to outrun the men.

The street they were in was a busy one with apartment blocks, shops, cafés, and bars on both sides of the road. Several of the apartment buildings had stairs leading up to entranceways. As she reached the first set of stairs, Ellie spotted that the heavy, black door at the top was ajar. Panting slightly, she scooped Suman up into her arms and ran up the steps as fast as she possibly could and in through the door. Not looking to see where she was, she shut the door with a loud clatter, wincing as the Yale lock clicked with a noise that sounded to her ears like a gunshot.

Ellie glanced around seeing behind her another set of winding stairs leading to the apartments on each floor. She stood still for a moment in case the noise had disturbed anyone above. She put Suman down on her feet and bent over to peep through the letter box on the door. Dismayed, she saw the two men had turned the corner and were beginning to search, looking into shop doorways, behind cars, under cars and anywhere someone could hide. She closed the flap of the letterbox quickly but softly, her heart racing. Listening very carefully at the door, Ellie heard the men mounting the steps towards her, whispering to each other until they were standing just outside the door, one of them trying the door handle.

Sick with apprehension, she silently pulled Suman out of sight of the letterbox, glancing up at the catch to double check it was locked.

Holding on to Suman tightly, she prayed the child would make no sound. After a moment, they heard the men descend the steps again hopefully to continue their search elsewhere.

They waited silently in the hiding place for what seemed an eternity with Ellie holding Suman's hand firmly for reassurance. Eventually, hearing no sounds outside, she plucked up the courage to peep out again through the letterbox. There was no sign of the men within her range of vision, but she was still terrified they would be further down the street, concealed, waiting for them to come out of hiding.

After another five minutes Ellie checked again, grateful that no-one living in the apartment block had appeared and no-one had come to the door. From the area she could see, it was still clear. Turning the lock as quietly as she could and opening the door a few inches, she peered out, trying to stay as invisible as possible. As she had hoped, there was no sign of the two men, and she opened the door a bit further. Ellie signalled to Suman to wait where she was and, leaving the door open, walked down the steps to stand for a few moments at the bottom. No-one came running out to grab her; the men seemed to have disappeared from the street. She ran back up the steps to collect Suman and together they hurried across to a side street, watching all the time for any sign of the two men.

Ahead of them, Ellie could see what looked like a few cafés with outside tables and chairs filled with people enjoying their coffees. She guided Suman past the first one they came to but stopped at the second, which seemed busier and noisier inside. Pushing her way past a group of people coming out, she clung tightly to Suman's hand and once inside, began to search around looking for the ladies' room. Unable to spot it, she hesitated. Two young women with coffee cups in their hands were sitting on stools at the bar and one of them reached out a hand to touch her arm.

'Ik ben alles goed met je?'

'I don't understand,' Ellie returned, glancing in fear at the door behind her.

'Is everything okay? You look worried,' the woman said with a heavy Dutch accent.

'We need to find the toilet, quickly,' Ellie replied, glancing down at Suman.

'Please follow me. I will show you,' offered the woman, laying down her cup. She led Ellie round behind the crowded café area and through a door into a corridor where the rest rooms were clearly marked.

'Thank you so much,' said Ellie.

As they turned away, the Dutch woman laid a hand on Ellie's arm for a second time and said, 'The little girl is badly hurt. Is there anything else I can do to help? I am a nurse.'

Ellie swallowed hard, wondering if she should take a chance and accept the offer of help. At this moment, she felt she didn't have a lot of choices if she was to get Suman to safety. She made a quick decision.

'We're running away from someone who will harm us. We desperately need to get away from this area. Could you help us do that?'

'I have a car nearby. Can I take you somewhere?'

Ellie nodded eagerly, breathing a very grateful, 'Yes, please.'

'Who are you running from?'

Again, Ellie hesitated. To tell the truth of what she was doing would, she thought, sound insane. She improvised.

'My husband. He beats us.'

'Oh, that is not good. Did he do this to the little girl? You must go to the police. They will help you. If you don't really need to go to the rest room, we can go upstairs from here. There's a cocktail bar upstairs and it has a separate entrance at the back of the building. If we go out by that door, he perhaps won't know to come and look there. My car is near that entrance, on the street.'

Ellie nodded and the woman led the way upstairs. About halfway up, the door leading into the café opened and from her position on the stairs, Ellie caught a glimpse of two men entering the bar from the street. She drew back instantly, suspecting it was Van Breda's men, still looking for them.

'Is that him?' the woman asked as they hurried up the steps.

'Yes,' Ellie whispered, terror in her eyes. 'And he has someone with him now.'

They rushed up the rest of the steps and into an upmarket, modern cocktail bar. The room was empty and they hurriedly made their way between the tables, out of a doorway at the far side and down another flight of stairs to reach the street.

'My car is just over here.' The woman pointed to a few cars parked across the other side of the road.

Once inside, she drove quickly out of the parking space and sped away from the bar area.

'I'm Caro by the way,' she said, turning to look at Ellie. 'And the friend I have left behind in the bar is Odile. I will phone her to let her know where I am in a moment. What is your name?'

Ellie opened her mouth and paused.

'Jo.'

'Well, don't worry, Jo. I will take you away from here. Can I take you to a police station?'

Ellie thought quickly. Where did she want to go? The longing to go back to her hotel and enlist Geoff's help was very strong, but she discarded this, feeling it could be dangerous. Although Van Breda and his men were probably unaware of who she was, Ellie didn't want to take any chances. Angena had called her by name, and she suspected this could lead to them discovering her identity. Arriving at a police station might not be a good idea either, she thought, suspecting they would immediately take Suman away. At this moment she preferred to keep the child with her until she knew it was safe to hand her over to someone. She had no way of knowing just how far Van Breda's influence stretched in this city and decided she could not gamble with the life of a child.

Aware she had been silent for some time, she apologised to Caro.

'My thoughts are so jumbled just now, and I hadn't planned where to go,' she explained, thinking that this was indeed true. 'I don't want to go to the police yet. If you could please just take us to a railway station, this would be good. If it's not too far.'

'It's probably only about three kilometres, about five minutes away. Do you have somewhere safe to go?' Caro asked curiously.

'Yes,' said Ellie, reverting to her improvised story. 'I'll go and stay with a friend. You've been so very kind to us, we can't thank you enough.' As she spoke, she glanced round at Suman, sitting silently beside her, huddled into Angena's cardigan, obviously feeling the cold.

'No problem,' said Caro. 'I hate to see anyone in trouble. And it's been a bit of excitement for me, coming to the rescue.'

After a slight pause, she continued, 'You must get your little girl to a doctor or a hospital. She needs her wounds treated.' The advice was given seriously, and Ellie was even more grateful that Caro had come to her aid.

As predicted, within five minutes they drew up at the railway station, and all three climbed out of the car. A quick hug was exchanged before Caro waved goodbye and set off back to the café.

Immediately, Ellie took off her leather jacket and knelt to button it around Suman. Like the cardigan, it was massively too big for her, but Suman stopped shivering quickly once it was on. Putting her wallet and phone into her trouser pockets, she took the child's hand and began to head towards the station entrance. As they walked, however, Ellie noticed in the distance a Holiday Inn Hotel, its name written large down the side of the building. It crossed Ellie's mind that this would perhaps prove a safer venue for them than her own hotel and she could make some phone calls once there.

Angena had been right in thinking that perhaps a white woman with an injured Asian child would attract attention and Ellie became aware of people's curious glances as they walked towards the hotel. Putting Suman in a holdall had not been at all practical, but Ellie did wish that they were not quite so conspicuous.

Crossing at a pedestrian crossing, she explained to Suman that she thought they could go and hide in the large hotel they were approaching and get something to eat. As she chattered away, she was aware that Suman probably did not understand what she was saying. However, feeling very protective towards the child, she was trying to make a connection and to make her feel she was in safe hands. Ellie knew no other way than to hold her hand and to speak to her.

They entered the large automatic doors of the hotel and approached the reception desk.

'Do you have a room available for tonight?'

She was in luck and the receptionist handed over a registration form for her to complete. Thinking hastily, she decided it would be better not to give her real details, hoping she would not be asked for identification or passport.

'May I pay in cash, please? It is just for one night.' Ellie did not want to use her Visa card and was very thankful that she had a good reserve of Euros in her wallet.

The receptionist nodded and took her payment with thanks, handing over the room key. They made their way to the elevator and Ellie pressed the button for the fifth floor. Finding the room easily, they entered the comfortable twin-bedded room and locked the door behind them.

Feeling safer than she had during the whole rescue, Ellie lifted Suman and placed her gently on the bed, her thin legs dangling over the side. She knelt on the floor in front of Suman and looked into the child's eyes.

'Hi. I'm Ellie as you'll have realised and I want to try to help you. You have been through a terrible time and Angena asked me to take you away from there and look after you.'

The dark eyes stared back; the little face expressionless. Ellie tried again.

'You...' she began, pointing, '...are Suman. And me, I'm Ellie. And I'm going to try to keep you safe.'

With no answer forthcoming, Ellie waited, unsure whether to continue. To her amazement, Suman slipped down off the side of the bed, shrugging off the leather jacket as she did so. Standing in front of Ellie, she slowly stretched out two small hands to Ellie's own and lifted them to her cheek. Ellie swallowed hard, her heart melting at this gesture of thanks and trust from the little girl who had been through so much. She tilted Suman's chin upwards and looked into her eyes.

'I will look after you and protect you, and I'll never let them get hold of you again. I know you don't understand what I'm saying, but I'll just keep talking to you and maybe soon you'll be able to speak back to me. But first, my darling, we need to get you all washed and cleaned up and some cream on these sore bits. How does that sound, eh?'

Undeterred by no reply from the child, she continued. 'A wee bath first maybe, then something to eat. You wait here and I'll go and run the bath. I might even put bubbles in if I can find some bubble bath.'

Ellie rose, watching Suman's face as she did so. She could see that Suman was listening intently and who knows, she thought, maybe even understanding some of what was being said. Consequently, she chattered on, making her way into the bathroom. Turning on the taps, she watched as Suman came to stand at the bathroom door to see what she was doing, or perhaps just to be near her. The water was warm, and Ellie added the hotel bath foam, swirling the water with her hand to increase the bubbles.

Speaking reassuringly all the time, she indicated to Suman to take her clothes off and was dismayed to immediately see a look of terror cross Suman's face.

'Oh, Suman, I'm so sorry,' she whispered quietly. 'I won't hurt you in any way, my darling. I just want you to climb in the bath to clean up all these sores you have.'

As she said this, she stood up, pointing first to Suman, and then to herself and thirdly to the bath. Trying to relieve the tension she had created, she pretended to climb into the bath and wash herself with the soft white facecloth provided by the hotel, making funny faces as she did so. Suman watched her in amazement for a moment before tentatively allowing a very tiny smile to appear on her swollen face. Moving slowly, she began to remove all the clothes she was wearing, before climbing in amongst the warm bubbles. To give her a feeling of safety, Ellie had wrapped one of the small towels in the bathroom around Suman's middle, and she kept it on while in the bath.

In the water, she allowed Ellie to gently and carefully wash away the dried blood from her injuries and to shampoo her long, matted hair. At times, she winced as a tender spot was bathed, but she made no noise, sitting submissively in the foamy water.

Ellie's eyes opened wide when she saw the extent of Suman's injuries, seeing open wounds, huge bruises and burn marks on the little girl's emaciated body but she made no comment about them. After drying her gently and wrapping her up in a dry towel, Ellie carried her carefully to one of the two beds and sat her up against the pillows.

'Are you hungry?' she asked, gesturing with her fingers as if putting food into her mouth. Suman nodded.

Accompanying her next words with gestures, Ellie told her that she would go downstairs to see if she could buy them something to eat and drink. Suddenly terrified as Ellie moved towards the door, Suman slid quickly off the bed, hanging on tightly to the towel, and ran to grab hold of Ellie's arm.

'I understand. You don't want me to leave you.' Ellie knelt and gave Suman a reassuring hug. 'Don't worry, I'll stay here. Let's see if there's anything to eat in the room then, shall we?'

Ellie opened the cupboard doors, looking for a kettle and tea-making facilities, Suman still by her side. She was pleased to find what she was after and delighted to see a small packet of shortbread biscuits on the tray as well. She pulled open the packet and handed one to Suman, who, after a moment's hesitation, put the whole biscuit in her mouth as if it was going to disappear before she ate it. Ellie chuckled quietly, handing over the rest of the packet and lifted Suman back over to the bed.

When the biscuits were finished, Suman dressed herself in the clothes she had taken off, and wrapped Angena's cardigan around her small body. Ellie had been fiddling with the TV set in the room, trying to find a children's channel. There were one or two and she settled on the Disney Channel, leaving the sound low. Suman sat on the bed again and stared, fascinated by the television and Ellie wondered if this was perhaps the first time she had ever seen one. She realised that she knew nothing at all about Suman and what her home life had been like.

Angrily she thought for a moment about the people who had hurt this lovely child and made a vow to herself that if she was ever given the chance, she would do everything in her power to bring them to justice.

Her thoughts turned for a moment to Angena and she frowned, unable to begin to contemplate what might have happened to her once they had gone. She knew that whatever had happened, it would be bad, and she saw again in her mind the fury on the face of the woman she had glimpsed rushing towards the open window as she climbed out. She shuddered, glancing over at Suman who was still watching the TV intently.

Ellie sat down on the other bed, leaning back against the pillows, and putting her feet up. The realisation that she was exhausted hit her at that moment, and her plans to begin making some phone calls for help faded into the distance as she closed her eyes.

A short time later Ellie woke with a start, aware of someone lying beside her. Looking down, she saw that Suman had changed beds and was lying fast asleep at her side, one thin arm stretched across Ellie's waist for safety and comfort. The room was bright with the sun streaming in the window and the Disney Channel was still playing quietly on the television set. As carefully as she could, Ellie removed Suman's arm, slid her feet over the edge of the bed and stood up managing not to wake Suman.

Lifting her mobile phone from the dresser, she tiptoed to the bathroom, softly pushing the door to. She glanced at her watch and saw with surprise that it was almost three in the afternoon.

Her first phone call was going to be to Geoff, but she hesitated before dialling his number. She wondered how safe it would be to use her phone. After a moment, she decided to take a chance. She was desperate to speak to him, to let him know that she was okay. Perching on the edge of the bath, she dialled his mobile.

Geoff answered his phone very quickly.

'Hello,' he said sharply.

'Geoff, it's Ellie,' she began.

'Oh, thank God,' he interrupted. 'Where are you? I've been worried sick.'

'I'm fine,' she said, her heart lifting at his words. 'I'm safe and well.' Ellie couldn't answer his question yet, not until she knew what was happening at his end.

'Where are you?' he repeated. 'Where did you disappear to? I know you're not in the hotel, there are people here searching for you. I'm in your room now, with two of them. Are you sure you're all right?' His voice was fraught with anxiety.

'People are looking for me?' Ellie's heart sank as she asked the question. 'Geoff listen, I'm okay, but who's searching for me? Who is with you?'

'Ellie, just tell me where you are and let me help you. I don't know what's wrong, but I want to help. They're saying you're in trouble and they must find you. Please tell me where you are.'

'You tell me first who the men are, Geoff. I need to know.'

'There is a police inspector here and...'

Ellie heard a commotion from the other end of the line and realised that someone had taken Geoff's phone from him as she heard an unknown voice come on the line.

'Ellie, this is Lucas from UBI. I met you the other day. You know me and can trust me, so please tell me where you are so that I can help.' The man's voice was friendly and reassuring, but Ellie was aware of a fast pounding in her heart as he spoke.

'Lucas? Lucas Decker?' she queried.

'Yes, it's me. Geoff will verify this. Tell me where to find you and let me come for you. You'll be quite safe.'

'Who else is with you?' Ellie asked him, ignoring his request.

'An officer from IPOL is with me. Tell me where you are.'

'What is the officer's name?' Ellie was persistent. Instead of an answer Ellie heard a muted conversation in the background and then a third voice spoke.

'This is Frank Levy, on the Dienst IPOL team. On Daan's team. You've got yourself involved in something you shouldn't, Ellie. You must tell us where you are before you get in any deeper. Where are you?'

Ellie's mind was in turmoil as he spoke, desperately trying to put the facts together. Knowing that Decker was there, the name Angena had given her, huge alarm bells were ringing in her head. And what was it Angena had suspected? That he was in league with someone at IPOL. Could this Frank Levy be the one, could he be involved with Van Breda as well? Her head was spinning as all these thoughts swirled around inside. She had no idea who she could trust and who she couldn't.

She switched off her phone abruptly and stood up. Pacing around the bathroom, she tried to figure out what she should do. How had they known she was involved in this? The information could only have come from someone at The Furnace nightclub, no-one else could have known she was there this morning.

To have discovered who she was so quickly was terrifying and she worried that with such a powerful organisation as this, she and Suman would be quickly traced. She knew they had to get away, far from Amsterdam, to somewhere safe, until she knew exactly who she could trust. She immediately thought of John, her boss back in Edinburgh. She would trust him with her life, but with Angena's warnings running through her head, she hesitated. Who would John contact? Of course it would be IPOL and Ellie knew IPOL, in the form of Frank Levy, was already trying to find her. At this moment, Ellie was sure of only one person who could possibly come and help her without drawing attention to the authorities. Only one person she knew would do as Ellie requested and tell no-one; her life-long friend, Sara.

Using the hotel phone, Ellie dialled Sara's mobile and held her breath, praying the phone would be answered.

She had almost given up when she heard Sara's voice.

'Hello?'

'Sara, it's me, Ellie. Are you alone?'

'Ellie? Great to hear from you. What do you mean, am I alone? I'm at work so there's me and my workmates here. Why are you asking that? Have you got a secret lover out there that I don't know about?' she asked with a laugh.

'Sara. This is serious. I need you to go somewhere no-one can hear what we say. I need your help. I'm in dire trouble.'

'Hold on. I'll go outside.'

Ellie waited a few moments until she heard Sara's voice again, this time not laughing and sounding worried.

'What's happened? What trouble are you in?'

'Bad trouble, Sara. I need you desperately. I'll tell you...'

'I'm on my way,' Sara interrupted. 'Where shall I go?'

'Hang on, hang on, it's not as simple as that. I need to tell you a bit about it, so just listen for a moment, and then I'll tell you where to come. Okay?'

'Okay, I'm listening.'

As concisely as she possibly could, Ellie gave Sara a one-minute outline of what had been happening to her, and an even shorter version of Suman's rescue. She finished by explaining the danger they were now in and why she needed to get them out of Amsterdam.

'I'll go and get a flight as quickly as I can,' promised Sara. 'How will I know where to find you?'

'I'm going to try to get to somewhere like Rotterdam this afternoon. I'll phone you from a public phone to tell you where we are as soon as I can. I'm worried about using my mobile in case they're able to trace it, and any credit cards I use too. If you can, would you bring a lot of cash in Euros, and maybe some food, and some clothes for me and warm clothes for a little girl about eight or nine years old? We've got nothing.'

'Will do. And you promise me that you'll stay safe and keep well hidden 'till I get there. I love you, honey, so you be careful.'

'I will, Sara. Love you too, and sorry to be dragging you into this.'

'That's what friends are for, El. See you soon.'

Ellie switched off her phone and began to make some plans, knowing she had to work quickly and be long gone before Decker or someone from Van Breda's organisation discovered where they were. She woke Suman gently, explaining that they were moving on.

Ellie gave a last look around the room before they left. For a short time, she had felt they were safe there, but as the minutes ticked by, she had become increasingly worried about staying in one place too long.

Stealthily they made their way along the corridor and into the elevator, where Ellie was relieved to see no-one. She checked the buttons and as she had hoped, there was a basement in the hotel, below ground level. Although marked 'Staff Only' she pushed the button and they began their descent. The passageway of the basement was gloomy and cold, with the overhead light dimmed to a pale glow as she searched for an exit door. Finding a fire exit, she quickly pushed open the heavy door, and holding tightly to Suman, climbed the few steps up to the pavement.

There were few people around the hotel and only the occasional car passing by. According to the information book she had come across in the room, a twenty-four-hour taxi rank was operating just two streets away and Ellie breathed a sigh of relief as she saw some empty cabs parked outside the office, waiting for passengers.

'Can you take us to Lelylaan Station please?' she enquired in the office. The man sitting behind the desk glanced at her appraisingly before answering.

'Forty Euros,' he said gruffly.

Ellie swallowed hard. This was a much higher figure than she had anticipated, and she knew she should really haggle for a lower figure. However, she desperately wanted to get them off the streets and out of sight of anyone searching for them. She had chosen Lelylaan Station to try to board a train out of Amsterdam as she felt that Central Station nearby could be where Van Breda's men would search for them.

Reluctantly agreeing to the forty Euros, Ellie and Suman climbed aboard the cab for the short journey to the station. Ellie was tense while walking through the station, afraid that Lelylaan was still too close for comfort to the dangerous people looking for them. Seeing a ticket machine on the platform, she paid the fare for tickets from Amsterdam to Rotterdam and was grateful to see that a train was due in just a few minutes. They hurried to the platform, Ellie still on the alert for anyone watching or following them.

The journey proved uneventful with no-one approaching or taking any notice of them and the forty-minute journey passed quickly. On arrival at Rotterdam, Ellie was relieved to be able to merge into the hectic throng of commuters milling about the busy station. On the street, she began to look around for a restaurant in which they could sit for a short time and have a quick meal while she planned their next move.

An Indian restaurant caught her eye and she thought this would be good for Suman. It was crowded but the waiter found them an empty table for two tucked behind some pillars and took their order quickly. The food arrived eventually, and she could see that Suman was pleased with what she had ordered. She watched Suman's face light up as she tucked into Kurkuri Bhindi and rice.

As Suman finished her plateful, she looked over at Ellie still watching her while she ate her own meal. Ellie leaned across and asked softly, 'Okay?'

To Ellie's amazement, the child slid off her chair to come and sit on Ellie's knee, her stick-thin arms winding their way round her neck. The two sat for some moments, Suman's eyes half closed and her body at peace. Ellie's eyes remained watchful as she rocked Suman gently to and fro, whispering words of comfort, and telling her about Sara coming to rescue them. Ten minutes passed by as they sat, undisturbed by anyone, and eventually Ellie judged it time to once again find a place to hide. A leaflet she had picked up in the station was advertising the Inntel Hotel at the foot of the Erasmus Bridge as a reasonably priced hotel and she hailed a taxi at the roadside to take them there.

She was relieved to find a room available, and booked in for one night, again paying in cash to the friendly receptionist on duty in the foyer. The woman on reception had asked about their luggage, and Ellie had replied truthfully that she hoped this would be arriving soon with her friend who was staying in the room with them tonight and would arrive later.

By now, what she had initially thought of as a large reserve of cash was almost gone and she knew she would have to be more careful with her few remaining Euros. Using her credit or debit card would be too dangerous, she reckoned, and like her phone which she had switched off completely, she kept them out of sight in her trouser pockets. Their room was on the sixth floor of the hotel, with a panoramic view over the city skyline and a lovely view of the River Maas, which was very picturesque, she thought, but of no current interest to her.

Once in the room with the door locked, she sat Suman on one of the three beds and tried to explain what was happening.

'We're far away from Amsterdam, from the people who hurt you, and hopefully we'll be safe here.' She smoothed the child's hair back from her face and looked into her eyes.

'There's a lovely, happy little girl with a great big personality in there, isn't there, my darling? And together, we're going to try to bring her back.'

CHAPTER 13

Amsterdam

Two men stood by a tall window in a large, modern office above The Furnace, the taller of the two looking out at the darkening panorama of the city in front of him, the second looking downward, checking an incoming text on his mobile phone.

'Rotterdam,' he informed Van Breda. 'I'll get the hotels checked out, pronto. Let's hope she stays long enough for us to get there this time.'

'I want them both out of the picture within the next few hours,' Van Breda ordered without turning his eyes from the view.

'I'm on it, Arne. Thus far, she's done us a favour by going it alone, means we won't leave any traces. The boyfriend's been trying hard to find her, but she's not returning his calls. Wouldn't have been so bad if she had, we'd have found her quicker.'

Van Breda sighed and turned back to his desk; boredom was written large on his face as he sat down.

'Just let me know when it's done,' he ordered. 'I don't need to know how.'

With a dismissive turn of his shoulder, he pressed a button on the intercom on his desk and spoke sharply into it.

'Send Geeta to me, now.'

The second man still hovered by the desk, nervously moving from foot to foot and Van Breda turned back to him.

'Stop worrying, Frank. Just keep a close eye on the boyfriend, and make sure the girl and the kid disappear permanently. Apart from having the youngster with her as evidence, as far as we know, she has nothing else to hang us with and if you do it right, there'll be no connection to us.'

'I don't know. UBI's reports are getting more and more dangerous for us, and with my IPOL team so heavily involved, they know this girl. I can't help worrying this is all going to open things up too much. I know you've suspended the whisky operation while we knew they were around, but they're digging pretty deep.'

'As long as we're one step ahead of your organisation, Frank, nobody's going to open anything up. And that's what I'm paying you for, isn't it?' he asked with a menacing hint in his deep voice.

As Frank Levy opened his mouth to reply, there was a quiet knock on the door.

'You look after your side and I'll look after mine,' Van Breda continued, and with a nod towards the door indicated that Levy should leave.

Shaking his head and with a troubled look on his face, Levy opened the door to admit Geeta and let himself out. His scowl deepened as he strode heavily along the corridor, the mobile phone back in his hand and his thumb already moving swiftly over the buttons.

Behind him in the office, an ominous atmosphere pervaded the room as Van Breda asked Geeta to account for the problems he was now experiencing.

'I never thought the girl, Angena, would turn traitor,' she tried to excuse herself.

'I don't pay you to trust people, Geeta, especially not the brats we buy in. I gave you a warning the last time about the new one giving us bother, and you ignored me. You failed me, Geeta, and you know I don't tolerate failures.'

'I had her punished. I didn't want to get rid of her at that time. They liked her for the films, and the punters liked her. So I gave her another chance. How was I to know Angena was going to do what she did? It won't happen again. And you'll get Suman and the one who took her, I know you will.'

'I shouldn't have been put to this trouble. You're losing your touch. I need someone who can do the job properly and who doesn't slip up.' Van Breda's eyes narrowed as he spoke.

'I'm not the only one to blame for this,' she replied, her voice becoming high and loud with fear. 'If your staff had answered my shouts for help before they did, the two of them wouldn't have got away.'

'The fault is entirely yours, Geeta. You've lost control of your girls and by the sound of what you did to Angena, you've lost control of yourself as well. Too messy, Geeta, too messy.' He pursed his lips and shook his head.

'It was that new one, the little bitch, Suman. I knew she would make trouble for me.' Geeta's face grew hot and her hands clenched as she spat the last words at Van Breda.

The slap on the side of her face knocked her sideways and she grasped a chair to stop herself from falling.

'Get out of here and get yourself under control. I'll decide later what to do with you, once 'the little bitch' as you call her, is disposed of. Meantime, go and get some of your other 'bitches' ready.' Van Breda's tone was sarcastic. 'We've got paying customers coming in shortly and I want their every need met. Is that clear?'

Geeta nodded but he had already turned away and was reaching for his phone by the time she began to move towards the door.

'Find Fairlady for me and ask her to come to my office,' she heard him command as she passed through the doorway and shut the door with a snap behind her.

Geeta's face stiffened and her lips tightened in fury as she realised the significance of what he had just said. Fairlady was an African girl who had been trafficked into the organisation a couple of years ago and was, she knew only too well, one of the favourites to take over the position Geeta held in the company. For the last six months, she had been answerable only to Van Breda himself and was already accompanying him to various 'business' meetings, in place of Geeta.

A wave of fear ran through her body, followed instantly by a feeling of intense hatred for her powerful employer. Thoughts of revenge flooded her mind. If I'm being taken out, she thought, I'm taking him with me.

She hurried along the corridor and up to the staff quarters above the huge nightclub, her mind full of revenge and thoughts of how to carry out his downfall. Knowing that Van Breda made no empty threats, she had already come to terms with the realisation that her end could be swift and brutal. Time was short and even though she had been carefully organising for this moment for a long time, knowing in her heart that one day it would come, she still had so much to do.

In the dressing rooms, she chose the girls at random and at speed, and told them to prepare for a busy shift with the clients who were coming in. About an hour later, as soon as the last client was satisfied with his choice and the work had begun, Geeta slipped silently up to her room. Knowing the building like the back of her hand, she climbed a set of stairs little used by anyone else and slipped furtively through one or two doors to reach her own room, making sure she was not seen by anyone. She opened the door with her key and locked it silently behind her. Once inside, she quickly packed a large suitcase with the items in the closet that she valued most, her designer clothing, bags and shoes. Then, returning to kneel and reach into the back of her cupboard, she turned the dial of a small safe three times, pulling the door swiftly open on the third click.

Reaching in, she lifted out a large velvet drawstring bag and carried it over to the suitcase. For a second she hesitated, her hands feeling the weight of the bag, her greedy soul swelling with pride at the thought of the uncut diamonds, the items of precious jewellery, the sparkling bracelets, rings and priceless watches she had collected over the last few years. With a sigh she tucked them carefully under some of the clothes in her suitcase.

Working swiftly, she returned to the safe to pull out a large manila folder tied tightly with cords, and a huge wad of banknotes secured together with a broad elastic band. Pushing the money in beside the diamonds under her clothes, she shut the case and zipped it up, inserting the manila folder into the large pocket on the front. Still moving fast, she slipped on her jacket, lifted a small digital camera from the dresser and put it into her pocket. Lastly, she collected her case from the bed and left the room as silently as she had entered.

Retracing her steps, Geeta made her way speedily back down the little used stairway to the basement. In the basement, she stopped on the way to open a broom cupboard, pushing her suitcase inside, and silently closing the door. She turned the key in the lock and placed it in her jacket pocket.

Moving more slowly now, she made her way to the warehouse where Ellie had come to meet Angena such a short time ago. With a quick look to see that no-one was around, Geeta pulled back a curtain to reveal a hidden door in the wall. The door had a secure entry system and Geeta keyed in four numbers, opened the door and slipped inside.

The large storage room was cold and dark but there was enough light for her to see her way to some huge cupboards along one wall. Using a key on her key ring, she unlocked the cupboard doors to reveal several pieces of industrial equipment and machinery of a bottling plant. She moved rapidly along, taking photos of the filling machines, packing materials, capping, labelling equipment and conveyers until she was satisfied she had enough.

Pocketing the camera, she hurried back upstairs. A row of doors stretched along both walls in the narrow corridor, and each door had a dull red, illuminated light above it. She passed quickly through the brothel area of the nightclub until she reached a heavy metal door at the far end of the corridor.

This door led into a film studio, which she entered by using her pass key. She knew that getting a picture of filming while in operation would be difficult, if not impossible, but she decided to try. Just inside the door, she removed the soft, silk scarf from around her neck, and taking the camera from her pocket, she switched off the flash and draped the scarf over it. Satisfied the camera was concealed, she picked her way through the lighting equipment and cameras on tripods that were strewn around and stopped near to where filming was taking place.

She nodded a silent hello to two or three of the men behind the cameras and stood back far enough to see the whole of the action taking place from a vantage point where she thought she might be as inconspicuous as possible. The appalling acts in front of her roused no emotion, her hard, dispassionate nature long inured to the abuse and violations suffered by those being filmed. Having been subjected to violence and degradation herself as a trafficked youngster, Geeta had completely lost her sense of empathy and compassion and the word suffering did not feature in her vocabulary.

Her thoughts were concentrated on how to take a photograph without the cameramen noticing and her chance came as a clumsy lighting boy tripped over a cable lying on the floor, falling flat on his face and uttering a loud yell.

As quick as a flash, while everyone's attention was drawn to the commotion, she seized the chance to move the scarf and take a hurried photo of the evidence she needed. Before anyone noticed, the scarf was once again draped over her hand, the camera hidden underneath. As soon as the filming re-started, she turned to go, pleased with her success, and feeling a vindictive satisfaction at the thought of the photographic evidence she now possessed against Arne Van Breda.

Back in the corridor, she strode quickly, making a call on her mobile phone as she walked. Being assured a taxi was on its way, she began to run, turning several times to check there was no-one following her. At the broom cupboard, she pulled her suitcase out and slipped the camera down into the front pocket beside the manila folder. She continued her frantic flight down the steps and into the basement, rushing along between the high, empty shelving units until she reached the exit.

Looking out, she saw only a few people on the other side of the road, but no sign of the taxi at the door. Breaking into an anxious sweat, she swore under her breath. However, a moment later, she was relieved to see the cab approaching and stepped out onto the pavement to wave it to stop.

'Schiphol Airport, fast,' she directed the taxi driver as she heaved in her heavy suitcase to the back of the cab beside her. As he drew away, she sat upright in the back, holding tightly to the handle of her case with both hands.

The cab had driven no more than a hundred yards down the road when a car travelling at great speed raced up behind and overtook them with a roar of its engine. It swerved sharply in front of the taxi with a screech of brakes, forcing the driver to skid into the kerbside, and hit his brakes hard. Without a seatbelt on, Geeta was thrown forward in her seat and onto the floor. Her eyes were wide with terror, knowing that the car in front was one of Van Breda's vehicles; her brain whirled as she panicked, knowing there was no chance of escape.

The taxi driver bought her a few seconds as he flew from his seat out into the street to confront the two men in the car in front, remonstrating loudly and wildly at their incompetent driving. During these moments, Geeta bent down and rapidly pulled out the manila folder and the camera from the front pocket of her suitcase. She threw these haphazardly under the seat in front of her and pushed them hard with her foot, straightening up as the men from the other car opened her door.

'Geeta, dear Geeta,' said the dark, unshaven man at the door with a sneer. 'I'm so glad we caught you in time.' He leaned forward and gripped Geeta's elbow tightly, pulling her from the car. Still holding on he turned to the cabbie and spoke.

'Sorry to give you such a fright, sir, but we desperately wanted to catch up with our friend here. There's someone who wants to see her before she leaves, and we just couldn't let her go without a proper goodbye.' He turned back to Geeta and smirked, 'Now could we?'

Putting his arm around Geeta, he manoeuvred her away from the taxi, turning to say quietly to his companion, 'Bring Geeta's case, Josef. I'm sure she'll need it.'

Geeta's eyes were like slits and her face a mask as she felt herself propelled towards the other car. She kept herself upright, turning only to see if Josef had found the file and camera. Maliciously pleased to see him bringing only the case from the taxi and shutting the door, she turned to stare ahead, knowing her fate was now sealed, but hoping beyond hope that someone would find the folder and camera and give it into the right hands. Geeta desperately wanted revenge on the man who had controlled her life for so many years.

The unshaven man, still holding her tightly, helped her into the back seat of Van Breda's car and climbed in, his grip relaxing only when he had pulled the door to. Josef put Geeta's suitcase into the boot of the car and walked around to climb into the driver's seat. Within seconds the car had driven off at speed, taking the road back to the nightclub.

'Tut, tut, Geeta,' the man at her side said with amusement in his voice. 'You should have realised he would have the doors watched. From the moment you left the building, we were ready to follow you and bring you back. You didn't really think he would let you go, did you?'

Staring straight ahead, Geeta made no reply.

CHAPTER 14

Amsterdam

Daan Meijer watched thoughtfully as Geoff paced backwards and forwards on the other side of the desk.

'Sit down, Geoff. We'll find her. It's just a matter of time.'

'You've been saying that all day and you haven't found her yet,' Geoff replied with a sigh as he sat down heavily in the chair. 'If only she would answer my calls.'

'That would certainly help us find her and help her too.'

'What's bothering me is *why* she won't contact anyone. Not me, not you. She must know she can trust you and yet she's not getting in touch at all. She hung up on Levy. Why didn't she want to speak to him? Could there be something about him?'

'I don't think so. He's one of our team; in fact, he's the one with the contacts inside the Van Breda organisation. Goes about the place and is known to them. Maybe she saw him there and doesn't trust him. I'll speak to him as soon as he comes in.'

'Is there anything at all I can do in the meantime? I find it so hard to just sit waiting for news.'

'It would be helpful if you could give us some more details of Ellie's background. Her family, her friends, that kind of thing. Anyone you think she might contact.'

'Unfortunately, I don't really know her well enough to tell you anything you don't already know. John Anderson knows her better than anyone and I know you've spoken to him.'

'I thought you and Ellie were an item, together as it were?'

'If only,' Geoff accompanied his words with a sigh. 'It's a bit one-sided, I'm afraid. I'm really just getting to know her better.' He stared into space for a moment, his thoughts elsewhere.

A sudden knock at the door brought him out of his reverie, and Daan's shout to come in made him swivel round in his chair to look hopefully at the door. However, his hopes were dashed as one of the

IPOL team popped his head round the door, shook his head at Geoff to confirm there was no news yet, and then asked to speak to Daan in private.

'Sure, come in.'

Daan looked across apologetically to Geoff but before he could speak, Geoff had risen and walked to the door.

Geoff turned. 'I'll go back to the hotel. You *will* phone if there's any news, won't you?'

'I will. Right away. And vice versa, if she contacts you, I want to know about it. And Geoff...' Daan paused, 'watch your back.'

Geoff left the office and hurried towards the elevator, keen to get out into the fresh air. As he left the building, he again tried to call Ellie on his phone, but as before, was unsuccessful. She was not answering his calls and as he had already left a few messages for her, he didn't feel he could leave any more.

In a room in the Inntel Hotel in Rotterdam, Ellie was just hanging up the hotel phone, having left a voice message on Sara's mobile to say where they were. Staring at the receiver before letting it go, she prayed that no-one yet suspected Sara of being involved and that Sara would be the only person to hear the voice message.

Turning around, she looked at Suman, avidly watching her from the chair in the room. Suman's swollen jaw was reducing marginally, but the vivid colours of a bruise were beginning to show, making her look more incongruous than before. Her eyes however, had a brightness now that they had lacked yesterday, and her body was losing its listlessness.

Time was dragging slowly for Ellie, waiting impatiently for Sara. Leaving Suman to watch the television again she had a shower and washed her hair, feeling much more refreshed and ready to face the next part of the race to safety.

Having time to think everything through and plan properly was also beneficial, and she realised that she was overlooking a few things in her plans, perhaps underestimating the dangers of such a powerful organisation as Van Breda's. She was deep in thought, her bottom lip receiving the usual attention it did when she was nervous, when a sudden knock on the bedroom door startled an exclamation from her. The effect on Suman was dramatic. The child was a picture of abject terror as she jumped up from the bed and ran as fast as a bullet to Ellie, clutching her fearfully and hiding behind her back. Her arms were gripping Ellie so tightly, that it was with difficulty Ellie prised herself loose enough to approach the door.

A second knock came to the door just as she leaned forward to peep through the spyhole, making her jump.

'It's me, it's Sara,' came a loud whisper through the edge of the door.

Ellie breathed a sigh of relief as she heard her friend's welcome voice. Still cautious, she asked a question of Sara before opening the door.

'Are you alone?'

'Yes, and I'm absolutely laden, so open the door,' came Sara's voice.

The fear and dangers that Ellie had already experienced made her take extra care. Leaving the chain on the door she opened it a fraction to check but was unable to see along the corridor. What she could see was Sara standing alone outside with a suitcase at her side, a haversack on her back and several plastic bags in her hands. She unclipped the chain and leaned out, swiftly checking both sides of the corridor, and then opened the door wide enough to help Sara in with all the luggage as rapidly as she could.

Once inside, the door was double locked and the chain back in place again before Ellie turned to hug and welcome her friend with profuse thanks.

'Never mind all that,' Sara interrupted. 'You looked so scared to let me in; you're frightening me. Is this really so serious, Ellie? Help me with the bags and let me get my coat off. Then I need to hear absolutely everything.'

As she spoke, Sara suddenly became aware of a small, dark face peeping round from Ellie's back. Laying the bags on the floor, she said quietly, 'And more importantly, there's somebody here I'm dying to meet.'

Ellie knelt on the floor and reached round to gently pull Suman from her hiding place. She put her arms around the little girl to make her feel safe.

'Suman, this is my best friend, Sara, who I've been telling you about. She has come to help us, to help me look after you and help get us away from here. Say hello.'

Suman stared at Sara, but no words came from her lips. She watched with wide eyes as the tall newcomer knelt on both knees, clasped both hands together as in prayer and said, 'Namaste, Suman.'

Suman's eyes lit up; copying Sara, she put her hands together and bent her head gently.

'I think she's accepted you, Sara. Well done and thank you.'

'No problem. And if you open that rucksack you've just put on the floor, I think you'll find some things in it for Suman. There are a few nice warm tops and trousers. Ellie, she must be freezing in that dress.'

'Sara, you're a star. She *is* freezing. You're wonderful, but how on earth did you get here so quickly. I wasn't expecting you for hours?'

'I got a flight really quickly after you phoned. Then I got your message on the way out of Amsterdam airport, so I just dashed to the station and got on the first train to Rotterdam. Didn't take long at all, just forty minutes. Then a taxi brought me right to the hotel and bingo, here I am!'

Ellie hugged her friend again, feeling much more confident now that Sara had arrived. Peeping into the bulging carrier bags, she was delighted to see a huge variety of snacks and sandwiches and drinks. Whatever else happened, they weren't going to go hungry.

The clothes for Suman were now piled up on the bed and Suman was happy to try them on. Thankfully the sizes were almost perfect. Dressed in a warm vest, with soft woolly jumper and trousers and new socks and shoes, she walked across to the full-length mirror on the back of the door and gazed at herself in disbelief, reaching out to touch the mirror. Bending down, she ran her fingers over the pink trainers she had on her feet, touching the glittering stars on them as if in wonder. Ellie exchanged a look with Sara but made no comment.

Leaving Suman to look through the other items of clothing, Ellie took the opportunity to bring Sara up to date with all that had been happening to them, and the conversation led to a discussion on what to do next. Sara voiced some very strong arguments in favour of contacting the local police in Rotterdam and it took all of Ellie's persuasive powers to explain why this was not a good idea. She outlined in graphic detail the dangers they faced from the Van Breda organisation, Frank Levy in particular, and from Lucas Decker, the man Ellie suspected of working for both Van Breda and UBI. She eventually managed to convince Sara that they had to get Suman to safety before contacting any of the authorities.

On one thing, however, both women agreed. Remaining more than one night in Rotterdam was not an option. Tomorrow early, it was agreed they leave and find yet another hiding place.

'Could I hire a car and maybe drive us into France?' suggested Sara.

Ellie shook her head. 'I think they'll check for car hires and if by some chance they know you're in Rotterdam, we'll be traceable that way. Remember, this is IPOL and maybe even Interpol we're dealing with. Levy is on the IPOL team and will be looking for us with all the resources they have at their disposal.'

Ellie put a hand to her forehead and closed her eyes for a second.

'I'm just not sure at all what to do and who to trust, Sara. I firmly believe that our lives are in danger. And although I desperately want to go to the police and ask for their help, if everything Angena and Daan Meijer told me is true, I can't do that. Van Breda appears to have close friends in high places so I can't risk it, not until I know it's completely safe.'

'How can we bypass this Levy? Is there not someone you can absolutely and utterly trust to go to Daan Meijer and tell him about your fears of this man?' asked Sara.

Ellie's cheeks reddened slightly as she replied to her friend's question.

'Well, I trust Geoff implicitly. I got to know him well last week and I would trust him. But how would I know Decker and Levy aren't with him or watching him? They might even have a trace on his phone, waiting in case I call him?'

Sara eyed her friend speculatively, wondering about the tell-tale blush and suspecting that there was something new in Ellie's voice as she spoke of Geoff, but for now didn't mention it. Their priority was to find safety and to find it quickly.

'Well, let's say they have got the ways and means of finding us, traces on phones and things like that; I believe the police can trace a mobile phone's use to within one hundred yards of where the call is made, which means they could already have an idea where we are. Do you not think we should be getting away from here and then working out who to contact?'

'Yes, I do think that. But where would we go, and how would we travel? I've been looking into…'

As Ellie spoke, the hotel phone suddenly filled the room with its strident ring, freezing the three of them into immobility. The two friends looked instinctively towards each other, alarm and fear on each face and Suman, petrified at the sound, immediately bolted across to Ellie to cling on tightly.

'Don't answer it,' Ellie mouthed to Sara, holding tightly to Suman but nodding to her friend to get the bags and get ready to go. In minutes, the suitcase was repacked, and the rucksack was again on Sara's back. The three of them were by the door, prepared for flight. With Suman still clinging to her, Ellie peered through the spyhole, frustrated at the narrow vision this afforded her but just about to open the door when another noise reached her ears. The lift door was opening on their floor and Ellie held up a hand, her eye still glued to the spyhole.

Distorted but recognisable, two men appeared within her vision, both dressed in black, one with a hat covering the top half of his face. On his mouth she could see the scowl that had caught her attention in IPOL's office. Frank Levy. At his side was Lucas Decker.

She turned to Sara, her face white as she mouthed the words, 'Levy and Decker.'

Sara's hand flew up to her face, and her eyes widened with both surprise and horror. Ellie drew back hastily from the spyhole as a knock came to the door. As still and silent as statues, they waited, Suman's face buried deep against Ellie's waist.

The knock was repeated, and a quiet voice spoke through the door.

'Ellie, it's Lucas, Lucas Decker. I've come to help you. Open the door; I know you're in there.'

Ellie's brain was working overtime. Silently, she pointed at Sara's handbag, slung haphazardly over her shoulder, and then made a mime of using a lighter to light a cigarette. Sara nodded her understanding and, making as little noise as possible, she opened her bag and dug about inside for her lighter. Finding it right at the bottom of her bag, she pulled it out and handed it to Ellie. Unclasping Suman's arms from around her waist she passed the girl across to Sara.

Decker was again knocking at the door as she tiptoed to the bed, climbed on top and stretched up to the ceiling to where the smoke detector was situated and lit the cigarette lighter. She glanced round at Sara, who nodded her understanding and encouragement. Ellie's finger began to feel hot, but she held the lighter in place for a few seconds more until the noise she was waiting for started, a deafening, clamorous alarm, echoing she hoped, around the whole hotel. The noise was terrifying, and Sara covered Suman's ears from the shrill wails in the room as Ellie clambered down off the bed and moved over to the spyhole to look out again.

At first, she could see nothing. Decker had moved from view, but she knew he would still be there, waiting. After a few moments, an elderly lady passed by their door, and some minutes later, a second woman came into sight. Ellie hesitated. A few more people began to pass the door, looking scared and pulling jackets around them.

As a family group came into view Ellie seized the chance to open the door, peeping out to look along both sides of the corridor. To her left, beyond the group she could see Decker standing about six rooms away, holding open a fire door for everyone to escape and directing them to come that way.

She drew back quickly but knew he had spotted her. She could see no sign of Levy.

'Decker's there,' she whispered to Sara. 'Wait 'til more people come by.'

A noise outside make her peep out the door again and she watched as several burly young men wearing matching rugby shirts noisily but cheerfully came out of two rooms and headed towards them on their way to the fire door. She opened the bedroom door fully and motioned to Sara to come. As the young men were passing, she spoke to the one at the front, praying silently that he understood English.

'Could you help us, please?' she said loudly, the din of the alarm still going strong above her head.

'Sure. What can we do?' he shouted back with a very marked French accent.

'Our little girl can't walk very far, and we have a heavy bag,' she replied, indicating behind her.

Within moments, Suman was scooped up and held by one of the kind strangers as his companion lifted the bag swiftly, smiling at

Sara and Ellie. Sara tucked her hand through the arm of the young man who had taken her case, thanking him profusely, and Ellie held tightly to Suman's hand as she was being carried. They all walked quickly to the fire door, Decker still in place holding the door, his cold eyes watching every move being made.

As they passed through and began to descend the stairs, Ellie glanced behind, seeing him come through and follow the group, leaving the door to shut by itself. Frantically thinking, she could see no way to get away from him but prayed that there would be a crowd of hotel residents gathered outside in which they could mingle. He would surely do nothing with so many witnesses around, she thought. Worried too about where Levy had gone, she kept her eyes peeled for him and stayed very close to the young man carrying Suman.

Stepping into the gathering darkness outside, Ellie was relieved to see a lot of people mustering on the strip of grass opposite the hotel and the staff appearing with clipboards, beginning to ask names and room numbers. The young men continued to escort Ellie, Sara and Suman over to the grass, Decker still on their heels. Once they were in the middle of the crowd they stopped, and Suman was lowered to the ground by the strong hands of the young man. Ellie and Sara showed their gratitude by shaking hands and offering profound thanks, trying to generate a conversation while remaining close to the lads, all too aware that as soon as this situation was over their lives were in imminent danger.

A fire engine arrived quickly on the scene and the crowd watched as several of the fire-fighters entered the hotel to begin a check on the building. A second fire engine was following, the increasing noise of its siren heralding its approach long before it came into sight. Standing tightly beside one of the young men for protection and with Suman closely wrapped around her again, Ellie watched the second fire engine draw in beside the hotel. Glancing behind, her eyes immediately encountered the watchful, threatening stares of both Decker and Levy. They were moving slowly towards her, inching forward, trying to be unobtrusive.

Ellie looked away quickly and realised as she did so that she couldn't see Sara. She turned in a circle, looking frantically all around, between people, above their heads, and over to the street. But there was no sign of her friend.

CHAPTER 15

Rotterdam

With her heart in her mouth and trying not to panic, Ellie turned to the young man at her side, asking, 'Did you see where my friend disappeared to?'

He looked around and shook his head, turning to repeat the question to his colleagues. Seeing each one shake his head, Ellie's hold on Suman tightened and beads of sweat appeared on her brow. She glanced back at Decker and Levy, dismayed to see that they had split up and were approaching from two different angles. Ellie's heart began to race as she bent to lift Suman up and hold her tightly. She began to walk backwards through the crowd, her brain telling her to run, run fast away from here while a voice inside her head screamed out, where are you, Sara?

The question was answered as from out of nowhere a white delivery van appeared, swaying from side to side on the road and plunging towards the crowd, the driver appearing to have lost control of the vehicle. Several people screamed as the van neared and scattered quickly out of the way. Ellie had turned and could see the words '*DBD Bloemen*' emblazoned on the side of the white van. The side door was open, offering a view of a host of shelves with flowers, buckets and debris, a lot of which had fallen to the floor and were rolling around inside. As the van screeched to a halt just feet from Ellie, she heard her name screamed out and knew at once it was Sara who was driving.

Holding Suman in a death grip, she lunged forward, reaching the van without looking behind to see if Decker was chasing, and swiftly threw herself in the open door, falling sideways as she did so, protecting Suman as much as she could. Keeping a tight hold of the little girl, she yelled, 'Go!' to Sara, in the driver's seat wrestling with the gear box.

Immediately the van screeched forward, ploughing its way over a small bed of flowers and a grassy banking very near to the crowd, causing more shouts and panic amongst the people as they scattered. Looking out through the door, Ellie saw Decker running quickly after the van, a gun held in one hand, pointed towards her. Immediately, she turned her body to cover Suman's and as she did so, there was a sudden explosion inside the van. Instantaneously she felt a hot searing sting in her shoulder, so unbearable that it made her scream out and clutch a hand up to the pain.

The scream terrified Sara, frantically trying to get control of the vehicle as it lurched from side to side. Looking in the wing mirror, she could see Decker chasing after the van and she pressed her foot even harder on the accelerator. As the engine gained momentum, she could see him begin to slow down, looking mutinously angry and waving the gun around.

In the back, Suman sat up, her eyes wide with fear. She moved in closer to put a protective arm around Ellie. Realising that Ellie must have been shot Sara was desperate to stop the van but knew she needed to get further away before she could look for a safe place. She shouted out, her voice shrill with fear.

'Suman, is she okay? Is Ellie okay?'

'I'm all right,' she heard Ellie's voice waver. 'I've been shot. Just keep driving and get us away.'

'Are you sure? Will I find a hospital?'

'No, just get as far away as you can. Suman is looking after me.'

Ellie looked up into Suman's eyes. Suman nodded, her small, thin arms holding on tightly and protectively. After a moment, she laid Ellie down and pointed to the open door of the van, asking with a gesture how she could shut it.

'Push it along with that handle,' Ellie indicated with her uninjured arm, her voice cracking slightly as she grimaced with pain.

Suman crawled over and with all her strength, pushed the side door of the van closed and clambered back to Ellie. Looking around the van, she seemed to realise that she had to do something to help. In a corner lay the suitcase, obviously thrown in haphazardly by Sara and Suman crawled over to it and opened it up. Quickly taking out a tee shirt, she began to fold it into a tight pad, her fingers working deftly. Ellie looked at the little girl.

'Clever girl.'

As she spoke, she felt the strong little fingers gently prise her own hand away from the wound at the top of her shoulder. The pad was then pressed hard against the wound and held tightly in place by a small brown hand.

Ellie looked at her own hand and saw that it was covered in blood. She suspected the bullet wound was quite a bad one and that she was losing blood fast. However, unable to move, she could do nothing but leave it to Suman who appeared to know exactly what she was doing, and Ellie lay back, closed her eyes and concentrated on not crying out again.

Sara was keeping up a running commentary from the front seat, her driving improving marginally as she steered the van through the back streets and nooks and crannies of Rotterdam. A busy city, she was glad she had no rush hour traffic to contend with, but faltered at crossings and traffic lights, unsure at first of protocol on the Dutch roads and desperate to push on and get as far away as possible. Glad that she had previous experience of driving on the right-hand side of the road, she was however unfamiliar with all the controls of the van. Her relief was immense when, eventually, the traffic began to lessen as they entered a quieter area of the town. Surmising they were near the outskirts of town, Sara watched carefully for signs to minor roads, trying to avoid the main motorways. Soon she began to see more open, green spaces and fields around her.

To begin with, when Sara had been asking questions, she had received replies from Ellie, but for a while now, there had been no sound at all from the back. Frequent glances behind told her that Suman was still holding a pad tightly against Ellie's shoulder and as soon as the van was a few kilometres outside the city limits, she judged it was time to pull up to see for herself what was happening.

Turning into a small clearing amongst some trees, she switched off the engine and climbed over the seats to get into the back. She knelt beside Ellie, shocked at the amount of blood there was on the pad and on the floor, and at the ghastly pallor on her friend's face.

Ellie's eyes were closed, and her face had relaxed, as if she no longer felt the pain from her injury. Sara leaned over, holding her breath, and checked for a pulse in her neck.

'Oh, Ellie,' she whispered, her voice breaking. 'I should have taken you straight to a hospital.'

Suman reached out and touched Sara's arm.

'Ellie okay,' a gruff, heavily accented little voice told her. 'Ellie need...' Suman pointed to the pad as she spoke. 'Blood stop now. Ellie need...'

The child hesitated, searching for the right word.... 'Wee bath?'

Suman's serious little face looked into Sara's with a question in her eyes.

In shock at hearing the child speak in English, Sara couldn't answer for a moment or two, her mouth hanging open.

'Well...are you going to get us to a wee bath or not?' came an amused voice from below and Sara looked down at Ellie who was smiling up at her.

'I certainly am,' she replied, a wide grin appearing on her face. 'You're in good hands.'

She turned to Suman. 'Thank you, Suman. Keep her well until I can get help.'

Sara scrambled back into the driver's seat and got the van moving again. As before, she continued to chatter, full of questions to the two in the back of the van.

'How does Suman know English, Ellie?' was one of her first questions.

'I think that's down to Angena. She told me that she was sure Suman could speak, even though she never made a sound.' Ellie looked up at Suman. 'So she spoke to you all the time in English, didn't she, Suman? She taught you English words so you could understand other people when they spoke.'

Listening very intently to Ellie's words, Suman nodded.

Sara's questions soon turned into a running commentary about the areas she was driving through, and she began to suggest stopping places. She tried to interpret the road signs they were passing but didn't really understand most of them. However, one of the signs caused an excited shout.

'A caravan site! What do you think? Would that do?'

Hearing a faint 'Yes' from the back, Sara began to follow the signs for the caravan site, driving the van down a small, twisty road and into some stunning countryside. The last few kilometres were far off the beaten track.

'Well, this certainly looks like an isolated place. There's a sign saying that the caravan park is two kilometres away, so not far to go. Hope we can get a doctor or some form of medical help when we get there.'

Driving much more slowly on the windy road, Sara was relieved to spot the entrance to the site and rows of static caravans in the surrounding fields. Once in, she realised she had turned into what appeared to be a small farm, and she drew up at a wooden hut with a sign outside stating that all visitors should stop there. A quick check with the two in the back told her that Ellie was still conscious and holding her own and that Suman was still sitting beside Ellie, applying pressure to the wound. Assuring them she would be quick, she jumped down from the side of the van, closed the door from any prying eyes and entered the hut.

Not long after, she re-appeared, hands full of leaflets and pieces of paper and a small bunch of keys dangling from her fingers. Quickly she climbed into the driver's seat and shut the door.

'Thank goodness I can still remember some of my schoolgirl French. The woman couldn't speak English but we both spoke a little French.'

'She was a bit surprised at us arriving at this time of night,' Sara continued. 'I told her that you had taken ill and that we had decided to stop for the night to give you a bit of rest. She was lovely after that, very helpful. She's given us a caravan in a shady spot, pitch number nine. We'll get you there in a couple of minutes, Ellie, and into a comfy bed, I hope. And then we can get someone to come and have a look at you and see what needs to be done. The lady gave me the number of a doctor. The road's a bit rough, but there's number eight, so that must be number nine next to it. Sorry about that,' she added, as the van bumped through a large pot-hole on the narrow track.

Sara turned to have a quick look behind, to make sure she had done no more damage to Ellie. Then, pulling gently into a space beside a rather ancient looking static caravan, she jumped down from her seat and ran around to open the side door of the van.

'Wait here a minute until I check out the caravan.' The two weary faces in the van nodded.

A hasty sniff told her that it was a little musty inside, but a glance round showed it was clean and well furnished. She closed all the curtains before hurrying back to help Ellie and Suman out of the van.

The transfer to the caravan was a painful ordeal for Ellie, her shoulder extremely sore as soon as she moved. Sara was dismayed to see the blood starting to flow again as she helped Ellie up the rusty steps into the caravan, with Suman holding on at the other side. Ellie's legs were weak and trembling, and dizziness made walking difficult, so she was grateful for their support up into the spacious caravan and onto one of the long seats by a window. As they laid her down, Suman immediately began again to apply pressure to the wound, having grabbed a towel folded on the worktop.

'I can take that over if you like,' Sara told Suman, bending over Ellie and checking her pulse.

'It okay. Blood stop,' Suman replied, lifting the pad off the wound to show Sara.

Both Ellie and Sara looked at Suman, still amazed to hear the rough, stilted voice from the young girl who for so long had been unable to speak to anyone.

Suddenly, a recognisable noise outside, very soft at first but growing louder, caused panic to appear on their faces.

'A helicopter! Oh, God,' said Ellie softly, 'please don't let them be looking for us already.'

Sara was already striding towards the door of the caravan, still wide open.

'I have to hide the van. I need to get it completely out of sight.'

She disappeared outside and they heard her starting the van and driving off. It was fifteen minutes or so before she returned, startling them as she pulled the door open with a clatter.

'I'm sure we're fine,' she said as she entered and laid down the suitcase. 'The helicopter was high up and miles away and the farmer has allowed me to put the van into one of his barns. I gave him a tale that I had borrowed the van from a friend and needed it under cover. Though my French is not that good; heaven only knows what I actually said to him.'

'You're doing brilliantly,' Ellie replied. 'Though you had me worried when I lost you at the hotel. What a fright you gave us. I didn't see you disappearing to get the van and panicked when I couldn't find you. And now you've got us safely away. Thanks, Sara.'

Sara knelt beside Suman and reached to have a look at the bullet wound, saying huskily, 'Don't be daft. I was just lucky that the laddie driving the van went off and left it lying wide open.'

She had taken the towel gently from Suman and began to try to move Ellie's jumper back from the area of the wound.

'Careful, Sara,' Ellie warned, 'It's really painful.'

'I'll be careful, don't worry. I just need a peek to be able to assess how bad it is and what we should do.'

Ellie gritted her teeth as Sara exposed the wound.

'Wow. It's a nasty one,' Sara confirmed. 'It's taken a chunk out of your shoulder, that's for sure. I really think you need stitches and some proper medical attention.'

'Well I don't know how we can do that. I can't put any of us at risk. I'll be all right if you just dress the wound.'

'No, Ellie. We can't just leave it. The farmer's wife told me there's a doctor living nearby in a village called...,' she stopped, reaching over to where she had laid the documents when she came in.

'*Rozenburg*,' she read out. 'She gave me his card and says that he'll come to the farm in an emergency although he doesn't actually work in this area. I'll go over to the farmhouse and use the phone there to see if he'll come and see you.'

Sara left them again, returning with the good news that the doctor not only spoke English, but had been very helpful and was willing to come soon and look at Ellie's shoulder. Suman, meantime, had rummaged through Sara's bag and given Ellie a drink of water, holding her up with one hand while helping her sip from the bottle. Sara saw that Ellie was looking a bit worse than when she had left and realised by her friend's face that the pain was obviously increasing, and the blood loss was having an effect. Although not sleeping, Ellie was lying with her eyes shut, a deep frown on her face and her bottom lip between her teeth.

It was another thirty minutes before they heard voices approaching and a knock on the door. The farmer's wife pushed her head into the van and announced the doctor had arrived. As Sara had predicted he was a kindly man, a fatherly figure who asked only a few questions about what had happened to Ellie. Although they fully realised he was sceptical about their replies, they were thankful he didn't push for the truth, appearing to accept their story of Ellie having fallen against a spiked metal fence.

The wound, he told them, was indeed a bad one. However, no major surgery was needed to repair it; he would clean it up and put in some stitches. He had brought his surgical bag with him and performed the procedure there and then. Sara, feeling a bit squeamish about watching, helped by ferrying through the boiled water and clean towels to wash up the wound, and putting the tiny kettle on to make a cup of tea for everyone once the gory bit was over.

Suman, on the other hand, acted as the doctor's assistant, supporting Ellie and holding tightly to her hand when the pain was severe as he cleaned out the wound. Once numbed with a local anaesthetic, he was able to insert the stitches without too much discomfort and in no time was applying proper dressings and a sling to minimise movement of the arm and shoulder. The child avidly watched every move he made, taking in every detail with no sign of squeamishness.

When the wound was neatly bound and Ellie's clothes back in place, Suman ran her thin little hand down Ellie's cheek, gazed adoringly at her and said, 'Ellie very brave girl.'

Although still in a lot of pain, Ellie couldn't help smiling. She realised instantly that this must have been something that had been said to Suman at the end of some ordeal she had gone through. She took Suman's hand and kissed it.

'Thank you, sweetheart,' she whispered.

The doctor, sitting with a cup of tea in his hand, watched the three of them closely. He cleared his throat and began to speak to them all.

'I do realise there is to more to you three than meets the eye.' Sara and Ellie exchanged a nervous look.

'However,' he continued, aware of the look, 'to put your minds at rest, I will not be informing the authorities that I had a bullet wound to deal with.' He held up a hand as Sara made to interrupt.

'No point denying it, young lady. I've dealt with this kind of wound before. I won't ask you any questions about how it happened as I suspect I won't be given the correct answer.'

He rose and laid his cup down on the table, turning to address Sara and Suman.

'I'm relying on you two to see that the patient stays as still as possible and gets as much rest as she can for the next week or so.'

He swivelled round to address his next remarks to Ellie. 'You are still very weak after your loss of blood, and I am leaving these pain-killers to help you sleep tonight. If you need me again, please telephone, but otherwise, please try to stay away from trouble. I wish you all well,' he added as he closed his bag and headed for the door.

Sara and Ellie both thanked him profusely and Sara went down the caravan steps with him to shake his hand.

'You know, we have a very good police department in this area. Good men if you need them,' he said to her with a nod.

'I know,' she replied. 'It's just very complicated, but we'll remember everything you said, and your kindness to us. May I ask? You didn't mention a bill or payment for your help. Do we owe you some money?'

'Young lady,' he answered acidly, 'if I had wanted money from you, I would have asked for it.' With a softened voice he added, 'I was happy to be of help to what I suspect are two very brave ladies. Good-day,' he finished with a nod, marching off towards the track to the farmhouse.

Sara returned inside.

'Well, what about some supper now?' she asked cheerily. 'I don't know about you two, but I'm starving.'

Around midnight, the small lamps in the caravan shone softly, casting a rosy glow over the faded upholstery and scattered cushions and creating a twinkle from the scrubbed stainless-steel sink in the tiny kitchen area. The curtains remained shut against the world and the door was locked. Ellie still lay on the long seat in the living area and Sara was stretched out on the opposite side. The seats had been made up into beds with sheets, blankets and pillows.

Suman lay between them, on a small makeshift bed on the floor, fast asleep. The two friends spoke quietly, their discussion concentrated on what to do next.

'I do agree with what you're saying, Sara, but you have to admit there's no way we can just hide out here even for a few days, let alone a week. It would be too dangerous. I know you don't like it, but my mind is made up. We've run far enough, and it's now time for me to go back.'

'Go back?' exclaimed Sara in astonishment. 'I can't understand that. Why would you go straight into the lion's den and put yourself at risk like that? You're not even strong enough to walk now.'

'I know, I know. But we both know that every police force in Holland could be on the lookout for the stolen van. And we can't just sit here and think that these lovely farming folks won't read papers or listen to news or speak to people. It won't be long before they start asking questions or talking and Decker will find us again. No, we need to come up with a better plan and I know what I want to do.'

'I can see your reasons, but at least give yourself twenty-four hours to rest,' Sara begged. 'Too much movement will burst the stitches and then you won't be able to do anything.'

'All right, I'll agree to that. Then I want you to take Suman by train over into France, and after that, if you can, get the two of you home to Scotland. I'll give you her passport; it's in my jacket pocket and we'll pray that it passes scrutiny and you can get home with her. Take her to my mother in Anstruther, tell her everything, and ask her to look after Suman until I get there.'

She hesitated before continuing.

'And if the worst comes to the worst and I don't come home,' she swallowed hard as she saw Sara close her eyes for a moment, 'then you'll try to get Suman back to India and find out where she came from, won't you?'

There was no reply. 'Sara, you will, won't you?'

'Of course I will. You know I will. But I'm not going to think about that because you're going to come home. In fact, you could just as easily come home now with us, and we'll sort out Van Breda from Scotland.'

'I can't. I've never been more determined about anything in my whole life. I know it sounds melodramatic, but Suman may well have saved my life today and you've seen what a special girl she is. She didn't deserve what happened to her and neither do any of the hundreds of other kids who fall into the hands of traffickers. They're just the scum of the earth, using kids like that for their own gain.' She stopped, realising her voice had risen and could disturb Suman.

'Sorry to be so angry,' she continued in a whisper, 'but you didn't see all Suman's injuries and what they had done to her. And God only knows what other damage they've done that we can't see. I've thought this through, and I feel she has a much better chance if we split up and she goes with you.'

She looked over to Sara and her friend recognised the determination on her face.

'You know I have to do this, Sara. I've got to stop Van Breda and his henchmen from doing any more damage to girls like Suman and Angena. So for the two of them, I'm going to try if it's the last thing I do. I'm quite certain I know where part of their operation is happening. I've got it in black and white if I can get hold of my files. I'm going back to Amsterdam to see Daan Meijer and help him get the prosecutions he needs. You will help me, won't you?'

'Well, that's the daftest question you've asked me in a long time, El. You know I will. Now, you need to get some sleep tonight; you're tired and we've got a busy day tomorrow. Loads to do, plans to make, find a disguise for you.' She stopped, waiting for Ellie's reaction.

'A disguise?' Ellie queried, looking strangely at her friend.

Sara looked back. 'We might have to dye that lovely hair of yours or cut it off to smuggle you back into Amsterdam unrecognised. And we've flights to book and a wee girl to explain everything to. I'm putting the lights off and you're getting some sleep. Doctor's orders.'

Ellie lay back against the pillows as Sara climbed out of bed over the sleeping Suman and began switching off the lamps. At last, quietness descended on the caravan while outside the crickets and night birds began to sing their songs.

'Proud to be your friend, El,' came a soft voice through the darkness.

'Ditto,' whispered an exhausted Ellie. 'But over my dead body will you cut or dye my hair!'

———————————————

CHAPTER 16

Edinburgh

'Sara's been off work for the last couple of days and she's not answering her home phone or her mobile.' Evelyn laid the phone down on its cradle and leaned heavily on the kitchen table, her face lined with concern. Her husband Matt hurried round the table and gently coaxed her to sit in one of the chairs.

She looked up at him. 'She's not answering her door, either. Someone from her firm went to her house. I'm seriously worried, Matt. John Anderson wouldn't tell me much either, but I'm convinced the girls are together and they've both gone missing. What should I do?'

'Well, we don't know that Sara's actually missing,' he tried to console her as he sat down. 'There might be a perfectly reasonable explanation why she's not answering. If she *has* gone off somewhere, there's the slight comfort that they're most probably together, wherever that is. You know yourself that if Ellie was in any kind of trouble, it's Sara she would call on.'

'I know, Matt, and I'd put my money on the fact that Sara's gone haring off to Holland to try to help Ellie. I'd give anything myself to fly there and help to find her. It's so hard not being able to do anything except wait for news. If only she would phone me.'

'No news is good news, Evelyn.' Matt was trying to offer comfort to his wife, and she was grateful for his support. Just out of hospital after an eye operation, Evelyn was feeling the frustration of being confined to the house, not knowing if her daughter was safe or in trouble.

She sighed deeply as she rose to put the kettle on and began to prepare mugs and biscuits on a tray, more to keep herself busy than anything else. As the kettle began to boil, the loud ring of the telephone cut through the bubbling noise and for a moment, she was flustered not knowing whether to reach for the kettle or the phone. The phone won, being a much higher priority in Evelyn's mind, and

Matt took over tea making duties.

'Hello?' she said hopefully into the receiver.

'Mrs Hamilton?'

'Yes, this is Mrs Hamilton. Who's speaking?'

'My name is Geoff Mendez and I'm a work colleague of Ellie, at UBI. I'm calling from Amsterdam. Mrs Hamilton, you don't know me, but I've been working out here with Ellie and I just wondered...' He halted mid-sentence.

Evelyn stepped in to finish his question.

'You wondered if I'd heard anything from Ellie. No, I haven't, and I'm worried sick. I thought maybe you were ringing to give *me* some news. John Anderson did mention you, Geoff, and Ellie told me all about you too, in the last phone call I got from her. That was a few days ago.'

At Evelyn's words, Geoff's heart skipped a beat. Ellie had mentioned him to her mother, had she? He listened carefully as she continued.

'Did John tell you that her friend, Sara, has gone missing as well? She seems to have taken off and we suspect she's gone to help Ellie. Have you heard anything at all about where they might be?'

'No, unfortunately not, although we're pretty sure Ellie is still in the Netherlands somewhere. Do you think we could contact Sara on her mobile, maybe?'

'I think lots of people have been trying to do that but she's not answering. I've been sending voice messages and texts to them both to let them know how worried I am.'

'Will you keep on trying, Mrs Hamilton?'

'Call me Evelyn,' she interrupted. 'Everyone does.'

She caught her husband's eye as she spoke and turned away quickly.

Geoff continued. 'Can you take a note of my number and let me know right away if you get any word from either of them? I'm desperate to find her and get her back home safely.'

'I will, Geoff. Can you tell me honestly, is she in danger? John didn't give me any details, just said that she got involved with one of her projects and they weren't sure where she'd gone; but I wasn't to worry too much. Are the police looking for her?'

Geoff realised that Evelyn must be unaware of the extent of the danger her daughter was in and hastened to reassure her that the authorities were doing everything they could to find Ellie. He added that he was doing his very best as well and was sure they would find her soon.

'Well, you *must* find her quickly, Geoff,' she pleaded. 'She's very precious to me and I need to know where she is. Please, phone me any time, night or day, if you have any news and I'll do the same.'

Assuring Evelyn that he would keep in touch, Geoff ended the call, praying that Ellie would be in touch with her mother soon.

In the kitchen, Evelyn was also hanging up the receiver and reaching for her handbag to search for her mobile. Again, she caught Matt's eye.

'What? No harm in getting to know him a wee bit, is there? You know I suspected Ellie of liking him a lot, the way she spoke of him.' Evelyn began to search her contact list for Sara's number and continued talking as she did so.

'Strange second name he has. Mendez. Wonder if that's Spanish? Do you think he's good looking?'

She located Sara's number and began to text another message, the worry back on her face again.

In his hotel bedroom in Amsterdam, Geoff tried to concentrate on the statistical documents in front of him, needing something to take his mind off his worries about Ellie and his frustration at not being able to help her when she needed him. He rummaged through the tidy bundles on the desk to find his own hand-written notes and checked them again. His laptop was open, a graphic chart on the screen, and he flipped through some of his other charts, reading and re-reading the information and making notes on occasion. He ran a hand through his thick, dark hair, and scratched the back of his head.

'I know I'm missing something. Something important,' he mused out loud. What was it? he thought irritably, going back to the piles of documents and starting again.

It was one in the morning when his heart began to race as he realised he had stumbled on something significant. In front of him, on a pad on the desk was a list of the bottles of counterfeit malt whisky which had been bought from the various Van Breda outlets and recently tested by Ellie in Amsterdam. Meticulously he began to highlight several bottles with the same brand name, all produced in the town of Campbeltown in Scotland, all 46 per cent proof, and all with the same distillation date. Ellie's notes recorded each bottle as having been distilled by a blending company called Hennie Scotch Whisky Company, Glasgow; not a company Geoff was familiar with.

The cask numbers of each of the bottles differed only slightly, a curious co-incidence but possible given that they could have been purchased together. These two facts, the unfamiliar blending company and the similarities in cask numbers were what gave Geoff his instinctive feeling that this was a strong clue.

For the next half hour, his back was hunched over his computer, researching each bottle by its distillation date and its phenolic level of malt. He included in this research Ellie's notes and statistical information from the other parts of the world she had visited recently. Bingo, the link was there.

Geoff turned to the blending company's details. It was not long before he discovered there was no such company in Glasgow or anywhere else. The tingle in his spine grew stronger. He knew, through his conversations with Ellie, that counterfeiters would not normally change details on labelling, only copy information that would ring no alarm bells. Why, therefore, would they use the name of Hennie, a name that didn't exist? he wondered.

Finally, his dogged determination paid off. He gazed at his screen in amazement as his long search brought up the name of a man, the main suspect himself, Arne Thomas Hennie Van Breda.

What arrogance and confidence in his own invincibility, thought Geoff. Not only was he counterfeiting expensive whiskies with a blend of cheap whisky, water and chemicals, he was having his own name added to the label. And by exporting his whisky to many other parts of the world he was expanding his counterfeiting operation into an international enterprise worth, it looked like, many tens of thousands of Euros each year.

Geoff's incredulity led his thoughts down another path. Was it possible that Van Breda was so self-assured, so certain he couldn't be caught, that he might even be producing and bottling his whisky somewhere here in Amsterdam? Could it be right under the noses of the customs and excise authorities, as well as the UBI staff, and the IPOL team at the Amsterdam Politie office? If so, Geoff surmised, could his assurance of his own safety point to his having control of people within these organisations, someone in UBI, and in IPOL, looking after his interests while lining their own pockets with illegal gains.

He turned to Ellie's notes on where the whisky had been bought locally. All outlets were within a five-kilometre radius of his largest nightclub, The Furnace. Certain he was on the right track, he reached for his phone and called Daan's number, knowing he was taking a chance contacting someone from Dienst IPOL and not knowing who he could trust and who he couldn't. He had to act on instinct, he had no other choice.

Within thirty minutes he was in the IPOL office, in front of a computer, deep in explanations and answering Daan's many questions.

The phone on Daan's desk rang and was answered quickly. On a pad in front of him Daan wrote the name 'Frank Levy' and slid it across to Geoff. From the conversation that he could hear, Geoff realised that Levy was reporting in to give an update on his progress in finding Ellie. He listened anxiously.

The conversation was mostly one-sided, with Daan giving a series of grunts and Frank doing most of the talking. It was only a few minutes before he hung up the phone and turned back to resume the scrutiny of the computer screen, saying nothing at all about the call. However, looking across at Geoff, the IPOL boss relented at the anguish he saw on Geoff's face.

'I can't tell you anything except that we know roughly where she is, and that from now there will be a much larger team assigned to look for her. Levy's being recalled. We need to get her to safety before Van Breda finds her and Levy reports he's had no sighting yet. We need more officers out there looking.'

'I heard you tell Levy you were alone in the office. Why didn't you tell him I was here?'

'He didn't need to know that.'

'Why has Levy been recalled? Has he been taken off the search?'

'Developments, Geoff,' said Daan curtly, indicating that they should return to their previous discussions at the computer.

Returning to his hotel room a few hours later, Geoff caught some sleep, eventually surfacing around nine and heading down for breakfast in the hotel restaurant. As he sat at the table waiting, he checked his phone for a message from Ellie. He was suddenly aware of an uneasy feeling, a feeling of being watched, and he turned to check out the occupants of the restaurant. An elderly lady sat with a child at a table close by and his eyes skimmed over her to the next table. Two innocuous looking young lads sat toying with their coffee, deep in conversation. They were dressed in scruffy jeans and jerkins, with rucksacks lying at their feet. Geoff dismissed them as two lads on holiday and continued his inspection of the rest of the customers. He saw no-one he thought suspicious, although the uneasy feeling persisted as he turned back to his phone.

Breakfast arrived in the shape of coffee and a croissant and he ate quickly, wanting to get back upstairs to make some phone calls. However, before he could rise from the table, his phone bleeped with a text message. Opening it, he saw it was from an unrecognised number but thankfully the sender had added her name. The text read, 'Call me straight away but only if you are *totally* alone. Evelyn.'

The underlining of the word 'totally' was not lost on him and he shot another glance around the very busy restaurant. Pulling his jacket off the back of the chair with haste, he strode quickly towards the door and out on to the street. Running fast, his feet pounded heavily on the pavement for a short distance towards the canal. He made straight for an empty bench near the banking and making sure there was no-one nearby to overhear his conversation, he pressed 'call' and lifted the phone to his ear.

'Evelyn, it's Geoff. Have you got news?' he asked as she answered her phone.

'Yes, I have.' Her voice was full of anxiety. 'Thank you for phoning so quickly. I've so much to tell you but they made me promise faithfully that I wouldn't say anything until you guaranteed you were absolutely on your own. Is there anyone called Lucas Decker or Frank Levy with you? Is there anyone with you?'

The names had startled Geoff. From Daan's comments about Frank Levy last night, he had suspected there was something about him to worry about, but Lucas Decker from UBI as well? That was a shock. He wondered if Daan was aware of Decker.

'No, Evelyn. I promise with all my heart, I'm alone. No Levy, no Decker, no-one at all.'

'Could they be listening in to your phone? Could this call be traced?'

'I don't think so. I'm not under suspicion, so there wouldn't be any reason to do that. Would you feel safer if I phoned you from a landline?'

He hoped she would say no as he was desperate to hear what the news was. However, he realised that Ellie would not have asked for such secrecy without a reason and he was willing to go along with anything she wanted.

'No, I think it will be all right. I'll tell you quickly what they told me and then we'll hang up and you can get in touch with Sara yourself.'

He waited, relief flooding his body now that he was within reach of making contact.

Evelyn continued. 'They are in a place near Rotterdam called Rozenburg, the three of them. Ellie, Sara and a little Indian girl called Suman that Ellie has rescued from traffickers. They are hiding from people called Van Breda, Lucas Decker and Frank Levy. Do you want me to repeat these names so you can write them down?'

'No, I know the names. Just go on, Evelyn.'

'They need your help, Geoff. I'll give you Sara's number and you've to phone her from a landline and she'll give you the address where they are. Ellie's hurt.'

She heard a groan from Geoff as she said this and continued swiftly.

'She's okay. I've spoken to her and she assures me she's fine. She said to tell you to trust no-one. Please get to them quickly, Geoff. Please get them to somewhere safe over there. Or bring them home.'

'I will, Evelyn. I'll get to them as fast as I possibly can. And thanks for trusting me. I won't let you down. I think a lot of your wonderful daughter,' he added.

'I know,' she whispered. 'Bring her home.'

Evelyn read out Sara's mobile number and then hung up the phone. Geoff sat for only long enough to return his pen to his pocket and then rose from the bench, walking briskly back in the direction he had come. A hotel caught his eye further down on the other side of the road, and he headed towards it, breaking into a fast run as adrenalin coursed through his veins. He entered the hotel, asking hurriedly at the reception desk if they had a public phone he could use and was directed to a booth at the rear of the lobby. He sped towards it, pleased to see it was in an enclosed phone box where no-one could hear his conversation.

Sara answered her phone on the second ring, and he spoke to her for only a moment before asking to speak to Ellie, his heart pounding.

'Geoff?' he heard her say.

'Ellie, thank God.' His head was bent over as he spoke, his eyes shut. 'Are you okay? Your mother says you're hurt. What happened and where are you? I'm coming to help you.'

He heard her soft laugh. 'Slow down. I'm fine. Lucas Decker fired a gun at me, he's one of Van Breda's men by the way. An evil man.' She stressed the word evil. 'You must tell Daan Meijer about him right away. The bullet took a wee bit out of my shoulder, but it's been stitched by a doctor and Sara and Suman are looking after me. Do you honestly want to come and help me? I'm going to come back to Amsterdam and would certainly appreciate your help. It's dangerous though, Geoff. I don't want to put you in danger, too.'

'I'm coming, Ellie. I've promised your mother I'll keep you safe so tell me where you are, and I'll come right now. Then we can return together.'

Ellie experienced a feeling of huge relief at his words, knowing that the journey back would be easier and less dangerous with Geoff at her side, especially with the wound and sling hampering her ability to move around easily. She realised too, without a shadow of a doubt, that hearing Geoff's voice and his promise to look after her had done strange things to her heart and she admitted to herself that her feelings for him were stronger than she had ever imagined. She warmly accepted his offer and gave him the address and directions to the caravan site.

It was with reluctance they said goodbye, Geoff's parting words causing Ellie to blush rosily as she turned to face her best friend's grin. On the other end of the line, Geoff knew an overwhelming sense of relief as he hurried through the hotel lobby to pay for the call with an urgency in his step and a warm feeling in his heart.

He hurried back to his own hotel. The dangers that Ellie, Sara and Suman were facing were now uppermost in his mind. He knew he had to contact Daan and tell him about Levy and Decker and he wondered about the best way to do this. Admitting he had spoken to Ellie would mean that Daan would want to know where she was, and he was not yet ready to share this with anyone. He wanted them safe first.

He decided he would delay getting in touch for the moment. He wasn't happy about this but couldn't think of anything better. He would call Daan the moment he felt it was safe to do so.

In the hotel lobby, he stopped to pick up a road map at the Concierge's desk and ask where he could hire a car. A quick dart into the hotel gift shop to buy a few essentials, and then he hurried upstairs to his room to grab a few things before making his way down again and out into the street. A taxi took him to the car hire building and, paying the sum asked, he received the keys for a large, black, powerful BMW with a navigation system installed. Instinct told him it would be safer and more reliable to have a car with a powerful engine and he thought that Ellie's injury might fare better with a comfortable, smooth running car. They faced a long, perhaps perilous journey back to Amsterdam and he was preparing himself for any eventuality they might face.

He thought long and hard about whether to try to acquire a weapon of some sort. Ellie's safety might depend on this. However, he was a peace-loving man who had never held a gun in his life except for sport and decided against arming himself in this way. He hoped he wouldn't live to regret this decision.

The call to Daan Meijer was made minutes before he set off. Giving Daan the information about both Levy and Decker as clearly and concisely as he could, Geoff let him know that he was going to be bringing a wounded Ellie back to Amsterdam and into the IPOL office as soon as he could. He demanded Ellie's safety by insisting that both Levy and Decker be held somewhere secure when he and Ellie arrived, threatening not to bring Ellie in if this wasn't done. He hung up abruptly as soon as Daan began asking about her whereabouts.

He drove fast. Unlike Sara and Ellie, his journey to Rozenburg was uneventful and he arrived at the caravan park in under thirty minutes. Following the same track as Sara had the day before, he noticed the wooden hut at the entrance to the farm but didn't stop. He was looking for pitch number nine as he had been instructed by Ellie.

However, rounding a bend in the track the uneasy feeling from earlier, the sensation of being watched, returned and he slowed the car to a stop. Twisting round to look behind he saw nothing; no car, no people, no movement. He waited a moment. Thinking back, an image of the restaurant came to his mind, of the two youths with their rucksacks, deep in conversation, the old lady with the child, the other diners. Could someone have been watching him, following him?

I'm being paranoid, he thought. No-one had followed him. He was certain of this although, like before, the strange feeling of not being alone remained with him. Staying alert, he put the car into gear and moved slowly on, turning his eyes to search again for pitch number nine. His bushy brows which had earned him his nickname of the Professor were once more furrowed into a frown.

———————————————

CHAPTER 17

Rozenburg

Pitch number nine was half hidden among some tall trees and bushes, and as Geoff neared, he noticed the curtains were drawn tight and no signs of life. To his right, he could see a couple of large barns in the distance with tractors and equipment lying around outside. Feeling it might be safer to conceal his car he turned down the pitted track and drove round to the back of the large barns to park the BMW. He climbed from the car, closing the door as silently as he could and walked cautiously back in the direction of the caravan. He kept a close look-out for anyone wandering around. As he neared the road through the site, the sound of voices reached his ears and, not wanting to be seen, he concealed himself behind a clump of bushes.

The voices grew louder as two people, a young man and woman, made their way along the road and passed by close to where he was hidden. They were chatting and laughing happily, unaware of anything but each other as they continued very slowly along the track hand in hand.

Geoff stayed as silent as possible, feeling like a peeping tom but not wanting to draw attention to himself. Impatient to get to Ellie, Geoff wished they would move a bit faster, but it was a good three or four minutes before they disappeared. He waited until they were fully out of sight before coming out from behind the shrubbery, checking all about him to make sure that no-one else was around. After only a few steps, the noise of a car coming along the track halted him for a second time. Again, he felt the need to hide, some instinct warning him.

The car rounded the bend as he hid behind a tall tree. Not slowing or stopping, it purred its way past and out of sight.

I really am paranoid, Geoff thought, giving himself a shake. He headed up towards the caravan but for a third time his walk was interrupted. From out of nowhere a man appeared in front of him wielding a large club in his right hand, a scarf wrapped halfway round his face. Taken aback, it took Geoff a second or two to react. Realising that the man was going to attack, his heart began to race, and adrenalin pumped through his body. His hands came up in a defensive stance and his eyes never left his attacker.

The man moved closer. Geoff edged sideways to get a bit of distance between him and his assailant. Out of the corner of his eye he noticed a stout log, short enough to be held in his hand and used as a club, and without taking his eyes off the man, he swiftly bent forward to pick it up. It was done in seconds. He now faced straight on to his unknown attacker.

'Hello, Geoff.' A soft voice from behind startled him and he flew round. His heart leapt into his mouth as he saw Lucas Decker aiming a gun at his chest.

'Thanks for leading me to her. I knew you would eventually.' The voice was sinister and menacing.

Geoff made no reply. Every sense was on alert as he watched Decker. A prickling sensation down the back of his neck warned him that his first assailant was right behind him. He turned around just as a club was swung towards his head. Geoff protected himself with the log, parrying the assailant's weapon, which fell to the ground. At the same time, the scarf which had been masking the attacker fell far enough to reveal the sinister face of Frank Levy.

'Don't even think about it, Geoff,' said Decker as Geoff raised the log to strike Levy. 'It'll be the last thing you ever do.'

Geoff's arm fell to his side. Quickly, Levy closed in behind, throwing an arm around his neck in a tight stranglehold. Geoff reacted instantly. With all his strength, he twisted round and brought his knee up between Levy's legs, at the same time pulling his opponent around between himself and Decker just as a muffled shot rang out.

Locked together, the two bodies jerked at the violent impact of the bullet and fell to the ground. Stunned, Geoff lay still for a second, his attacker's body lying half on top of him. As realisation quickly dawned that he was okay, he heard the click of the slide on Decker's gun being pulled back, ready to fire again. Suddenly, Decker was right up beside him and again, Geoff saw the gun being aimed at his chest.

Instantly, Geoff lifted the log he still held and crashed it into Decker's outstretched hand. The gun flew upwards and landed a few yards away. Decker sped after it, falling to his knees to find it amongst the leaves and twigs on the ground. As he raised it and turned, a clenched fist caught him on his chin. He reeled backwards at the impact. A second punch followed the first. Decker's head hit the ground with a bump.

Jumping on top of him, Geoff closed his hands round Decker's neck and held them there. There was no movement from Decker, no resistance at all. Staying astride Decker's body, his every sense on the alert in case it was a trick, Geoff carefully lifted one hand and removed the gun from Decker's grip. Still unsure if the man was alive or not, Geoff put his fingers on Decker's neck to check for a pulse. At first, he could find none, but after a few seconds he detected a faint throb and knew that the punch had merely knocked Decker out.

Aiming the gun at the unconscious man, Geoff moved over to the second man on the ground. With his foot, he rolled Levy over. A dead man's eyes stared up at him. Geoff shuddered and immediately turned back to the unconscious man. Still keeping the gun aimed at Decker, he managed to take out his phone with his other hand, and quickly called Ellie's number. There was no reply and he realised her phone must be switched off. He tried Sara's number and was rewarded after a few seconds with a quiet voice replying, 'Hello?'

'Sara, it's Geoff,' he explained rapidly. 'I'm outside, in the wood opposite your caravan and I've got Decker here unconscious... and Levy dead. I need you to bring some sort of strong ropes so I can tie Decker up before he comes round. Can you hurry?'

There was a pause at the other end of the phone, Sara being stunned into silence at this unexpected call. As Geoff began to repeat his request, she jumped to her feet, and handed the phone to Ellie who was propped up on her good elbow watching Sara's face intently.

'Tell me that's definitely Geoff,' she said to Ellie. 'He says he's outside and needs help. It might be someone else. I don't know Geoff's voice.'

With a worried look on her face, Ellie lifted the phone to her ear. 'Hello, who is this?'

'Ellie, it's me, Geoff. Can you tell Sara to hurry and bring me some rope or something to tie up Decker?'

'Okay,' she replied, her face still looking puzzled. She looked over at Sara. 'It's definitely Geoff, and he wants you to...' she stopped abruptly as Sara leapt to her feet.

'Tell him I'm coming,' she shrieked, as she frantically began to search through drawers and cupboards in the caravan. Under the sink, she unearthed some clothes ropes amongst a few laundry items. She grabbed these and hurried to the door, all the time giving Ellie a breathless account of what Geoff had said on the phone.

'Be careful,' shouted Ellie as Sara swung the door open and jumped down over the step. The next minute she was gone, the door slamming behind her.

Suman, sitting at Ellie's side, tugged on her sleeve.

'Don't worry,' Ellie reassured her. 'It's just Sara gone to find a friend of mine who is coming to help us. Everything's fine.'

She peeped out the side of the curtain but could see nothing, feeling the frustration of knowing there was nothing she could do but wait. She longed to be able to get up and go to help Sara and Geoff and see for herself what was going on.

It seemed a very long time later when they heard a car drawing up outside the caravan and the engine being switched off. Fear that it might still be Levy or Van Breda's men made Ellie hastily order Suman to hide in the bathroom and lock the door. She looked around for some form of weapon and her eyes alighted on a tall vase of artificial flowers. Despite knowing it would be little protection against any assailants, she grabbed it anyway and sat ready to throw it if necessary.

The car doors shut, and footsteps approached the caravan door. She lifted the vase higher. The door was pulled open and Sara appeared first, followed by Geoff close on her heels. They stopped suddenly, both gazing in wonder at Ellie with the tall vase of tulips in her raised hand.

'Flowers, Ellie?' said Sara, highly amused. 'Is it your birthday, Geoff?' she asked, turning to look at him, her eyes full of laughter. He grinned at her comment, though his eyes never left Ellie's face.

'I thought it might be Decker or Levy. How was I to know it was you? And there was nothing else to hand but the vase,' Ellie ended sheepishly, turning to lay it down.

Turning back, she looked up and met Geoff's eyes, staring at her with the most loving expression she had ever seen. Their eyes locked, and Sara watched in awe as the two of them seemed, in that one moment, to be exchanging their love with one another. She stood still with her mouth open, watching the romantic scene in front of her.

After a few moments she cleared her throat, with reluctance breaking the magic spell in the air and bringing the two of them back down to earth with a bump.

'Right then,' she said, looking at Geoff. 'You sit down and tell Ellie what's happened to Decker and Levy, and what we think might be our next step. I'll keep an eye on the car in case Decker comes to. Where is Suman hiding, Ellie?'

'She's in the bathroom,' Ellie replied. Raising her voice, she called, 'Suman, you can come out, it's quite safe.'

The lock was pulled back and the bathroom door opened. The small face peeped round and Ellie beckoned for her to come out.

Suman ran to Ellie and curled up beside her, staring at the newcomer.

'Suman, this is Geoff. Come and sit down and speak to her, Geoff. She understands what you say.'

'Hello, Suman,' he said slowly, moving to sit on the opposite seat. 'I'm very pleased to meet you. Sara has told me all about you and I know you saved Ellie's life. And because she's my friend, I want to say thank you.'

He dug deep into his pocket and brought out a tiny parcel.

'This is for you,' he said, holding the small gift out to the child who was watching him closely. She looked up at Ellie, not knowing whether to take the parcel or not.

'It's okay, honey,' said Ellie, nodding. 'Take it.'

Suman reached out shyly, taking the little parcel with one hand. She drew it in close to her chest and held it there.

'You can open it up, see what's inside,' urged Ellie.

Suman looked down at the parcel then back to Geoff, still unsure of him, and Ellie began to help her open it. Between them, they removed the wrapping paper, finding inside a silk padded box which contained a child's silver charm bracelet, hung with little hearts and flowers. Suman stared into the box, not moving a muscle.

Geoff reached out and lifted the bracelet while Ellie raised Suman's hand up towards him. He fastened the bracelet around her wrist.

'This is especially for you, Suman,' he said. 'Because I think you're a very special person.'

He turned a wry face to Ellie. 'Sorry, this was all I could find in the hotel gift shop.'

'It's beautiful, isn't it, Suman?' Ellie asked.

Suman stared at the bracelet, holding out her wrist and twisting it round and round, the bracelet glinting in the light.

Eventually, she leaned closer to Ellie.

'Is it mine?' she whispered in her ear. With a kiss on the top of her head, Ellie replied, 'Yes. It's yours.'

A huge smile appeared on Suman's face and her eyes shone with delight. Moving across to Geoff, she reached out and touched his face.

'Thank you,' she said clearly.

A quiet sob from the doorway broke into the emotional moment, as Sara reached for her hankie. Ellie and Geoff grinned at one another, while Suman jumped down from the bed and ran the few steps to hurtle into Sara and give her a hug. She held up the bracelet excitedly for Sara to see and began to chatter.

'Thank you, Geoff,' said Ellie quietly. 'That was so thoughtful.'

'I'm glad she likes it.'

Geoff's voice changed. 'Tell me how you are, Ellie. Are you in a lot of pain?'

'No, I'm all doped up with painkillers and not feeling it very much at all. I'm fine, but desperate to know what happened out there. Tell me.'

'Well, I was obviously followed here although I didn't realise it at first. When I got here, I drove past your caravan and decided to hide my car down behind the barns, just to be on the safe side, and then walk back here. On the way back I was ambushed by Levy and Decker. I managed to get behind Levy just as Decker shot at me. The bullet went into his chum, I'm afraid. So Levy's dead. And somehow or another, I managed to knock Decker unconscious.'

Ellie's eyes had widened at the tale and she gasped in horror.

'You could have been killed.' She reached out and grasped his hand, holding on tightly. 'To knock out a man like that must have taken some courage and strength.'

He gave a lopsided grin. 'Well, I do work out occasionally, you know. Got to keep in shape. There's someone I work beside that I'm trying to impress.' He stared into her eyes. 'And I think it might be working.'

She blushed rosily as she smiled. 'Enough of that just now, tell me what happened next.'

'That's when I phoned you. Decker was unconscious on the ground and I needed to tie him up before he came round. With Sara's help I got the dead man into the boot and Decker all trussed up like a turkey and into the back seat before he started to regain consciousness. He's there now tied up to one of the seats. What would you like us to do with them both? Personally, I'd like to put a bullet in Decker for what he did to you.'

Ellie nodded slowly, her mind taking in and weighing up all the information Geoff had given her.

'Daan Meijer, where does he fit in? If we go back and hand Decker over to him, what do you think he'll do? Is there any chance he might let him go? And Levy's body. Could you be charged with murdering an IPOL officer? He might not believe us when we tell him about this; it's only his word against ours.'

'I can't say for certain, but I suspect Daan knew about Levy before I left Amsterdam. They had recalled him back to headquarters, but he obviously wasn't going in before he found you.' He paused. 'Probably best that I phone Daan before we do anything else.'

'I agree, though I'd really like to discuss Suman with you first. Presumably Van Breda's still at large and I want her safely out of his reach. The further the better. Once we've decided how we can do this, you should phone Daan. I'm still not a hundred percent sure who to trust, Geoff. There could be more of Daan's team working for Van Breda, or even Daan himself, though I don't think so.'

Ellie, watching Geoff, saw him shake his head.

'No, I don't think so either. I found him a very honest man. I liked him and would trust him.'

'Okay, but we must be sure before I hand Suman over. We'll see what he does about Van Breda. I'm sure I've got evidence of his illegal operation working both here and in India. I found links between the counterfeit alcohol in Amsterdam and what I discovered in India when I was over there.'

Geoff nodded at this. 'That bit he will certainly believe. I gave him evidence of this before I came here.'

'Great. And there's more. I need to re-check, but I think I'll be able to identify where the bottling and labelling is going on. The more I think about it the more convinced I am that it's happening right there, in the nightclub in Amsterdam. Angena took me through the hidden bits of the building and at the back entrance there's a huge warehouse. Could easily be used as a bottling plant. Ideal space.'

'I think you're right. My findings will certainly tie in with that. So, let's discuss Suman. How are we going to keep her safe while we go back and confess what we've been up to?'

―――――――――――

CHAPTER 18

Amsterdam

With the kettle on and Suman in charge of the kitchen, setting out the biscuits, Ellie and Geoff sat around the table discussing their plans.

'I want Suman hidden far away. Scotland would be best. Somewhere Van Breda can't get to her. I'm sure my mother could help us, and I think I know a way we could get Suman and Sara on a flight to Edinburgh with no suspicions raised.' Ellie glanced round to the others.

'Evelyn would definitely help, but don't you feel it's wrong to take Suman out of the country?' Sara queried. She had pulled her seat over near to the door as she kept a beady eye on the man tied up in the back of the car. 'Should we not get her to a safe destination here and find an organisation in the Netherlands that helps trafficked children get back home?'

Ellie looked thoughtfully across to Sara. 'Angena warned me that Suman might not be able to return home. I'm not sure if this is true or not, but one way or another, she's still in a lot of danger. Van Breda's running a huge criminal enterprise, trafficking children and counterfeiting spirits and goodness knows what else. He's not going to let Suman or any of us spoil that for him. He'll have many more people working for him who would do what Decker and Levy tried to do.'

'I think you're right,' agreed Geoff. 'We are all still in danger, so tell me how you think we could get Suman to Scotland. She would need a passport to board a plane.'

'Yes, and I have one for her; Angena gave it to me. It's a forged one that I think they used to get her into the country when they brought her over from India. If it got her through Dutch passport control, it will hopefully get her into Scotland. What's worrying me is that the airports may be watched by Van Breda's men, and a little

Indian girl along with a white woman is what they'll be looking for. I've been thinking hard about this while I've been lying here and that's where my mother could help.

She has a good friend, a lady called Devyani who is from India but has lived in Scotland for many years. It crossed my mind that Devyani might be willing to help us. If she was to fly across to, say, Paris, and we got Suman and Sara to the airport there, she could fly back with Suman to Edinburgh, pretending she is her grandmother. It would be much safer for Suman if she appeared to be with someone from her own family. And Sara, you could fly home separately on the same flight, to keep an eye on them. What do you think?'

Sara answered. 'If Devyani would do it, it would be a great idea. What do you think, Geoff?'

'Maybe,' he replied, looking pensive. 'Let me check out the journey to see how it could be worked out.'

He glanced across to Sara. 'We'd need to get you both to Paris somehow. It's probably a journey of about four or five hours from here by road. Could you drive my hired car?'

'No problem. I've had plenty practice driving on the wrong side of the road.'

'Okay. That would leave us the van to get back to Amsterdam with our 'passengers'.' Geoff pointed outside with his thumb as he spoke. 'Let me check out the details and timings and then you can phone your mother.'

The phone call to Evelyn was made a short time later and as expected she was more than willing to help with the plans once everything was explained. After about twenty minutes, she phoned back to confirm that Devyani had enthusiastically agreed to do her part in the rescue. Hearing the tale, Devyani has said she'd be delighted to help and had already checked out flights from Edinburgh to Paris for the following day.

With plans for Suman's safety taking shape, Ellie began to feel happier, and turned her attention to organising the return of Decker and Levy to Amsterdam. It was early evening when the decision was taken that it was time to let Daan Meijer know what was happening and Geoff reluctantly took out his phone and dialled IPOL's number.

In the IPOL building in Amsterdam there was a buzz of activity. The senior officer's room was crowded with people, some sitting behind their computer screens and some huddled in groups round their desks in rapt discussion. Daan Meijer sat at his desk, head bent over a pile of paperwork. He had been in his office since the meeting with Geoff on the previous day, surviving on coffee and the occasional snack brought to him by a member of staff. Apart from a few surreptitious yawns, he gave no sign of fatigue, his eyes alight with the enthusiasm of a man on the edge of a breakthrough on one of the biggest and most important cases in which he had ever been involved.

A table in one corner had been cleared of its normal contents and spread with a vast array of documents and photographs, each one being meticulously examined and catalogued by members of the team. A digital camera also lay on the table, attached by a USB cable to a large computer screen on the wall. Two of the team were closely observing this and making notes about the images portrayed on the screen.

Through the hubbub of voices, a phone could be heard ringing and Daan reached out quickly to lift it to his ear. He listened for a second.

'Stilte,' he called tersely across the room. 'Silence. It is Geoff.'

An instant hush descended on the office as all heads swivelled round to look at him. Minutes passed with the only sounds to break the silence being a series of grunts from Daan into the mouthpiece. Eventually he spoke.

'You stay where you are, and we'll come and get you. Van Breda's still out there so I need you all under my protection immediately.' He stopped and listened again for a few moments.

'I do believe you, Geoff. We know it's all true, both Levy's and Decker's involvement. You have my word that we'll keep you both safe. Just tell me where you are.' Again, there was a pause while he wrote directions on his pad.

'Right,' he continued. 'Sit tight, keep hidden and we'll be with you as quickly as we can. I'll phone you when we get there, so if you don't get my call, don't open the door.'

He hung up and turned to look out at the faces around him.

'He's only got Levy's body in the back of a van and Decker trussed up like a turkey! Wonder if he'd like to come and work for us?' Daan's words were received with amazement in the office.

Picking a team swiftly, he barked orders at his men who rose to carry out his instructions. The others returned to their cataloguing and inventories.

Around nine in the evening, the IPOL cars arrived in convoy at the caravan park and soon Geoff and Ellie were being driven through the deserted streets of Rozenburg on their return to Amsterdam. Daan was in front alongside the driver and Geoff sat with Ellie gathered protectively under his arm in the back seat. Levy's body had been removed by some of Daan's team and local police had been called in to help, some of whom were now scouring the park for evidence to corroborate Geoff's story.

Decker was being driven in a separate car, still bound up and although now completely conscious, was saying nothing. Of Sara and Suman there was no sign, no indication that they had ever been there. Daan was most unhappy about this but for the time being, could do nothing about it as neither Ellie nor Geoff was prepared to say where they had gone. Worried about the dangers still present from Van Breda, the IPOL boss had tried several times to convince them that the child and Sara would be safer under his protection. However, it was to no avail. Geoff and Ellie remained obstinate in refusing to disclose their whereabouts.

The evening traffic was light as the cars drew to a halt in front of the IPOL premises and Ellie and Geoff were quickly hustled inside and up the stairs into Stefan Janssen's large office. Seats were produced for the two of them and coffee and snacks ordered.

Janssen appeared and shook hands with them both and explained that he was having to go out but was leaving them in Officer Meijer's capable hands.

'Daan has some good news for you. I think you'll be happy about it. Well done both of you and hope that shoulder gets better soon, Ellie.'

After a few words with Daan, he left the office and Daan sat down behind Janssen's massive desk.

'Ellie,' he began, leaning forward on his arms, 'first, I'm delighted to have you back under our protection. You've had a bad time and I am going to need a full statement of everything that's been happening to you, right from the start. However, before we do that, I think you deserve an update on what's been going on here. The good news our chief mentioned.

Late last night, we got a phone call to say that some files and important items had been handed in to the central politie office. Items that had been left, deliberately it would appear, in one of the local taxi cabs. These were brought to our office. They were files, meticulously kept over the past six years or so, as well as photographic evidence, of all Van Breda's nefarious businesses, both here in Amsterdam and in other parts of the world, including Mumbai.'

He turned to look at Ellie whose eyes had widened at this news.

'Which, of course, ties in with your findings from the same area. The evidence seems to have been collected over the years by a member of his staff, obviously a trusted member working closely by his side. As well as Van Breda, it names many names. And can I add here that Archie Wallis' name was not on the list and from all the evidence we have now, we are positive that he wasn't working with Van Breda at any time. Unlike Lucas Decker from UBI and Frank Levy from our team.'

Geoff and Ellie exchanged relieved glances. This was excellent news and Ellie was particularly pleased, for Archie's wife's sake.

Daan continued his story. 'As you can imagine, what we've got, if it's genuine, is going to blow his whole empire apart. Alongside your evidence, Ellie, and your calculations, Geoff, we've got everything we could ever want to put him and many others away for a very long time indeed.

A lot of what you've been telling me in the car is being substantiated by what you see out there.' He pointed through the glass to the general office where all the cataloguing was taking place. 'Might take us many months to get through it all. It's a staggering amount.'

He leaned back in his chair, clasping his hands behind his head.

'Anyway, more about that later. Right now, let's hear your story. I want the lot, every intricate detail. I'll record it as you speak, but please don't worry about that. This will help when you come to making statements and reports. Now tell me everything, right from when you were both here, in this office.'

Ellie's account took a considerable time to tell, and was listened to avidly, interspersed by many questions. Trying to include everything, she gave a very detailed description of the last couple of weeks, beginning with her chance meeting with Angena and ending with Geoff's phone call to Daan.

Geoff took over at this point to give his account of events. The only details omitted by both Ellie and Geoff were the present whereabouts of Sara and Suman. Daan was a fair man and understood their reticence in this respect.

'Until we have Van Breda and many more under arrest, I've no choice but to accept your way of keeping Suman hidden. But once the suspects have been brought in, I'll need to know where she is. Then we can discuss what's to be done with her.'

He hesitated as Ellie shifted uncomfortably in her seat, adjusting the sling on her arm.

'Are you okay? Is your arm sore?'

Ellie shook her head. 'No, it's fine, just stiffening up a bit. The doctor did a good job patching me up. I've to get the stitches out in a few days and it'll be easier then. If we're still in Amsterdam, I'll get your advice on where to go to get them taken out.'

'Sure, we'll sort that out for you. You *will* still be here; there's so much happening, and I need to keep you around and safe. As we speak, my team have begun a search of all the Van Breda outlets, not just in Amsterdam but in Germany as well. We need to move quickly, before he gets wind of what has happened to Levy and Decker although he most likely knows already. He's a very dangerous individual.

I need to get him and all his entourage under lock and key as quickly as possible. Therefore, it's safer if we look after you. Tonight, once I get the okay, we'll take you back to your hotel. Both your rooms are still being held for you, with all your belongings. We'll be putting security in to be with you until this is all over.'

He stood. 'Come, I'll introduce you to some of the staff and show you what they are doing. Then we'll find you a comfortable place to wait.'

CHAPTER 19

Amsterdam

It was in the early hours of the morning when Ellie and Geoff eventually reached the hotel and were accompanied up to their rooms by bodyguards. Ellie was shattered, the events of the last two or three days beginning to catch up with her, and she was glad they were to be given the opportunity of a good night's sleep. Looking anxiously at her as they parted, Geoff pulled her in close for a moment as he said goodnight. Although both were desperate for a chance to be alone together, there was a mutual understanding that tonight was not going to be the best time and, with reluctance, they drew apart.

'Sleep well, Ellie,' said Geoff quietly as he tenderly ran his hand down her cheek, acutely conscious of the security men standing close by. 'You know my room number. Any problems, just phone me and I'll be there.' His voice dropped low as he said, 'I promised Evelyn I'd let her know when you were safely back.'

She smiled at his use of her mother's first name. 'I'll do it,' she whispered back.

Next morning, refreshed from a difficult shower trying to protect the dressing on her shoulder, Ellie spoke briefly to check in with the security guard outside her door and then sat down to wait for Geoff. The restful sleep that she had enjoyed had been made possible by the receipt of a short text from Sara, confirming that she and Suman had arrived safe and sound. No names, place names or details were included in the text, and Ellie was grateful to Sara for maintaining caution for the time being. She had climbed into bed, and dropped straight into a deep sleep, waking only to the ring of her alarm clock in the morning.

Geoff's knock came soon after she had dressed and she opened the door, her heart lifting at the sight of him. They ate breakfast in Ellie's room, Daan having insisted that they stay away from the public rooms in the hotel for the present time. Informed that a car awaited them downstairs, they made their way to the entrance and out to an IPOL car purring gently at the side of the road. By ten o'clock, they were once again in the IPOL offices, seated in separate rooms to begin dictating their official statements.

During the day, at various intervals, reports continually came into the department on the searches and arrests taking place and Ellie and Geoff were astounded and, at times, appalled at the information being received. With the permission of Daan, today they were being allowed to stay within the main office, feeling part of the investigation and included in a lot of what was going on.

From their previous visit, they had learned that Daan's team were working in partnership with the KLPD, the *Korps Landelijke Politiediensten*, the National Constabulary of the Netherlands. The extra men and women drafted into the office to assist the team were from the Special Investigating Department of the KLPD and the two of them watched in admiration the efficient way the teams worked together.

All Ellie's professionalism was needed during the day as she struggled at times to deal with some of the horrifying details emerging within the reports. The picture opening-up to them was one of a massive trafficking empire stretching over many countries, including India, Bangladesh, Thailand, Malaysia and parts of China. Linked to the trafficking, evidence of a sickening pornographic film industry was uncovered, and several files full of names and details of paedophiles throughout the world were brought into the office, to be catalogued and dissected by the busy team members.

Fighting back feelings of revulsion, Ellie learned how small children like Suman were bought for tiny sums of money, taken from their homes and trafficked to different parts of the world, Amsterdam being one of the main places. Some of the children brought to the Netherlands were being used to make the pornographic films or put to work as prostitutes in the hidden rooms of Van Breda's nightclubs. Also emerging from the files were details of children of all ages who had been sent to cities in Argentina, Canada and India, to work for pimps in red light areas of some of the major cities. Evidence showed that some of the exploited children were as young as six years old. Figures revealed the enormity of the human trafficking business being run by Van Breda and his corporation as well as the money being made from it. It was extremely difficult information to take in, with worse still to come.

Ellie discovered that some of these trafficked children, after being used and abused, were then dispatched to unknown destinations, with no recorded details of what had happened to them. In other words, some were disappearing never to be heard of again.

On hearing this, Ellie's mind flew back to the story of the fire in the basement of The Furnace Nightclub that Angena had told her about, and her heart leapt in terror. She sought out Daan and repeated Angena's tale to him.

'We'll certainly check it out,' he reassured her, noticing the anxiety etched on her face. 'Try not to think about it too much. It's a hell of a lot to take in. Are you coping with it all here or would you like to go back to the hotel? You don't have to put yourself through this.'

'I do,' she replied quickly. 'I'm fine. It's the thought of little girls like Suman, and boys as well, having to go through this. Just innocent children, having their lives destroyed. I need to help. How can people like Van Breda do this, Daan? How do they sleep in their beds at night?'

'They sleep soundly with no conscience knowing they are amongst the very wealthiest people in the world,' he stated angrily. 'Human trafficking brings in billions of dollars each year, Ellie. One consolation is that at least we're putting a stop to this criminal empire. We're leaving no stone unturned.'

He paused. 'Over a hundred people have been arrested already, you know. All in custody, all being interrogated and many more to come. And you'll be pleased to hear that the children and the girls from the nightclubs have been taken to one of our hospitals where a wing has been set aside for them. They're going to be taken care of and, once this is all over, hopefully some will be returned to their homes. It's often difficult to return these kids to their own homes, but those that are left with nowhere to go, they'll be looked after, we'll make sure. So there's good news as well as bad.'

Ellie sighed. 'These poor children. Angena told me about the difficulty of getting them accepted back into their own communities, especially in India. And speaking of Angena, is it possible for you to find out if she is amongst the ones taken to hospital? I'd love to know if she's safe and go and visit her. I suspect she would be punished in some way for what she did, but hopefully not too badly.'

'I'll find out for you,' he assured her. 'Oh, and did they tell you a large whisky bond was discovered, just as you said, in the basement of The Furnace? The bond had been cleared of all evidence, but the machinery, bottles and alcohol were all found on the premises, waiting for the hue and cry to die down before starting production again. There was photographic evidence of this as well.'

'We were right; it was going on here in Amsterdam. I knew it!' she exclaimed. 'And what about Van Breda himself?'

He looked at her with an apologetic expression. 'That's not good news. I was hoping you wouldn't ask until we had some more information. Currently, there's no trace of where he is. He obviously got wind of us coming and has gone into hiding. Please don't worry; he's our number one priority. We'll get him,' he promised.

Mid-afternoon, sitting at a desk in the main office with a cup of coffee cradled in her hands, Ellie felt a hand on her shoulder. Turning around, she looked up into Daan's serious face.

'May I speak to you for a moment, Ellie? You too, Geoff.'

He nodded across the desk to where Geoff was in conversation with an officer. They rose and followed Daan to another room where he closed the door quietly behind them.

'Sit down, please,' he invited. 'I wanted to give you an update from The Furnace, specifically on what we spoke of this morning, Ellie. The real furnace, down in the basement.'

He stopped a moment, as if he didn't know how to continue. Taking a deep breath, he began again.

'I hate to have to report that you were correct. Our officers discovered the large kiln down underneath the building and have begun an initial search amongst the debris and ashes. It's still to be confirmed but they believe they have found evidence that the furnace was used to dispose of bodies. Many bodies.'

Ellie gasped and covered her face with her hands. Geoff's comforting arm reached around her shoulders.

The hardened IPOL officer continued, like them obviously moved by the distressing news he had for them.

'A lot of the staff at the club have already been questioned at length about it including the business manager, a man named Stefan Peters. He, with others, confirmed that many people were murdered, and their bodies cremated in the furnace, including Angena who was killed for letting Suman escape. I'm so sorry, Ellie.'

As the enormity of this information hit her, Ellie began to weep, an overwhelming sadness filling her body at the thought of such a horrible fate for the beautiful and caring girl who had saved Suman. Geoff pulled her close and held her tight.

'I'm okay,' she said at last, wiping her face with Geoff's handkerchief. 'I knew her for such a short time, but realised she was very special. She didn't deserve this.'

'I know,' Daan nodded, his voice subdued. 'However, you must always remember that her very brave, selfless act in saving Suman has sparked off this whole investigation and will save countless other children from the same fate.'

'Yes, thank you, I'll remember that. She would be happy to know that. Please go on with what you were saying.'

'Well, something else that might upset you. We've had a confession from one of Van Breda's men about your UBI colleague, Archie Wallis. Apparently, Van Breda had ordered various measures to try to frighten you and your organisation into discontinuing your searches for counterfeit spirits and when these failed, he ordered the murder of the boss of the UBI Amsterdam office. Archie was lured to the customs and excise offices by Lucas Decker.

It was supposed to look like a case of terrorism, and he was hoping your company would recall you back to Scotland. It appears he thought you were getting too close to discovering his counterfeit operation.'

In Ellie's mind she saw again Archie's kind face, and hot tears again pushed through her lashes.

'I know this is all very upsetting, but there's two other important bits of information,' Daan continued gently after a pause. 'The first concerns a woman named Geeta, one of Van Breda's close confidantes. We believe her to be the person who collected all the evidence against him over the last few years, and for some reason, decided to betray him. She hid the evidence in a taxi on her way to the airport, obviously trying to get away. We suspect, from pieces of her jewellery found, that she was disposed of in the furnace as well.'

His voice slowed as he looked at the two faces gazing at him. 'One last thing. This has still to be confirmed, but a ring known to be Van Breda's, a heavy gold signet ring inscribed with his initials, was found on the floor of the basement, very close to the furnace. It was reported that he never removed this ring. We'll need further proof, but we think it might just be possible that he too met his end in the furnace.'

Ellie's eyes were like saucers as she stared at Daan. After a moment or two, it was Geoff who broke the silence.

'A fitting end, if it's true,' he said quietly.

———————————————

CHAPTER 20

Edinburgh

The car taking them back to the hotel sped rapidly through the evening traffic. As before, they were not alone, the two bodyguards following them through the narrow door and up in the lift to stand guard outside their rooms. Daan was continuing to take no chances.

'I'll see you at seven for dinner, Ellie.' Geoff reached out to touch her hand as they parted at her door. She nodded and entered her room, locking the door with a click. For a moment she stood still, the turbulent thoughts of the highly emotional day running through her head, images of death and evil hard to banish from her mind.

She was tired, both physically and mentally and her shoulder ached, the stitches pulling as they healed. She crossed to the mirror on the wall, removing the clasp from her hair and allowing it to fall free. As she stared at her reflection, not aware of it, her thoughts turned to Suman and she wondered how she was doing, and if she was coping with yet another change in her life. Surprisingly, she found herself missing the child with something like an ache in her heart and knew that she would give anything to be able to return home soon to look after her and keep her safe.

Giving in to her feelings, she lifted the phone and dialled the number of her mother's house in Scotland. Matt answered and called to Evelyn to come and talk to Ellie. Assured that Suman was safe and well physically but not so good mentally, her low spirits plunged deeper. She gathered from her mother's words that without Ellie around, Suman had returned to her mute state again, refusing to talk to anyone. The description of a little girl curling herself into a ball to rock back and forth, hugging her knees, caused an anxious frown to appear on her forehead. Evelyn, realising Ellie's concern, kept the conversation short, asking instead how Ellie herself was faring and when she was coming home.

'I'll come as quickly as I possibly can. I'll speak to Daan tomorrow and see if he will allow me to go. Can I speak to Suman?'

'She's not here. Sara has taken her to the swing park along the road for a wee while. Just get here as soon as you can, Ellie.'

'I will,' she promised.

A bath and change of clothes did much to restore a little of her normal optimism and she busied herself tidying the room and putting a few things into her suitcase until she heard Geoff's knock.

'Come on in,' she said, opening the door. 'We'll just phone down for dinner and then we'll chat. Do you know what you'd like?' she asked, picking up the room service menu and handing it to him.

'Yes, but you're not on the menu,' Geoff teased.

Ellie chuckled, her mood improving now that he was with her.

'Well, I might be,' she flirted. 'Dish of the day, all yours.'

His eyes softened as they gazed at each other, locked fast in the strength of the attraction they were both feeling. Moving closer, he reached out his hands to cup them round her face.

'Do you know how much I want that to be true, Ellie?'

She couldn't reply at first, his nearness and the warm look in his eyes taking her breath away completely.

'It is true.' With her words came the release of the tensions that had been building up all day and, instinct taking over, she melted against his body with a sigh.

Geoff drew her face up and his lips closed on hers, the emotions he had kept in check for such a long time released in his passionate kiss. Ellie's body began to react as he tightened his hold and her lips parted beneath the kiss. The evil world they had been introduced into faded into haziness as she felt the moisture of his mouth and returned his kiss with a passion she had never known before. As the kiss ended, his lips moved softly to her face and down her neck. Her soft breaths quickened as his hands pulled her even closer.

Laying her gently down on the bed, Geoff looked into her eyes, knowing her beauty, her soul and her very being were everything he ever wanted. He ran his hands through her radiant hair, lying loose with abandonment on the silk cover of the bed, the lights from outside catching its beauty. Covering her body with his own, he felt the heat between them and the anticipation in her responses.

As they finally joined together as one, all thoughts of the day disappeared from her mind. They gave themselves wholly to each other, the distant dream that Geoff had long cherished finally coming true and his prayers answered.

'I love you, Elizabeth Douglas,' he whispered. 'I have loved you since the moment I first saw you and I will love you for the rest of my life and beyond.'

Her arms tightened around his naked body and her lips drew close to his again.

With wonder shining from her eyes, she breathed softly, 'I love you, too.'

They slept that night in each other's arms, waking occasionally to come together again, unable to resist the magnetic pull of their attraction and their love for each other. As the sun rose, they lay close for a while, happy and content to be where they were but knowing they had another emotional day ahead of them. By seven thirty, breakfast had been ordered and both were dressed and ready to go, expectation of the difficulties they faced made easier and less stressful knowing they would face them together.

During the morning, Ellie found an opportunity to talk to Daan about Suman and about going home. Sitting in his office, she decided it was time for a frank and truthful discussion with him about Suman's future, and the mental anguish and problems that the trafficking and abuse had caused the child. She explained about the bond that they had formed and the responsibility and affection she felt for the little girl. Ellie told him how it had taken so long to get Suman to speak and how she had now regressed back into silence again, away from Ellie's comforting presence. Daan was thoughtful as he listened to the story.

'I understand what you are saying, Ellie. I've seen trafficked children and I know the effect sexual slavery can have on them. Tell me, what are you asking of me? What is it you want me to do?'

'Well, I seem to be the one that Suman responds to and trusts. What I'd like is for you to say that I can keep her for a while, just to care for her until she's over the trauma a little, and then, with your help, I can take her home again to her village in India.'

'That's a distorted picture you've imagined in your mind.' He shook his head. 'The reality for these children is not like that. Huge numbers of children are trafficked each year in India. I think the figure is something around ninety thousand, and of the small percentage that are rescued, many are unable to return to their homes.'

'Angena told me this when she asked me to take Suman. Why can't I take her straight home?'

He leaned back in his seat, a serious look on his face.

'Lots of reasons. She would have to be taken into care while the authorities decide what to do with her. There are government shelters to house trafficked victims until their futures are sorted out. Sometimes it's impossible to discover where they have come from, and sometimes it can be that they are not accepted back because of the stigma attached to girls who have been raped or abused. There's a name for them, *paro* meaning purchased, I think. And with that name comes great shame. In India, quite often it's the victim who becomes the accused, and once a girl is no longer a virgin, she may be unacceptable for marriage in her village and her family will refuse to take her back. I've come across this before. Girls in some parts of the world are very expendable, Ellie.'

'That's despicable.' Her voice rose in anger. 'It's not the child's fault. Why should she be punished like this?'

'I can't answer that apart from saying it's been my experience that some Eastern countries don't provide a good protection service to their children who have been trafficked abroad for sexual exploitation. I don't understand it any more than you do. Rescued children like Suman are usually put into government shelters, but often receive little or no medical, psychological or legal assistance. She may be there for a long time waiting for courts to agree release.'

'You see why I'd like to keep her with me for a while, Daan. I can provide these things for her. And once I feel she's strong enough, I'll take advice about getting her back to India somehow to begin a search for her family.'

His voice softened. 'Suman sounds to me like a very remarkable little girl. And after the ordeal you have both been through, it is understandable that you want to look after her. I agree she would be far better off remaining with you for the moment, so leave it with me and I'll see what I can do. It may be that we can 'fail to find her' for our investigation. We have so much evidence against the Van Breda organisation already. Let me have a think about it.'

'I need to know quickly, Daan. I desperately want to go to her.'

He nodded. 'Okay, I'll talk to some colleagues and get back to you.'

He was true to his word and that afternoon, Ellie and Geoff were called back to his office to be told that they would be released from their enforced stay in Amsterdam and allowed to return home as soon as they wished. There was a proviso that they should stay in touch, and that they would return at any time should they be needed during the investigation. And when the time came, they would be called to testify at the court cases that would take place in the Netherlands' courts of law.

As far as the little girl was concerned, Daan Meijer would apply to the authorities for permission for her to stay with Ellie for an indefinite period, to allow the child to recover from any post-traumatic stress disorder symptoms she might show following the suffering she had endured at the hands of her traffickers.

Unable to resist, Ellie threw her arms around him and hugged him tightly.

'I can't begin to thank you.'

'It is I who should thank you, Ellie. You're a very brave lady. But one piece of advice. If Suman had stayed here with the other rescued children, she would have received a medical examination to determine if she was HIV positive, or if she had been raped and had any injuries, internal or external. I would suggest that you do this for her as soon as possible. Some of these children can be badly injured and need repair work. For some it can mean the destruction of their internal organs, meaning they can never have children.'

Ellie stared at him, a feeling of nausea threatening to surface.

'Another reason their families won't take them back,' he added.

It was in an angry mood that she left the building around four, clutching tightly to Geoff's hand. Daan's words had caused a violent reaction in her heart and she found herself hating the perpetrators of trafficking and the child pornography industry with a passion.

If I had my way, she thought furiously, the people responsible would all be sentenced to the Van Breda furnace. How dare they destroy so many innocent lives in this way?

Back at the hotel, they managed to book a flight home the following morning and packed their cases in readiness for an early start. Ellie was grateful that Daan had also organised a visit from a local doctor during the evening to remove the stitches from her shoulder and apply a light dressing to the wound which was healing well. Their last night in Amsterdam was spent in each other's arms, waking early in anticipation of the journey home at last.

The flight touched down late morning at Edinburgh Airport and they queued for a taxi to take them to Geoff's home in Musselburgh to pick up his car. The driver stopped in front of an attractive Victorian house in Linkfield Road, and as she climbed out of the cab, Ellie admitted to a strong curiosity to see where and how he lived. She followed him through the gate across the road from which she could see the racecourse and, in the distance, the Old Golf Course, a well-known landmark in Musselburgh.

Nice, she thought, admiring the neat garden and eye-catching azalea bushes lining the path.

'One day I'll carry you across the threshold, Ellie,' he vowed as he unlocked the door.

'Oh, you will, will you?' she replied saucily. 'We'll see.'

He led her into an impressive hallway, glimpsing a beautiful ceiling with ornate cornicing in a sitting room on the right. Smiling as he watched her glance all about, he told her to have a look around while he put his case into the bedroom. Geoff's indelibly male aura pervaded each room, but Ellie was impressed by the spaciousness and the neatness of the whole place.

'Glad to see you keep it clean and tidy,' she informed him with a twinkle. 'And with a few designer touches here and there, I might even come back and stay soon.'

As she spoke, he swept her up in his arms and kissed her lips, held up invitingly. With slight reluctance, they eventually made their way to his car outside and began the journey to Anstruther, their bodies close together in the car. An hour and a half's driving took them within sight of the harbour and marina of the town and Ellie gave him directions on how to reach Evelyn and Matt's house. Approaching the door, Ellie found herself very nervous about the reunion with Suman, feeling both excitement and anxiety and hoping the little girl would begin to speak again once they were back together. As far as she knew, Evelyn had not informed Suman of their arrival, and she opened the door quietly, hoping for the element of surprise.

There was no noise at all in the house and for a moment she thought there was no-one in. But going through the hall to the back of the house, they were drawn to the sound of voices in the garden outside. She hurried through the open door with Geoff close behind, and stood there, taking in the scene. The large, colourful garden was spread out in front of them, with the sun glistening on the ripples of the water of the Firth of Forth in the background.

Ellie was oblivious to the stunning view, and to the other people in the garden. She saw only Suman, sitting on a mat on the grass, a Barbie doll cuddled to her chest and her knees pulled up close making her look even smaller than she was. Her face wore a serious, almost desperate expression as she stared out across the garden, her thoughts miles away. Ellie's heart thumped and a lump made its way into her throat.

'Suman,' she called softly.

Suman's head flew round and for a few seconds she stared at Ellie and Geoff in the doorway. Ellie opened her arms wide. The next moment the doll was thrown to the ground as she leapt up and bounded across to where they stood.

The squeal took everyone by surprise as Suman found her voice. It was followed by a howl and the tears began as she threw herself into Ellie's arms and wrapped her own tightly around Ellie's neck.

'Elleee, Elleee,' she cried, tears pouring from her cheeks.

Ellie comforted Suman, holding her tightly and lifting her up from the ground. She moved with her over to where her mother sat with Matt on garden chairs, both anxiously watching the scene. She lowered herself down onto a vacant chair and sat Suman on her knee. It was a few moments before Suman's sobs began to subside and Ellie spoke soothingly to her the whole time. When the tears had stopped Ellie, holding her close, began to question her, speaking gently.

'I think you must have missed me. Are you happy to see me?'

Suman nodded.

'And have you been good while you've been here?'

Again, Suman nodded.

'And have they been looking after you, and...' Ellie paused.

'...Well,' she continued in a surprised voice, 'I can see you've got a lovely new dress. Did Sara give you this, or did...'

She looked across at her mother. '...Auntie Evelyn?'

Suman sat up on Ellie's knee, looking across to Evelyn with a perplexed frown.

'Nan,' she corrected in her gruff little voice, pointing.

Hearing Suman speak, Evelyn's eyes filled with tears and Matt reached over to clasp his wife's hand.

'Oh, it's Nan, is it?' Ellie grinned as she hugged Suman closer. Her heart soared as she looked at the child's face, so relieved and delighted to hear her speaking again.

'And what have you been doing with Nan?'

Ellie's question received no answer for some long moments. Eventually, Suman spoke.

'Will you take me to Aayi, Ellie? I want go home.'

'Oh, Suman.' Ellie hugged her even closer. 'Is that your mother? Is Aayi your mother?'

Suman nodded.

'Well, I'll certainly try as hard as I can to take you home. It might take me a little time to find her, but we'll make you all better while we search for her. Would you be happy to stay with me while we search? And I promise I won't leave again if I can possibly help it.'

The child nodded. 'With you,' she confirmed.

'And Geoff?' Ellie asked tentatively, her eyes meeting and holding her mother's rather watery ones.

The question brought about an abrupt change in the child. Suman turned to look at Geoff standing a little way off and she jumped down to run to him, shouting his name. She hurtled herself into his arms and he lifted her high and swung her round and round high in the air. Her squeals of delight rang out through the air.

As he laid her gently back down on the grass, she held out her wrist. 'See, see,' she said. 'Suman bracelet. Thank you, Geoff.'

Turning around, she addressed herself to Evelyn.

'Geoff love Suman, Nan. Geoff love Ellie, too.'

Evelyn let out a hoot of laughter as she rose to greet the abashed young man with a warm hug. Matt chuckled softly while Ellie's face took on a pink glow.

Pleased with the reaction that her words had caused, Suman continued, watching all the faces as she spoke. 'And Ellie love Geoff.'

The laughter rang round the garden and continued long into the afternoon as they caught up with each other's news and played with the child. Towards six o'clock, they were joined by Sara, with more hugs, kisses and tears. Sara stayed for tea, cooked noisily in the kitchen by Evelyn, Matt and Suman. It was much later in the evening, when Suman was in bed and fast asleep, that the serious explanations began. Astounded and dismayed to hear of the ordeals that her daughter had been through, Evelyn was nevertheless proud of the actions that Ellie had taken in rescuing Suman.

'She's wonderful, Ellie. What's going to happen to her now?'

'Well, I've been given permission to keep her for an indefinite time, during which I'll be able to give her all the support I can to get over what they did to her. The bastards,' she added angrily. 'Sorry, Mum, I know you don't like me swearing, but that's what they are.'

Fully understanding her daughter's feelings, Evelyn ignored the lapse and asked, 'And then what?'

'Then I'll take her to Mumbai, possibly to a government shelter that looks after trafficked children, and I'll stay for a short time to see if it's going to be possible to get her back to her village. Daan Meijer has said he'll help with this.'

'How are you going to look after her and still work, Ellie?' asked Matt.

Ellie looked round to Geoff, beside her on the sofa.

'Geoff's going to help, and I'll work slightly shorter hours at UBI. I'm hoping maybe I can ask you two to help as well, and Sara.'

Sara nodded her head vigorously, delighted at being asked to help.

'John Anderson is giving me some time off for a few weeks,' Ellie continued. 'He's being supportive. We'd like to try to teach her to read and write a little bit in the short time she's here. It's what she wants more than anything, so we'll search for a teacher who speaks Marathi, and we'll coach her in English as well. I think it's the best thing we can do for her.'

'We're more than happy to help.'

'She's very bright, Mum. And very determined.'

Suman's determination and her quiet intelligence came to the fore in the next few weeks as she very speedily soaked up everything she was taught. Evelyn's friend, Devyani had guessed well in thinking that it was Marathi that Suman spoke, and a tutor was found quickly to teach Suman the basics of reading and writing in Marathi. Her English improved dramatically as well, and she developed a huge love of the children's programmes on television and repeated many of the words and phrases she heard there.

The very difficult task of booking a medical examination was done in the first month of her stay with Ellie. Knowing it would be a horrific experience for Suman, Ellie insisted on a female doctor, and she explained in detail exactly what Suman had undergone and what it was that had necessitated the examination.

Dr Joan Marshall was very gentle and patient with her. With Ellie present throughout, a detailed examination was undertaken, Suman being tested for HIV/AIDS, Hepatitis, TB and a frighteningly long list of urinary tract and sexually transmitted diseases. She was given x-rays and scans on different parts of her body and the understanding doctor made her laugh while searching her hair for any sign of lice, by searching through her Barbie doll's hair as well.

With Ellie by her side, Suman submitted well to all the tests, only reacting badly to her internal examination. Panic was written clearly all over the little girl's face and, holding her tight, Ellie was shocked at the desperation and utter terror in her eyes. Dr Marshall suggested doing the examination under anaesthetic and, feeling that only the truth would help, Ellie explained as simply as she could that they needed to see if the bad people had hurt her inside, and if they had, Ellie and the doctor would make her better.

'They did hurt me,' Suman whispered in Ellie's ear. 'They gave me something horrible to drink and...' She stopped, turning her face away, unable to say any more.

'I know, I know,' said Ellie gently, holding her close as she sat on the bed. 'But I love you so much and won't let anyone else hurt you. Dr Joan just wants to help you too. The same as you helped me when I was hurt in Amsterdam.'

The tests were carried out under a general anaesthetic with Suman asking multiple questions all through the procedure of putting her to sleep. The results came through quickly and Ellie was summoned a few days later to speak to the doctor.

'I'm pleased to say,' Dr Marshall began, 'that, although Suman has undergone the worst mistreatment I've ever seen in a child, her internal organs are still intact and beginning to heal. She has tested negative for HIV and for most of the STD's but there are signs of an infection still hanging around. I'll give you some antibiotics for this. We also found that three of her ribs had been broken but all other x-rays are okay. That's the good news.'

'Good news?' gasped Ellie. 'Oh God, I hope there's nothing worse.'

'Well, although I said her internal organs are still intact, they have been badly damaged. Whilst I'm hopeful that her ability to carry a child one day has been unimpaired, I can't promise this. I have to say, Ellie, Suman's body has been through the most horrific abuse. Internally and externally. She has burn marks all over her body, healing nicely, but she might be left with light scars. She's also got the remnants of bruises and cuts everywhere, and I noticed her jaw slightly out of alignment. I hope to hell these people are all prosecuted for this,' she finished vehemently.

'I hope so, too,' agreed Ellie. 'I'm doing my best to help with that.'

'You said the child had been trafficked.'

Ellie nodded. 'Yes, she was. There are kids like Suman being stolen or bought every day of the week and trafficked into sexual slavery to be used and abused. The figures are something like two to four million children every year. It's mind-blowing.'

The doctor shook her head. 'And we all thought slavery had been abolished.'

'No, it's worse now than ever before. Rescuing one is a drop in the ocean, but she's become a very precious little drop in the ocean to me. I wish I could do more for her.'

'Are you organising psychological help or counselling for her?'

'I'm not sure if I'll have her with me long enough to do this, but I will if you think I should.'

'I think the help you're giving her yourself is probably what she needs most right now. Maybe in the future she may need more professional help, but time will tell.'

'Well, I'm hoping to be involved in her care right up until she's returned to her mother. So I'll take advice as we go.'

The doctor looked at Ellie with respect and admiration in her eyes as they shook hands and wished her well.

CHAPTER 21

Mumbai

It was after a stay of around nine months and with a very heavy heart that Ellie began the planning and organisation of the trip back to India. Daan had been in constant touch with them regarding the court cases taking place, and at the same time, gave advice on where Suman should be taken in Mumbai and the legal paperwork necessary to get her back into India.

The flight and accommodation were booked by Geoff, unable to accompany them but desperate to help. The hotel was near to the area in which the chosen government shelter was situated and Geoff had reserved a room in the hotel for seven nights, knowing that Ellie would wish to remain in Mumbai for at least a week, maybe more, to make sure that Suman's welfare and future were being taken care of properly. Ellie was dreading the separation and very anxious about how Suman would react when she was eventually left in the shelter without support. The best thing would be if they could find Suman's home village quickly and return her to her mother and family, thought Ellie, even although she knew this was what Daan had called 'a distorted picture of reality'.

Suman, now aged ten, was aware of everything that was being planned for her and her anticipation of going home grew every day. Her goodbyes to Evelyn and Matt were tinged with sadness as well as excitement, and the evening she said goodbye to Geoff and Sara was heart-wrenching, with many tears and cuddles being shared well into the evening. Her bag was packed ready with all her new clothes and gifts, and on the top, she lovingly laid new books that Ellie had given her. Zipping up the suitcase, she laid it at the bedroom door in readiness for the journey in the morning.

Geoff drove them to the airport, coming in to spend some time with them as they waited in the restaurant for their flight, and then waved them off through the departure gate to begin the long arduous flight to Mumbai, via Dubai. He was disappointed at not being able to go with them but work at UBI since he had joined the anti-counterfeit team had grown too busy to allow him more time off.

Daan had been in touch regularly with him at UBI and kept them updated on the investigation into the Van Breda empire. A huge number of arrests had been made, far and wide, with many influential politicians, police and government workers also taken in for questioning about their association with Van Breda. Initial court cases had already begun.

Of the head of the empire himself, there was still no sign and it was felt safe to assume that their first suspicion that he had met his end in the furnace at the nightclub had been correct. However, until this was proven, he was still on the Interpol wanted list. His empire was all but gone but it would be many months, even years before all loose ends were tied up. Until it was, and until proof of Van Breda's death was confirmed, Daan still recommended caution in everything they did.

Ellie was conscious of this as they took their seats on the Boeing 777 to Dubai, checking out their fellow passengers on the way down the aisle. A nervous passenger most of the time, she made a huge effort to appear unconcerned for Suman's sake, so successfully that the young girl was unaware of Ellie's anxiety and chattered non-stop for the first hour of the flight, until she fell fast asleep in her seat.

No mishaps occurred during the flight and the transfer of planes at Dubai Airport was achieved with no hitches. At last, after almost twelve hours of flying plus their stop in Dubai, Ellie heard the words she had been waiting for.

'Ladies and Gentlemen, we are beginning our descent into Mumbai and will be landing at Chhatrapati Shivaji Airport in twenty minutes. Please make sure you have all your belongings and your passport and visa ready to show at customs.'

Memories of her last trip to India came flooding back and it was with amazement that Ellie remembered how much had happened in her life since then. After collecting their luggage from the reclamation area, the pair made their way outside into the warmth of the Indian sun and the hustle and bustle at one of the busiest airports in the world. An auto-rickshaw took them to nearby Antheri Station to catch a train to central Mumbai, the bumps and rattles of the rickshaw over the rough patches on the roads making them giggle together. The train they caught was a fast one and seemed to take no time at all to reach the centre of the city, where a local taxi took them to the hotel Geoff had chosen for their stay.

In the large, imposing Marriott Hotel, the air conditioning was a welcome release from the muggy heat and dust of the city. Suman's eyes were round with wonder at the sumptuousness of the décor in the hotel and at the staff so willing to gratify their every need. Ellie gave a hug as the overwhelmed Suman moved in close to her side. Their room was spacious and nicely furnished and Ellie was glad that Geoff had insisted on paying a bit more to ensure their comfort.

Weariness began to show after they ate a light evening meal and Ellie decided that an early night would do them both good.

'Will I sleep in this bed, Ellie?' Suman asked as Ellie began to run a bath for her. 'It's huge.'

'Yes, and I'll be in the other one, right beside you.'

'Wow!' said Suman as she climbed up on the bed and began to bounce up and down.

Ellie laughed, peeping round the door of the bathroom.

Bathed and clad in new pink pyjamas, Suman climbed into the bed and pulled the covers round her neck tightly. Ellie knelt at the side of the bed aware that the dark eyes were staring out at her with a very worried expression. She smoothed the stray hairs back from the beloved face and whispered, 'Sleep well, my darling. We've got an important day tomorrow.'

'If I don't like this place, this shelter, can I stay with you?'

'We've spoken about this, honey, and you know that the people from the shelter are going to try to help you get home to your mother, to Aayi. You know you want to go home, to see her and your father, and your brothers and sisters.'

'Yes,' Suman whispered softly. 'But I want to be with you, too, Ellie.'

'I know, and I want to be with you, too. I'll stay here for a while so that I can see you every day, and then, you know that Geoff and I will come back to India very soon to see how you are. And just think, when you're home in your village, I will come to see you and meet Aayi and all your family. You can show me where they live and introduce me to all your friends.'

'What if Aayi sends me away again?'

Ellie swallowed hard. 'Suman, my darling, she will never send you away again. Only to Scotland to visit all of us.'

As Suman nodded, Ellie bent her head and planted a kiss on her forehead, her own eyes lowered to hide any anxiety she was displaying about the next day.

'Love you, Suman,' she whispered.

'Love you, Ellie.'

The morning came too quickly. Awake as soon as the sun began to stream through the curtains, Ellie lay for some time with many different thoughts chasing through her head, until, at last, she heard Suman stir in the bed next to her. Preparations began for this momentous day. Trepidation was on both faces. Ellie's voice was cheerful but forced as she dressed and helped Suman to re-pack her belongings into the new suitcase she had been given by Geoff. Breakfast was eaten in the opulent dining room of the hotel although neither had much of an appetite for the rich foods set before them.

By nine, they were standing in the hotel lobby, waiting for their taxi to arrive. Ellie was finding it increasingly difficult to maintain her earlier air of cheerfulness and she gazed into the small face, knowing how very hard it was going to be to leave her in the shelter and no longer be responsible for her safety.

An Uber cab drew up at the entrance to the hotel and the driver entered the lobby and called out Ellie's name. The journey to the shelter took them just over thirty minutes, the heavy traffic of Mumbai delaying their progress and bringing them many times to a standstill.

Suman gazed from the window, taking in the hubbub of the city, the throngs of people walking on the streets and pavements, the shops and businesses by the side of the road and the beggars at every corner the taxi turned. During the journey she turned to look at Ellie several times for reassurance.

The car came to a stop outside a fenced garden, the gate padlocked against intruders and no-one in sight. A notice on the side of the dilapidated looking building informed Ellie that they were at the right place, and for a moment her spirits plummeted as she took in the obvious neglect and derelict state of the house and grounds. The taxi pulled away and they stepped forward to the padlocked gate.

Ellie began to rattle it to attract the attention of someone inside.

She shouted out in English, 'Hello. Is anyone there?'

At first, there was no movement or sound to be heard, but in answer to her second shout the door of the house was pulled open slowly from within. An elderly man came out and seeing the two at the gate, he shuffled forward to where they stood. He spoke to them in Marathi and Ellie asked Suman to translate his words.

'He said, 'What do we want?'' said Suman quietly.

'Can you tell him that we have an appointment at ten o'clock?'

Suman translated Ellie's answer and the gate was opened to allow them access. A scowl on the man's face gave them no encouragement to think they might be welcome, but they followed him inside, jumping slightly as the heavy door swung to behind them with a clatter. The inside of the building did nothing to put Ellie's mind at rest and as they walked along a musty corridor and up a flight of stairs, her heart grew heavier and heavier. The man showed them into an office at the top of the stairs, pointing to a chair for Ellie to sit on and ignoring the child completely. He said something to Ellie as he turned to go, and Suman again interpreted his sharp command.

'He told us to wait here,' she said, in a rough imitation of the man's gruff voice. They giggled together; Ellie pleased that Suman appeared to be taking everything in her stride.

After a few minutes, the door opened to reveal a middle-aged woman, elegant in her turquoise sari and long scarf, her dark hair parted in the middle and drawn back into a roll on the back of her head.

'Good morning,' she said. 'I am Lavani Mandal and you are Ellie Douglas, I believe?'

The woman stretched out a hand in welcome and Ellie stood to shake it warmly, glad to hear her speaking perfect English.

'I am. And this is Suman.'

Suman stood close beside Ellie holding on to her arm.

Lavani nodded but neither looked at nor spoke to Suman.

A knock on the door was followed by a second, younger woman joining them in the office. Introduced to Ellie as her assistant, Ria, Lavani explained that Ria had come to take Suman to her dormitory to meet some of the other children while she and Ellie had a talk.

Suman's hold on Ellie's arm tightened and Ellie became anxious as the assistant took a firm grip of Suman's hands and pulled her away. Ellie stepped forward, a reflex action to protect Suman, but Lavani put out a hand in front of her, blocking her way.

'It will be fine, Miss Douglas. You will see Suman shortly and see how quickly she will settle in with the other children and the older girls. Please sit down, Miss Douglas.'

Suman was taken out of the room at speed and Ellie could do nothing but obey the curt command. She sat down again on the chair and looked towards Lavani. The woman pulled another chair out to sit close to Ellie, resting an arm on the desk at her side. She began to question Ellie, asking about the child's trafficking experience and the circumstances that had taken her to Scotland. Ellie tried to answer her questions as best she could, and to ask some herself, but these were ignored by the stern older woman.

Her frustration grew as the questions continued and after another few minutes, Ellie decided enough was enough.

Putting her hand up, she said firmly, 'Please stop. I'm so very sorry but I wonder if I could please see Suman so I can be assured she is okay. She has been through such trauma and I want to be with her until she settles here. Once I've seen her, I can answer any more questions you have.'

Lavani's face stiffened, her bewilderment clear to see.

'That's ridiculous, Miss Douglas. The child is now in our care and I can assure you she will be fine.'

'I'm sorry, but I need to see for myself,' Ellie replied, quietly but firmly.

There was quite a pause before the woman rose in silence to lead Ellie back down to the ground floor and round behind the stairs. Several closed doors were visible, and Ellie could hear the chatter of children's voices behind each one that they walked past. At the fourth door, Lavani stopped, opened the door and held it wide for Ellie to enter.

As she walked into the dormitory, the first thing Ellie was conscious of was a rank odour which she recognised as stale urine and without thinking, she raised her hand to her mouth to mask the smell. Lavani's disapproving demeanour increased as she followed Ellie into the room and shut the door.

With a plummeting heart, Ellie looked around the dormitory, seeing two long rows of bunk beds lining the walls, but no other furniture or embellishments in the room. The bunk beds were very close together and she was a bit taken aback at the number of girls sitting on each of the beds. On one or two, the girls were asleep, and Ellie noticed, with a shock, that they appeared to be sharing the beds.

Looking closer she saw that the one cover on each bed was ragged and dirty, and there were no pillows in sight. The children's noise had stopped abruptly as they had entered, and each of them was staring silently at Mrs Mandal with what Ellie would swear later was fear in their eyes.

Standing beside one of the beds was Ria and another member of staff, both holding on to Suman's arms to keep her sitting down on the bed.

Immediately she saw Ellie, Suman began writhing to try to free her arms, and get over to Ellie standing just inside the door.

However, the staff member had too firm a hold of Suman's arms, keeping her where she was, and Ellie's anger boiled over as she rushed forward to free Suman and hold her close. Lavani followed quickly, her anger showing as she took command of the situation.

'Miss Douglas,' she began, her voice condescending. 'We do realise how very difficult this is for both of you. And I must apologise. I see that I was wrong when I thought that a short, sharp separation would be best for the two of you. We were given certain information about Suman in advance and I surmised, rightly I see, that some form of bond would most likely have been formed between you. It is our task to break that bond. If we are to look after Suman and try to get her back to her parents, then she must learn quickly how to fit in here, in our shelter, and obey our rules. This is always hard for the children who can't understand why they are not allowed to go home right away, and I thought it would be less painful, not just for her but for you too, to separate you quickly. Perhaps not such a good idea after all. Please come back to the office and bring Suman with you.'

Back in the office Ellie was again given a chair while Suman was ordered to sit down on the floor. The tone of the command was that of a strict schoolteacher and Suman seemed afraid not to obey the authoritative voice and sat down at Ellie's feet.

Ellie began. 'This is not turning out as I had hoped, Mrs Mandal. I think perhaps I should take Suman with me until some other arrangements can be made for her.'

'What exactly did you expect?' Lavani asked curtly.

'I'm not sure,' Ellie admitted. 'I certainly did not expect such dilapidated conditions with what looks like gross overcrowding of the girl's dormitory. Are all of these children here because they have been rescued from trafficking, as Suman has?'

The woman inclined her head. 'Of course. That is what we are, a rescue home for trafficked children.'

'There are so many of them. And I was surprised that the children were so unkempt, and in such raggedy clothes.'

'I know it is not a very salubrious place, Miss Douglas. We are a government organisation, sadly underfunded and yes, overcrowded. However, the children are fed and clothed to the best of our ability with the resources that we are given. And we have staff here whose job it is to try to locate the children's home villages and towns and return them to their families. This takes up a lot of our limited funding and the rest goes towards the upkeep of the children. You will find most of the rescue homes have the same problems as we do.'

'I'm sure you're right,' Ellie agreed politely, reaching down and laying a hand on Suman's shoulder. 'And I'm sure you and your staff are doing the best you can. Tell me about the protocol here. Will Suman receive any education while she's here? I've begun to teach her English and I am hoping this will continue.'

Mrs Mandal's answer was spoken in a very arrogant manner. 'Education is compulsory in India, so Suman will be sent with the other children to one of the local schools.'

'Will she continue to be taught English?'

'She will receive the same education as the other children,' Lavani replied, not answering Ellie's question. 'And the same care, as well as her board and lodgings. In return, we expect obedience and respect from the children. Most of them have been here for quite some time and life can be very hard for any who do not obey the rules and learn to appreciate the fact that they are very fortunate to be here.'

Ellie found she could not reply to this statement and changed the subject quickly.

'I'm going to be around for at least a week. Will I be able to come in every day and see Suman?'

'I think not. My advice would be to go home, Miss Douglas, and allow Suman to become used to our way of life as quickly as possible. She will fit in better with the other children and feel more at home if she is not singled out for any favours or benefits. Life will be easier for her if she accepts this gratefully.'

Mrs Mandal rose and held out her hand. Taken aback, Ellie stood up as well and took the proffered hand, realising that the conversation was at an end.

'Well,' she began firmly, 'contrary to what you advise, I am afraid I'm not prepared to leave Suman here. My apologies for this, but if you would be good enough to give me back Suman's suitcase, we will say goodbye.'

Mrs Mandal shook her head. 'No, Miss Douglas. I'm afraid this is not possible. Suman has been assigned to our care and this is where she will stay. It would be a big mistake for you to try to take her away. I have the authorities behind me and will not hesitate to call them in if necessary.'

The advice was given in a threatening manner and Ellie deemed it prudent to agree for the moment.

'Very well,' she said.

Suman had risen as well and was looking at Ellie with eyes as wide as saucers. She grabbed Ellie's hands and clung on tightly. Ellie freed her hands and gently took Suman in her arms.

'You stay here, darling, just for tonight, and I will be back very soon. Mrs Mandal will look after you and...'

'No,' Suman interrupted, holding on tightly to Ellie.

'Yes, Suman. Just for a short time. See how it goes and I will be here tomorrow to see you.'

She knelt beside Suman and gently unclasped the child's hands. 'I promise. You know I keep my promises. And, in the meantime, you must tell them all about yourself. Give them the name of your village and describe it to them, where you think it is. And tell them about all your parents and your family. You never know, you could be home in no time.'

She leaned forward and gave Suman a kiss on her cheek then stood abruptly, glancing round and inadvertently catching a glimpse of Lavani's stare before it disappeared. She pulled herself up to full height and looked straight into the woman's disapproving eyes.

'I'm trusting you to look after Suman as if she were your own, Mrs Mandal. See that she is treated well, or I will be informing those same authorities that there is something wrong with your management of the shelter.'

With these words, Ellie strode to the door, unable to look behind at Suman's face, even when she heard a heart-breaking sob coming from the child. With her face set rigidly, she walked back along the corridor and out into the bright sunlight, the tears beginning as she closed the gate behind her.

As fast as she could, Ellie sought the quiet sanctuary of her hotel bedroom, shedding tears into the bedcover before recovering her composure. Sitting up and drying her tears, she lifted her phone and dialled.

'Hello, my name is Ellie Douglas. May I please speak with Officer Daan Meijer?'

CHAPTER 22

Mumbai

Following a sleepless night, Ellie rose early, worry lining her forehead as she dressed and headed down for breakfast. The phone call last night had been to no avail. Daan had been away from his office in Amsterdam and had proved to be out of phone contact with his staff. Unsure of who else to speak to, Ellie had no option but to leave a message that he phone her as soon as possible. She was going to have to wait for that call before she could try to remove Suman from Mrs. Mandal's care.

With great resolve, Ellie forced herself to visit a nearby shopping centre and spent an hour or so wandering around aimlessly, not for a moment interested in the beautiful silks and hand sewn saris and the intricate Indian jewellery offered for sale in the many boutiques and shops. Her mind was elsewhere.

By lunch time, however, she was in such an anxious state that she gave up and hurried outside to flag down a motorised rickshaw to take her to the shelter.

The same man as yesterday appeared in answer to her shout at the gate and as before, ambled over to unlock the padlock and let her in. She hurried through the neglected garden and into the house, pushing the door wide as she entered. Just inside she paused, momentarily taken aback by what sounded like a riot coming from the back of the house. There was crashing and banging, as if someone was throwing furniture about, and horrendous shouts and screams mixing with someone's high pitched wails.

Sensing instinctively that the noise was coming from the dormitory where Suman had been taken yesterday, she rushed into the room to be met with the distressing sight of Suman being held tightly by two members of staff and Lavani Mandal standing watching. Suman's feet were off the ground, lashing out as if trying to kick her captors and her body was flailing around, her head thrown back and her mouth open wide in a soundless scream. One of her captors was smacking her hard on her bottom, the thumps coming hard and fast.

The room was in chaos, a couple of the beds thrown over in disarray, and the dirty mattresses and covers scattered around the floor. Girls were in huddles on their beds and against the walls, wailing and crying while the women were shouting at the tops of their voices.

Seeing Suman being hit, with a strangled cry Ellie rushed across to her. Just as quickly, Mrs Mandal moved forward to block her way, pushing her backwards to the door. Ellie pushed back, but Mrs Mandal was hastily joined by other members of staff, and she was no match for them as they forced her out of the room.

'Miss Douglas, Miss Douglas,' she heard Mrs Mandal say. 'Please get control of yourself.'

'I must go to her. I must get in.' Ellie tried to push past, but the women blocked her way.

'No,' said Mrs Mandal with finality. 'You have to allow the staff to take care of the situation.'

'I can't. I must go to Suman,' Ellie cried again.

'I can't allow that.' The woman's strident voice forced Ellie to take a deep breath and calm herself down. She submitted to being led out into the fresh air of the garden.

'Suman is reacting only as other children do,' Lavani began. 'The children are damaged when they come here and we are ready and able to deal with situations like this. You must give her a chance to settle down and reach an acceptance of the fact that this is her home now. If you continue to come, this will be harder for Suman. You must see that yourself.'

Ellie lifted her head and stared hard at the woman.

'And you think beating her into submission is the answer?'

'No I don't, but these children need to be controlled the same as any other child, sometimes even more. Some of them are out of control. Suman has just vandalised that room in there, Miss Douglas. She needs to be punished.'

Ellie replied softly, through gritted teeth. 'Suman has had enough punishment to last her a lifetime. When she is with me, she does not react like this and does not need to be controlled, as you put it. She's rebelling against being left here and needs re-assurance, not violence.'

'That is your opinion, Miss Douglas. It is my experience that children like Suman need a firm hand. I've seen it with others that have come here. We'll give Suman something to calm her down and make her sleep. She hasn't slept since she arrived and is now over-tired and overwrought.'

'You will not give her any drugs,' Ellie stated, anger making her voice strident.

Mrs Mandal made no reply.

Getting control of her temper, Ellie continued, 'Is she talking? Has she spoken to anyone?'

'No, but that will come.'

Ellie put her hands over her face, distraught that Suman had again lapsed into silence. After a moment, she looked up into Lavani's face.

'I have to take her away. I'll keep her with me in the hotel and bring her back when she's ready for it.'

'You know that is not possible. Suman is now registered with us and will stay here under our control. There's no way round that and you will just have to accept it.'

'Then I need your absolute assurance that Suman will not be hit again or hurt in any way. And I need to know that she will get some professional help, child counselling or something similar.'

'We are very experienced and will be able to take care of Suman ourselves. There's no funding for anything like that, but please be assured that we can cope with this rebellion, her temper tantrums.'

'They are not temper tantrums,' Ellie returned irately. 'Suman has a lovely, gentle nature and is only rebelling against the abuse she's gone through and the abandonment she feels.'

'I repeat, Miss Douglas. We are well able to take care of Suman ourselves. Go home and do not worry about her. In fact, I think it would be best for Suman if you never visit again.'

Ellie's breathing slowed as she nodded slowly, the inner workings of her brain wrestling with what she was hearing. No, she thought, biting her lip furiously, that would not be best for Suman. I need to get her away from here, but I need help to do this.

'Okay.' The word was long and drawn out, Ellie's mind elsewhere.

After a moment, she continued, 'I have some of Suman's belongings in the hotel. May I return to give these to you?'

'Of course, Miss Douglas. Please ring beforehand to let me know when you are coming. I'm sure you understand.'

Ellie turned and walked away from the building, keeping her footsteps at a steady pace. Once out of sight of the shelter, she ran quickly to the corner of the street to hail a rickshaw which returned her to the hotel. Back in her room, she lifted the phone.

'Long distance, please,' she said clearly and precisely to the voice on the other end.

Putting her through to the number she had requested took many minutes and she waited patiently, the only sign of agitation being a pulse throbbing above her eye. A sigh of relief burst from her as she heard the voice she had been waiting for.

CHAPTER 23

Mumbai

At four o'clock that afternoon, an Uber cab stopped a short distance from the Government Shelter for Trafficked Children and Ellie climbed out from the back seat.

'Thank you, dhan'yavada,' she said to the driver. 'Please wait here, I won't be long,' she added, pointing to her watch.

To her relief, he nodded.

She made her way swiftly across the busy, congested road. A man was standing by the gate, his peaked cap and khaki shirt identifying him as a police officer. Ellie approached him and shook his hand. They exchanged a few words before she turned and called out for someone to open the padlocked gate.

The now familiar face of the doorman appeared through the door and walked towards her, his eyes full of suspicion. He mumbled under his breath as he unlocked the gate and allowed her in. The police officer followed, and Ellie almost smiled at the consternation on the doorman's face.

Once inside, the man pointed up the stairs, asking if she wanted to go the office, but she shook her head and pointed to the back corridor. With a loud grumble he left the two visitors to make their own way to the dormitory and quickly vanished into his own part of the house.

As expected, Mrs Mandal appeared in the corridor, breathless from hurrying and shouted to Ellie to stop at once. Her eyes took in the police officer at Ellie's side. Ellie waited while they conversed and saw the officer produce an official looking document from his pocket which he handed to Lavani.

She read the document with growing indignation and then turned and walked away her fury blatant as she slammed the door behind her.

Entering the dormitory, Ellie could see that Suman was lying fast asleep on the bed, the dirty, torn cover crumpled beneath her body.

The stench of the room again met Ellie's nostrils and she wrinkled her nose in disgust. The room, as before, was filthy and untidy, with dust thick in clumps against the walls.

A group of girls were sitting around on their beds and their conversation halted as they stared at Ellie making her way towards Suman, the uniformed policeman at her side. Every dark eye watched their progress, but no-one moved or made a sound. Ellie knelt beside Suman's bed and gently shook her by the shoulder. The young girl stirred, her hazy, sleepy eyes opening to stare up into Ellie's face. There was no sign of recognition in her eyes as the lids gently lowered once more and she turned her face away.

'It's Ellie. Everything's okay. It's only me, honey,' Ellie whispered softly as she lifted the child from the bed. Realising that Suman had been heavily sedated, she drew her close and turned towards the door. An offer from the police officer offering to carry Suman was accepted with a thank you. A wave to the group of girls and they were gone, moving swiftly along the corridor. She stopped only to pick up Suman's belongings from Lavani's office before leaving the building.

She found her heart was racing like an engine as they walked towards the waiting taxi, but she knew a huge sense of relief when she looked at Suman in the policeman's arms. This was the second time she had 'stolen' Suman and she vowed to herself that this would be the last. By the time they reached the Uber cab, her heart was back to its normal beat. How easy that had been after all, she thought. All the worry for nothing. Mrs Mandal had capitulated without a fight and there had been no-one else around to stop her in her tracks, no-one to even question what she was doing.

Thank goodness for Daan who had arranged for the police officer to accompany her in the rescue. The paperwork he had produced had been a temporary document as there had been no time to apply for a full warrant to remove Suman, but it had served the trick. The official, signed document would be available in a few days' time.

The cab driver, sitting on the kerb smoking a cigarette, jumped up hastily when he saw them approach, throwing open the back door to let the officer lay the child down on the seat, still asleep. Ellie turned to the officer, and being unable to express her gratitude verbally, she gave the man an enormous hug and a kiss on the cheek, causing both embarrassment and a huge beam to appear on his face.

'Dhan'yavada, thank you with all my heart.'

He lifted a hand to wave goodbye as he walked away, happy to have been of help to Ellie.

She turned to the cab driver who was watching avidly.

'Back to the hotel, as fast as you can.'

As the taxi roared into life and shot off down the road, the driver tooted his horn continually at anyone unwise enough to move in front of him and slow him down, enjoying the drama of what he imagined was a high-speed chase. In the back, Ellie looked down at the sleeping child and then leaned back in her seat and allowed herself a contented smile. That's the last time I'm doing this, she thought. Not good for my nerves!

Reaching the hotel in record time, Ellie climbed from the cab and turned to pay the driver his fare, along with a very generous tip.

His eyes shining, he stared at the rupees in his hand. 'Dhan'yavada, thank you, thank you veree much, Auntie.'

Pointing to the sleeping child in the back, he said, 'Mi vahuna?' He slapped his chest as he spoke and indicated a carrying position.

'Yes, please,' replied Ellie. 'She's getting a bit too heavy for me these days. If you could bring her inside that would be great.' Ellie looked round towards the hotel entrance.

Inside, he carried Suman all the way up in the lift to Ellie's room and laid her gently on the bed. Waving goodbye, he left them there, with more thanks for his huge tip.

Ellie sat down on the bed beside Suman and, checking that the child was still okay, still breathing, she filled the kettle with some water and put a tea bag into one of the mugs on the tray. She sat down on the bed to wait for the kettle to boil and began to think about booking flights to go home. Beside her Suman stirred, half wakening from her deep sleep. A noise came from her lips and Ellie leaned over to hear what she was saying, noticing as she did so some fresh bruises on the little girl's arms.

'Sorry, Ellie. Please, no more shelter.'

Ellie, with tears in her eyes, cradled the child on her knee.

'No more, my darling,' she whispered, rocking Suman back and forth in her arms. 'No more. No-one will hurt you any more. I promise.'

CHAPTER 24

Edinburgh

The aeroplane landed at Glasgow City Airport with a thud and, as usual, Ellie breathed a silent prayer of thanks for the safe journey. With Suman by her side, they left the plane, Suman carrying a new red handbag over her shoulder, her face alight with anticipation.

'Wait 'til Geoff and Nan see my new bag and the presents we got for them,' Suman said excitedly. 'They'll be happy to see me come home, won't they? Geoff, will he be happy?'

'He's going to cry like a big baby, my darling, when he sees you. He'll be *so* happy.'

'No!' mouthed Suman, slowing her steps. 'Men don't cry, Ellie. Only girls cry.'

'You just wait,' warned Ellie with a laugh in her voice. 'We'll see if he cries.'

At the baggage reclaim area, while waiting for their cases to come around the carousel, Ellie took out her mobile phone and pressed a button.

'It's me again, Daan,' she said softly into the phone. 'We're home, safe and sound. No problems at passport control. I can't begin to thank you for what you did except to say I'll take the greatest care of her that I possibly can.'

Daan Meijer held the receiver to his ear. 'I know you will, Ellie. Glad to be of help. I've cleared everything at the Mumbai end and the authorities there know where she is and where she'll stay. They won't come chasing after you. The only communication you should get is when they eventually locate Suman's home and family. Then you can take her home yourself.'

'Daan, there are no words to show you how happy you've made us. I'll send you some photos soon and you can see for yourself. Just to change the subject slightly, how is the investigation going?'

'Brilliantly, Ellie. All the sleaze-balls from here to China are being ousted from their hiding places and we're rounding them up, one by one. Except Van Breda, of course. We haven't yet had confirmation about what happened to him, but we will. The world's a safer place, thanks to you and Suman.'

Collecting their bags from the carousel, Ellie and Suman turned to walk to the exit doors, both eagerly scanning the waiting crowd for two familiar and very dear faces. Suman saw them first.

'Geoff, Nan,' she shouted at the top of her voice, waving her hands in the air.

As she ran towards them, her suitcase left behind, the tall man bent down to catch Suman in his arms. Evelyn moved forward to help Ellie with the luggage, enveloping her daughter in a warm embrace.

'You've brought her back,' she whispered, tears in her eyes. 'I'm so happy.'

'Me too, Mum.'

Freed from her mother's hug, Ellie turned to meet the eyes of the man she loved so dearly and had missed with all her heart. The long, lingering look they exchanged said everything they both needed to know.

Suman, still in Geoff's arms, pulled herself back from his strong grasp to stare at his face. With both hands, she turned his face right round until he was looking straight into her eyes, his mouth in a lopsided grin.

With her eyes opened wide, she turned to Ellie.

'You were right, Ellie,' she said in amazement. 'Geoff is crying.'

Epilogue

The plane landed safely in the breezy warmth of the morning at Mumbai's Chhatrapati Shivaji airport. The long line of passengers filed along the corridor to Immigration, tired and weary after the lengthy journey from Scotland, broken only by a three-hour stopover at Dubai.

Ellie and Suman linked arms as they walked, the bond between them stronger than ever. At fifteen, Suman was blossoming into a beautiful girl, on the edge of womanhood. Still small and delicate, she made an eye-catching picture, her glossy hair attractively cut to shoulder length and scooped up into a twist at the back of her head. A typical teenager, she loved experimenting with different looks and colours, and right now, the natural raven black of her hair was highlighted with fair and auburn streaks. The colours accentuated the darkness of her eyes, even darker this morning as she struggled with lack of sleep. The apprehension and excitement of the journey had been too much to allow her to close her eyes.

Once they had cleared customs and immigration, they walked along to the baggage reclaim area. Ellie was also attracting admiring glances in her sleeveless shift dress, the vivid blue colour standing out amongst the darker colours of the other travellers. She had taken off her jacket as soon as they landed, already conscious of the heat seeping through into the seating area of the plane. The bags had been taken off the carousel by the porters and they quickly found their labelled luggage, already placed on a trolley by these helpful assistants.

One of the porters led the way to the exit, pushing their trolley.

'Taxi or bus? You want taxi, ladies?' he asked.

'No thank you,' replied Ellie. 'We have a hired car and driver waiting.'

Amongst the crowds of people milling about the airport, Ellie spotted several drivers holding signs in front of them, waiting to collect their passengers. She located the driver holding her name and she greeted him warmly.

Once outside the building he hurried off to get his car, giving them the opportunity to stop and take in the scene in front of them. It was a hubbub of noise, smells, sights and colours as people loaded their bags into vehicles and families pushed their loaded trolleys to wherever they had to go. There were queues everywhere, people of every nationality all waiting for who knew what. The scent of India filled the air, a hint of incense mixing with the heady aroma of flowers and oriental plants growing along the bankings and the strong pungent smell of curry and spices wafting in the gentle breeze. They drank it in as they stood patiently waiting beside their trolley.

'I'd forgotten how much I love the hustle and bustle of India,' said Ellie.

'Me too,' whispered Suman.

Buses, taxis, cars, lorries, minibuses, rickety old trucks, rickshaws and bikes all passed by, all in a hurry to get on their way. From out of the melee, their driver drew up in front of them, jumping from the car to stow the cases into the boot and usher his passengers safely into their seats. As he pulled away, Ellie turned and saw a worried look on Suman's face.

'You okay?' she asked softly.

'I can't believe I'm back again,' Suman whispered back.

'I know. It's kind of surreal, but I'm right here beside you.'

Suman nodded, turning slowly to gaze out of the window to take it all in. Her emotions were in turmoil; a mixture of disbelief, amazement, anxiety and excitement all vied with each other inside her as the car travelled for many miles and many hours. At first, it crawled through the overpopulated roads of the city and then increased speed as they reached the countryside of Maharashtra. Their destination was Pune, cultural capital of the state, about a four-hour drive from Mumbai. Halfway along the Express Highway, the driver pulled into a roadside rest area to allow time for his passengers to have a quick coffee and snack. Fifteen minutes later, they were back on the road, heading for Pune and their hotel, the Marriott on Serapati Bapat, a popular area for tourists and businessmen visiting the city.

It was around three in the afternoon when they finally checked into the hotel, badly in need of a shower and a freshen-up once they had unpacked their cases. Ellie had booked an early meal in the hotel's rooftop restaurant, knowing they would be tired after the flight and the long car journey. Just before six, rested and changed, they made their way up in the lift and out on to the roof terrace. They ate their meal under the stars twinkling down on them from the balmy evening sky, enjoying the calm atmosphere of the restaurant. Both were acutely conscious of the emotional ordeal ahead and both had their own private, searching thoughts.

Ellie was thinking back over the years since Suman had entered her life. The time seemed to have passed in a flash, with Ellie loving being able to take care of Suman. The years had had their ups and downs, as Ellie supported Suman through horrific nights when the memories of her time in capture invaded her dreams, and through the health problems she experienced, a remnant of the abuse she had suffered at the hands of the traffickers. These were thankfully in the past now, and Ellie knew that with the patience, love and support given by all the family and Sara, Suman was growing into the confident, happy, young woman she deserved to be.

Knowing that this lovely girl was only 'on loan' to her, Ellie had made sure that Suman learned as much as possible about her own birth country, taking her to many Indian exhibitions in the National Museum of Scotland to pore over the displays and to learn about the Hindu religion of her childhood and a lot of the cultural aspects of India. The family celebrated the festivals of Diwali, Holi and Dahi-Handi with Suman and her friends from school and with the help of family friend Devyani, who had played a part in her rescue, Suman had the opportunity to continue to speak Marathi. She loved her visits to Devyani's house, the Indian influence there a strong reminder of the world she had left behind for the present time.

These thoughts and many more were running through Ellie's head as they shared their rooftop meal in Pune. She thought also of her wonderful husband, Geoff, so supportive in everything she did and still as loving as he had always been.

It had been his idea to send Suman to Ellie's old school in Edinburgh to be given a good all-round education and she had soaked up all her lessons like a sponge. Within months of coming back to Edinburgh, she was speaking English fluently, and she proved to be a keen student and popular girl with all her classmates. Now at secondary school, she dreamed of studying for a medical degree in the future, setting her sights on becoming a doctor, her interest in helping and healing people never waning as she grew.

Last month they had celebrated Suman's fifteenth birthday. Not knowing the exact date, it had been decided that her birthday would be celebrated on the day of her return to Edinburgh from Mumbai. To mark this latest one, the family had organised a wonderful surprise party at Evelyn and Matt's large rambling house in Anstruther. It was exactly a week later that the letter had come, with the news they had almost given up hoping for.

After all this time, it was shock, a shock which speedily turned to anticipation and excitement as the days passed. The decision for Ellie and Suman to go on the journey alone had been Suman's. The family understood her decision and knew that it was Ellie and Ellie alone who would give her the strength to cope with what lay ahead, whatever the outcome.

For Suman, the parting from Geoff and Sara had been as emotional as the last time, loving her new family and her new life so dearly, and now terrified that her dreams and the people she adored so much were about to disappear. Twisting through these thoughts was the deep longing and excitement bubbling inside at the thought of seeing her mother again after all these years.

Ellie too had a deep longing, a longing to keep Suman at her side, under her care, but this wish had to be kept at bay. She knew that the decision for Suman to come to India was the correct one, the timing was right. Looking across at the face in front of her, Ellie saw with misty eyes the feisty, determined, stubborn little girl she had first met through the grille of an air conditioning unit in Amsterdam. The little girl she might have to say goodbye to. Was this how Kanya had felt when she had been parted from her daughter, she wondered.

Suman's voice brought her troubled thoughts to a swift end. 'When does the car come for us tomorrow?'

'Nine o'clock. We're going to need two or three hours to get there.'

Suman turned her head away slightly and closed her eyes. Get there, she thought. Get where? What would it be like now? Would anyone remember her? Would they want her? And if they did, could she go back to living in the village?

She thought of Kanya, bent over the fire and stirring the rice for the evening meal. She saw the face of her mother as she had been, but the faces of her brothers and sisters were hazy and she struggled to bring clear images into her mind. What she did remember vividly was the river, the crisp, cool waters where she had splashed happily with her friends and carried home the heavy pots of water on her head.

Opening her eyes, she looked into the tender blue eyes of her best friend, her protector. With no words necessary, they reached out to each other across the table and linked hands, both realising that, no matter what happened, they would always have each other.

At nine sharp next morning, they climbed into their waiting hired car, the engine purring softly and the cool breeze of the air conditioning inside so welcoming. Ellie gave the driver the name of the village and the district, and nodding his understanding, they began the last lap of their long journey.

Both had taken extra care with their appearances, both needing the little boost of extra confidence that comes when looking your best. Ellie had opted for a short-sleeved tunic dress in navy and white with matching soft leggings, choosing her clothes carefully to honour the local custom of covering her legs and the tops of her arms.

Suman had also taken longer than normal that morning, nervous of what her mother would think of her. Her first choice of outfit had been rejected in favour of a much-loved pair of denims and a soft pink, frilled top. On her wrist she wore her silver bracelet, the gift Geoff had given her at the caravan. Two or three links had been added and rarely did she face a day without the treasured gift around her wrist. Her hair had been brushed until it gleamed, and a pair of tiny studs in her ears completed her outfit.

It was no wonder the driver had stared in admiration when he had collected them from the hotel in the morning and he drove with care through the busy, bustling streets of Pune. The heavy traffic seemed to converge from every corner, making progress slow. The rule of driving on only one side of the road did not seem to apply in this part of India and both Ellie and Suman caught their breath on several occasions as the small, motorised rickshaws, so abundant on the streets, weaved and dodged in and out, narrowly missing their car by inches. Vying for space on the road was like a competition and it was with relief that they realised the car was leaving the congested streets of the city and heading for the quieter roads leading out to the suburbs and the countryside of Maharashtra.

The surface of the road deteriorated quickly the further from the city they drove, the main highway giving way to less well-maintained roads which in turn led on to narrow tracks which barely had room for two cars to pass. Even worse were the stony, single-track roads they negotiated as they climbed high up into the hills and the journey got bumpier and more uncomfortable.

The driver apologised for the state of the roads, double checking his map to ensure he was going in the right direction. Re-assuring him that the village name he was attempting to find was the right one, Suman knew by instinct that they were nearing their journey's end. She sat bolt upright in the car, holding on with one hand to the strap by her shoulder. Tense and nervous, she kept her eyes straight ahead, taking in every detail of the scenery unfolding in front of them.

Rounding a wide bend, the slopes opened out onto a plateau where they could see all around for many miles. The area was stunning. On the left, far into the distance, they spotted a river snaking its way down to the valley from the hills, richly carpeted with an abundance of soft pink and white flowers. As they drew closer, Ellie stared in awe as the countryside changed, taking on a bright blue hue from the clusters of wild delphiniums growing tall amongst the trees and swaying in the gentle breeze.

Having pored over the computer with Suman trying to locate the village once they had been told its name, Ellie knew that the area was described as the 'nurseries of heaven'. Seeing it now, she understood the reason for the apt description.

'It's beautiful,' she breathed.

Suman nodded, looking way past the bright coloured flowers and pointing out a village with a shaking finger. Unconsciously, they drew closer together in the car.

For another ten minutes or so, they made their bumpy way over hillocks and grassland until finally the car came to a standstill on the exact spot where the green, dusty truck had stood all those years before. Suman caught her breath as she opened the door slowly.

Ellie spoke quietly to the driver who nodded his agreement to wait as long as was necessary. She followed Suman out, staring in wonder at the sight of the compact, little village with its mud huts and small wooden or brick houses. From this distance, they could see some women congregated around a tap sticking up from the ground, some washing their pots under the running water, some squatting on the ground, waiting their turn.

Ellie had the strong feeling that she had stepped back in time, fascinated by the aura of gentleness and peace pervading the scene. She reached out to Suman, this time needing the child as much as the child had ever needed her. Together they began the walk down the dusty track through the centre of the village, their steps slow yet purposeful.

Suman walked as if in a trance. She knew the path like the back of her hand, surprised that it was just as she had remembered it many times in her thoughts and in her dreams. In her mind's eye, she saw again Kanya's face, the look of horror and fear in her eyes as her eldest daughter was lifted from her side and taken away. The same look had been mirrored in the faces of her sisters and brothers, too young to understand why Suman was being put in the truck.

For a second she shuddered, remembering her own terror at not knowing where she was going. A tear pushed its way unbidden from the corner of her eye and rolled down her cheek. Her footsteps stopped. I can't do this, she thought, blinking fast and wiping the wetness away with the back of her hand.

'You can do it.' The words were said firmly.

She looked round into Ellie's eyes.

With a swallow she began to walk forward, her footsteps becoming more determined with every move and the small house at the bottom of the track edged closer.

Several villagers had stopped what they were doing to watch the two strangers. Some children were playing around the house and as Suman and Ellie approached, they ran inside, calling out in excited voices. A moment later they appeared again at the door, pulling a woman by the hand, a woman who looked as if she was annoyed at being interrupted in this way. On seeing the two women a few steps away from her door, she gasped and lifted her shawl to wipe the grime from her face and hands.

Kanya was perplexed, staring at the two people in front of her, one a young Indian girl in western clothes, and the other a white woman.

She took a step forward to greet them and invite them in, flustered and confused but happy to welcome the two strangers to her home. Suddenly her eyes met Suman's. Abruptly she stopped, her body turned to stone. Her heart began to pound so hard she could hardly breathe. She stared harder into the face of the young girl and the blood rushed to her cheeks, her breath suspended.

A moment later she whispered the name she had been forbidden to mention for many long, heart-breaking years. 'Suman.'

Mother and daughter looked into each other's eyes for an eternity. Then Suman ran forward into the outstretched arms with only one word.

'Aayi.'

ABOUT THE AUTHOR

After a varied career working in banking, administration and education, Avril Duncan was employed for many years in management within the charitable sector, with WRVS, NHS (Macmillan Cancer Support) and with Crossroads Caring for Carers. She studied at Perth Academy and through long-distance learning with Lampeter University, Wales.

Diverted Traffic is her first novel although Avril has been writing poems and short stories most of her life. She is a member of Scribblers Writers Group, in Perth, Scotland, where she lives with her husband, Bill.

Both her working life and her personal life reflect her interests and values of human rights for all, with memberships of Soroptimist International and Amnesty International. As part of Girlguiding UK and Trefoil Guild UK, Avril is a County Vice President of Girlguiding Perth & Kinross and a trustee of the Annie Unwin Trust.

THE FREE TO LIVE TRUST

Avril is a founder member of The Free to Live Trust, a charity working to rescue victims of human trafficking and to raise awareness of modern slavery. Through Girlguiding UK, Avril has been visiting India regularly since 2003, staying at Sangam Guide World Centre in Pune, Maharashtra, to work with street children and vulnerable young people. Founded in 2015, The Free to Live Trust has built two children's homes near Pune to house the rescued offspring of victims of human trafficking who are being held in the red-light area of the city as sex slaves.

With the help of the Church of Scotland Guilds, the Trust has set up a feeding programme to provide a hot meal daily for many of the children still trapped in the red-light area of Pune. Work is under way to rescue many more of these children and to free and rehabilitate victims themselves out of sexual slavery. To find out more about this work, visit **www.freetolivetrust.org**

TIPPERMUIR BOOKS

Tippermuir Books Ltd (est. 2009) is an independent publishing company based in Perth, Scotland. It runs on a not-for-profit basis and is a non-hierarchical collective. Proposals for books are always welcome. LULLABY PRESS is an imprint (fiction) of Tippermuir Books.

OTHER TITLES FROM TIPPERMUIR BOOKS

Spanish Thermopylae (2009)

Battleground Perthshire (2009)

Perth: Street by Street (2012)

Born in Perthshire (2012)

In Spain with Orwell (2013)

Trust (2014)

Perth: As Others Saw Us (2014)

Love All (2015)

A Chocolate Soldier (2016)

The Early Photographers of Perthshire (2016)

*Taking Detective Novels Seriously:
The Collected Crime Reviews of Dorothy L. Sayers* (2017)

Walking with Ghosts (2017)

No Fair City: Dark Tales from Perth's Past (2017)

*The Tale o the Wee Mowdie that wantit tae ken
wha keeched on his heid* (2017)

*Hunters: Wee Stories from the Crescent:
A Reminiscence of Perth's Hunter Crescent* (2017)

Flipstones (2018)

Perth & Kinross: A Pocket Miscellany:
A Companion for Visitors and Residents (2019)

God, Hitler, and Lord Peter Wimsey: Selected Essays,
Speeches and Articles by Dorothy L. Sayers (2019)

The Piper of Tobruk:
Pipe Major Robert Roy, MBE, DCM (2019)

The 'Gig Docter o Athole':
Dr William Irvine & The Irvine Memorial Hospital (2019)

Afore the Highlands: The Jacobites in Perth, 1715-16 (2019)

'Where Sky and Summit Meet': Flight Over Perthshire –
A History: tales of Pilots, Airfields, Aeronautical Feats, & War
(2019)

Authentic Democracy: An Ethical Justification of Anarchism
(2020)

ALSO BY LULLABY PRESS
A Little Book of Carol's (2018)

FORTHCOMING

If Rivers Could Sing: A Year in the Life of a Scottish River
(Keith Broomfield, 2020)

A Squatter o Bairnrhymes (Stuart Paterson, 2020)

William Soutar: Collected Poetry
(Kirsteen McCue and Paul S. Philippou (eds), 2021)

Tippermuir Books Ltd can be contacted at
mail@tippermuirbooks.co.uk.

TIPPERMUIR
· BOOKS LIMITED ·